Brooklyn Bones

Brooklyn Bones

An Erica Donato Mystery

Triss Stein

Poisoned Pen Press

Poisoned
Pen
Press

Poisoned Pen Press
6962 E. First Ave., Ste. 103
Scottsdale, AZ 85251
www.poisonedpenpress.com
info@poisonedpenpress.com

Printed in the United States of America

To the memory of Marilyn Wallace

Borrowing the great words of E.B. White,
"It is not often that someone comes along who is
a true friend and a good writer."

Acknowledgments

Thanks first to my writing group. Sometimes we have so much fun we forget to talk about writing, but you are the people who advised and prodded, encouraged and told the truth: *the late* Marilyn Wallace, Meredith Cole, Jane Olson, Mary Darby. There are not enough ways to say thank you.

Thanks to Phyllis Cohen, who knows why; to Lee Lofland and Linda Fairstein, who generously share their expertise with members of the mystery community; to Michele Martinez, who was the very first reader; to forensic anthropologist Amy Zelson Mundorff, who provided some crucial facts; to the members of Mystery Writers of America and Sisters in Crime, organizations that mean home for mystery writers at all stages of their careers; *and to the team at Poisoned Pen Press, who saw something in this book and made it happen.*

Thanks, as always, to Bob, reader of contracts, fixer of computers and proofreader in chief, and to Miriam and Carolyn, my cheering squad.

Chapter One

It began with a sobbing phone call from my daughter, the kind of call every parent dreads. All I made out was that something terrible had happened; she was terrified, would never get over it. It was all my fault.

Chris is fifteen. Pretty much everything is all my fault, and yet—and yet—her voice told me it was more than teenage hysterics. Maybe.

With my heart in my mouth—oh, yes, some of those old clichés are dead accurate—I slapped a note on my desk to say I was out for the afternoon, ran out of the museum where I was an intern, and hustled across downtown Brooklyn at an undignified half-run. I was in and out of the subway and running up the stairs to my house less than half an hour from the moment the phone rang.

"Oh, mommy." She flew from the back room and threw herself into my arms.

Well, I thought. She hasn't done that in years.

"What's wrong?" I used my best time-to-stop-the-hysterics mom voice.

The contractor who is renovating my house appeared behind Chris.

"Come on." He patted her curly hair. "You know you're all right. Here's your soda. Drink up now. No one can drink and cry at the same time."

She shook her head, hard, without lifting it off my shoulder.

Meeting my eyes over the back of her head, he said calmly, "Erica, we do have a problem."

Joe, my friend, my biking buddy, my contractor, is big, dark, deliberate. He's always calm. He says I will be too, when I get another decade down the road. I tell him not to treat me like a kid sister, and that he's learned to be cool because it was necessary to his work. He has to be calm, dealing as he does with stressed-out homeowners in the throes of expensive, complicated renovations of century-old houses.

I sat down on a drop cloth-covered sofa, Chris in my lap. In the tiny part of my mind not crazed with anxiety I wondered when was the last time she'd let me hold her like this?

"We do have a problem," he repeated. "Chris, do you want to tell or should I?"

As his quiet voice got through to Chris, the sobbing subsided.

"If someone doesn't tell me something, right now, I'll be hysterical myself," I said.

A muffled moan came from my shoulder. "We found something today when we broke through that wall." Joe pointed to broken plasterboard, and behind it, what looked like a long-hidden, crumbling fireplace.

Chris shuddered, as she whispered, "It was awful."

"Damn it, Joe!"

"All right, Erica. Brace yourself. We found some bones behind the wall."

His seriousness chilled me. "I don't understand. Mouse bones? That's what this is all about?"

He shook his head. "Not mouse. It's human, and Chris found it." The sobbing on my shoulder renewed its intensity.

"OK." I took another breath, a little shaky this time. "Let me get this straight. Chris is all right. And you were working on the house, like always, and you were taking down that wall and you…"

"Me!" Chris suddenly sat up. "It was me. I found them. And if you hadn't made me take this dumb job working for Joe, I never would have. And now I'll have nightmares forever." She jumped up from my lap and ran upstairs. I was too stunned to move.

Joe smiled sympathetically. "She'll get over it, but I have to tell you, it shocked both of us."

I didn't want to discuss my daughter's emotional state, so I turned to something safer. Plain facts.

"Tell me again. I can't quite take it in. I have heard stories like this, but I never believed any of them."

"Urban legends, right?"

I nodded

"Yeah, I guess I've heard those tall tales, too, but I know a guy who really did find a skeleton behind the wall in an old house. It was an infant, probably someone's secret baby, from way back when."

I shuddered. "And this?"

He hesitated. "I'm no expert, but it's not a baby, and not so old, I guess." He saw me turn pale and added quickly, "No, no, it's not a recent corpse. Only bones. Mostly bones, anyway. But I had to call the police."

"Of course," I said, absently, still in shock.

"We ought to leave it alone, not touch it, until the police come."

"I won't touch it, but Chris has seen it. You show me too."

He pointed to the jagged hole Chris had smashed in the wall, and gave me his flashlight. I took a deep breath and stuck my head in. It was a walled-over fireplace, all crumbling brick and tile. A musty, sour smell filled the space. Mice, I thought, and yes, the flashlight beam caught a few tiny bones, then a flash of silver.

It was a human body all right, folded up to fit the space, but neatly arranged and partly dressed, and pathetically small. I knew the living person had probably been bigger, that the skeleton tends to collapse. Even in the dim flashlight, I could see there was more there than bones. The body was wearing what was left of a tie-dyed t-shirt, and it was wrapped in the shreds of an Indian print cloth. She, he, it must have been wearing jewelry. The flashes of silver

shone from among the wrist and finger bones, and near the head
where the ears might have been. The bones of one arm may have
been wrapped around a large teddy bear. Neatly arranged along
one side of the body were colorful tattered squares, magazines
perhaps, and a twisted object made of metal piping.

The sight took a minute to sink in, and when it did, I
stopped breathing. I was looking at the remains of someone
young enough to hug a teddy bear. Old enough to wear jewelry.
I thought of Chris' room, with her stuffed animals still lined up
on her bed, and her vast collection of earrings, and my eyes stung.

It was warm and dry in there, Joe was explaining in a voice
that seemed to come from very far away. A heat pipe ran behind
the back wall and the dry heat preserved a lot.

Yes, I could see that.

"So you can see why I think it's not that old?" Joe's voice
came from behind me.

I nodded. "Relatively modern stuff. Sort of 1960s, maybe."

"That metal thing is a bong."

"I never saw one like that."

"You fill it with water and get a nice, soft smoke."

My astonishment must have showed in my face, because he
said with a dismissive gesture, "Ah well, it was all a long time
ago, in my wild youth."

"Joe." My voice shaking. "This looks like a burial, doesn't it?"

"Afraid so. Hey, you look kind of pale. Do you need to put
your head down on your knees?"

"No, no, I'm OK. It's not the bones so much. I took an archae-
ology course. I've seen bones. It's the teddy bear. And the hair.
Dear lord, Joe, did you see that? There's still hair on the skull.
This was once a real person, with light hair and a teddy bear."

"Here, take this. Sugar's good for shock."

He handed me Chris' still cold soda and I touched the icy
metal to my face as he gently guided me away from the wall.

"You know," he went on matter of factly, obviously trying
to distract me, "Chris is doing fine on this job. She's been a lot
of help, and she's really earning her paycheck."

He went on talking, but I didn't hear him. This was all my fault, Chris said, and in a way it was true. I had insisted she take this job, and I knew exactly how she felt about it. She made sure of that by leaving a resentful e-mail to her best friend up on the computer screen. Only someone who'd never heard of Freud could think that was an accident.

Joe disappeared into the back of the house, and I paced up and down around the mess in the room, trying to figure things out.

My daughter was upstairs crying, and I didn't know what to do with her. Or for her. She was so angry, I didn't know if she would let me near her.

Not so long ago, there would have been no question about what to do. I've been a mother since I was twenty, and I was thrilled right from the start. My husband was too. I guess we were too young and dumb to be scared. And all these years after he died, years when it was only Chris and me, we were the best of friends, our own little family of two.

I used to know what to do; I used to have answers. Lately, I only have questions. We aren't exactly friends these days and we aren't exactly a happy family.

I decided who was in charge—me —and started up the stairs. Then the doorbell rang.

There were two young officers in uniform, who looked so much like guys I knew when I was young that it hurt. They identified themselves and politely asked me to take them to the "situation."

Joe and I stood nearby watching, keeping an eye on them and at the same time curious to see what they would do.

When they poked their heads into the hole in the wall, one of them said, "Holy shit!" then he looked at me and muttered a quick "Sorry."

"It's ok. I've heard it before."

"Jeez," he said to his partner, "it looks like a burial or something."

"You said it. We've got to call detectives in, crime scene, the works."

The other one nodded. "They're going to drop their teeth when they hear this one." He turned to us. "We need to ask you some questions, and we're gonna tell you not to touch a thing until the experts show up. Got that?"

"Of course."

"I need names, addresses, phone numbers, occupation." He whipped out a notebook and pen. "So you live here? What were you doing when you found these bones?"

"Mrs. Donato wasn't here," Joe said emphatically. "She was at work. I'm her contractor. We started to break down that wall and there it was."

"So you found it?"

"Not exactly. I was here, but Mrs. Donato's daughter, who's working for me, was the one who actually uncovered it."

"Oh yeah? And where is she? We'll need to talk to her."

"She's upstairs, but please," I begged, "she's only fifteen and she's really upset. Can't you just talk to us?"

"No, ma'm, we can't." He smiled. "I have a younger sister. We'll be nice, don't worry, but let me get straight on these other questions first. Now, do you own or rent? Anyone else live here, besides you and your daughter? And how long have you been here?"

"Own. Ten years. It's only us right now. We used to rent out the garden floor, until we started all this construction."

"And you're fixing it up now?" He turned to Joe. "And you're in charge of that?"

I said, "Of course he is. You don't think we...."

"Nope, not thinking anything, just asking questions about stuff the detectives might want to know. OK, let's get the young lady down here."

I hesitated, wanting to argue, then gave in and went to get her. I found her curled up on the top step. She lifted her face from her knees and said, "I can't. I won't."

"There is no choice here. You have to. If you don't come down, I'm sure they'll come up to get you. Wouldn't that be worse?"

She gave me a considering look and went clattering down the stairs.

I followed, braced for more hysteria, but the young cops kept their promise and treated her gently. She described how she broke through the wall with a sledgehammer, and they teased her about not being that strong, and she offered to show them. Standing near the broken wall, looking in again, one of them said to the other, "Tell you something. I think that's a kid. Not a little kid, but a young girl."

The second cop said, "You can't tell all that from bones!"

"Yeah, you can. The experts can, anyways. Bet you anything it turns out to be female and young. Ever know a guy with a teddy bear?"

Chris looked ready to cry again, but I knew they were merely being young cops, covering up their discomfort. Either that, or they were jerks. I barely got the words out —"Have a little respect here!" —when the bell rang again.

A crowd filled my steps, men and women, some in plain-clothes, some in uniform. They came in, identified themselves, conferred with the cops already here. We sat in a corner, quiet and out of their way, and they forgot about us. In the blur of their intense activity, I never did figure out exactly who was who. Some were detectives, some maybe from a crime scene unit. They went right to work, carefully enlarging the hole Chris had made, taking pictures, taking samples, bagging up everything they found.

One would say, "Chain bracelet, silver-color," and the other wrote it down. "Record albums here—Rolling Stones, *Sympathy for the Devil.* The Doors. Just called *The Doors*, I guess. Jefferson Airplane. *Surrealistic Pillow.* Real oldies. I mean, when do you see records at all any more?"

"Man, this is a weird one. I don't see the head bashed in, we're not finding bullets here. Sure looks suspicious, but there's no obvious cause of death."

Another voice said, "ME's gonna have a field day with this one."

Chris covered her ears.

Joe watched what they did, asked and answered questions, but I sat with my daughter, stroking her hair. Then someone handing out the objects gave a low whistle and muttered, "I'll be damned." Everyone looked his way as he carefully held up a broken piece of brick and said, "There's writing on it. RIP. Then it says 9/16/72.

Over Chris' hidden head, Joe and I stared at each other as one of the cops said, "Not a cover up, a freakin' burial," and another said, "Or both."

Eventually one of the men in plainclothes come to us and double-checked all our answers to the questions of the first cops. He said to Joe, "Joe Greenberg? Office at 533 Bergen? We'll want to check out your contracting license numbers," and to me, "Can you verify when you moved here? And where you lived before? We might want that, but it can wait."

He turned to colleagues and said quietly, "If everything checks out, they're OK. This situation looks way older than their residence."

At last, they gently placed the body in a bag and wheeled it out, placed a bright yellow crime scene tape across the hole in the wall and started packing up their equipment. I hadn't moved from the sofa but looking through the front window I could see a crowd gathered outside, curious neighbors, a few cars stopped to see what was going on.

I heard a familiar voice saying, "I live next door. Just checking to see if everything's OK with Miz Donato. Anything I can do?" Mr. Pastore, my grandfatherly next door neighbor.

A cop replied, "Yeah, she's all right. You can come back later. No one's coming in right now."

The plainclothes officer who seemed to be in charge came back to us and said, "We're going to check out everything you told us, but for now, relax."

Chris looked up. "Checking us out? Do you possibly think we had anything to do with that….that….those bones?"

He smiled slightly. "No, young lady, we don't think that, but we have to ask, you know."

"Well, I do know. My uncle —well, almost uncle—is a retired detective. And he would know better!"

"Oh? What's his name?"

"Sergeant Rick Malone," she said proudly.

"Could be I've met him. Now, listen." He glanced sternly from me to Chris to Joe. "No one, and I mean no one, touches anything! That's what the tape is for, to keep everyone away. Don't even touch the tape! Don't even work *near* there. Don't even *think* about it. Got that?"

We did.

"Good." He looked up to see his crew gathered at the door. "Here's my card, in case you need to get in touch. I'm Russo. I'll be in touch with you, if we need anything else. That's it for now."

And they were gone at last. Chris, Joe, and I stared at each other. Then Chris stood, said, "This is too gruesome!" and disappeared upstairs.

Chapter Two

Joe asked me if I were all right, but I waved him away and he left. He needed to get on with his evening plans and I needed to collapse.

I found a cold beer in the fridge and fell into my favorite chair.

I could barely take in what I had seen. There was a body in my house. It had been there, unknown, all these years. It was not scary, not physically threatening, and I don't believe in ghosts, but my own little house that I loved so much now felt different to me. And not in a good way. Plus I might be dealing with the police for a long time to come. As if I did not have enough on my shoulders already.

The phone broke into my muddled thoughts. It was my best friend Darcy.

"Can you come meet me for a bite of dinner in a little while? I want a glass of wine and girl talk."

"Oh, no, not a chance, not tonight."

"Try to change that to 'yes of course.' I'm a free woman and I want to make the most of it. ALL my kids are out doing teenager things and Carl is on a business trip."

"I don't know…"

She abruptly stopped her torrent of conversation. "What's wrong? I hear it in your voice."

So I told her about the discovery in our house and she was appropriately shocked. "And Chris was hysterical? Of course she was. You poor thing! But who can blame her? How are *you* doing?" Then she said, carefully, "Maybe it would be good for you to get out tonight. Don't you think? Be with people, have some distraction."

"But I can't…Chris…"

"Chris will be fine." She said it with the confidence of one who had survived three teenagers.

"No, Darcy, I don't think…not tonight…."

Then, the sound of teenage chatter came drifting down the stairs.

"Hold on a minute."

Standing at the bottom of the stairs, I could easily hear Chris. Our house is tiny for the neighborhood, with a separate rental apartment, now empty, on the garden floor and only two narrow stories for our own use. Her high voice came floating out of her room, rising and falling.

"Oh. My. God," she said. "Oh my god! I hit the sheet rock with a hammer and it crumbled and there was this skeleton. It was the scariest, creepy…" Pause. "No, I am not kidding! How could you even think that? They were totally real bones and sort of dried skin too. And hair! Honest."

Her voice fell again, and I could only hear the sounds, not the words, but it didn't matter. She was working her own phone, processing the events of the day in her own teenaged way, with her friends. I said thank you to someone out there, some patron saint of parenthood.

I returned to my own call, told Darcy I would call her back and went upstairs. Before I could knock, Chris' door opened. She had changed her clothes and was in mid-makeup.

"I've got to get out of this house. It's too creepy."

"I hear that. Where are you going?"

"Meeting Mel for pizza." Her tone was sulky but her expression was pleading. I thought time with her best friend might be good for her.

"Then I might have supper with Darcy. You have your phone? Be home by ten."

"Whatever." She closed her bedroom door.

I wanted to smash the door down, even though I knew she was just trying to get control of her shock. Because I am a mature adult, I called Darcy instead, jumped into the shower, dressed quickly in a cool sundress and sandals, skipped makeup, and left the house. The ten-block walk to the restaurant, a cute patisserie with light meals, would give me time to compose myself. At least I hoped it would.

I stopped to exchange a few words with Mr. Pastore, assuring him I was fine, and Chris was fine, and promised to tell him all about it later. I stopped his flood of questions by admiring the magnificent roses he was pruning, and hurried down the block to our main avenue.

Before I got there, a voice called to me from across the street. It was Mary, our neighborhood crazy lady. Sometimes she was Ellen or even, occasionally, Zsa Zsa.

Of course we all teach the children to say the more correct "mentally ill." Some days she was incoherent, weeping, ranting, clearly unwashed and smelly, and probably off medication. Other days we have had wholly rational conversations about the changing color of the leaves or who was moving in and out, but she has never told me exactly where she lived, or where she comes from. I was pretty sure she was alone in the world, but even that was only a guess.

Today looked like a somewhat lucid day. She called out, "Everything all right, dear? I saw police at your house. They scared me."

I only gave her what I hoped was a friendly wave and an "Everything's fine." I didn't want to be unkind, but I didn't have the time or energy for her tonight.

I turned the corner into the crowds on the avenue. My modest house is on what used to be the far raggedy edge of Park Slope, this famously beautiful, historic neighborhood. But the neighborhood keeps spreading. Sometimes I miss the butcher and the sprawling, shabby toy store, so handy for last minute gifts, and even the tired corner bars where old men drank beer at eleven a.m. Coffee bars that offer four-dollar cappuccinos are replacing them all.

Actually, I was powerfully tempted when I passed one of them. The stress from this strange day was rapidly sinking in. Something sad and ugly had happened right there, in the home where Chris and I had been living our ordinary lives. It didn't feel quite so much like our shelter any more. Caffeine and sugar to go suddenly seemed like a wonderful idea.

I exercised self-control on the coffee but could not control my thoughts. Was there someone out there in the world wondering about the dead girl all these years, or was she one more of the city's tragic lost souls? I thought of my own child and I shuddered.

At the same time, I walked along through the warm summer night, skirting a chattering group of Chris' friends, who smiled nervously, no doubt wishing to be invisible to parental eyes. Outside the car service storefront, I passed the South Asian drivers, smoking and lounging, who always pretended I was invisible myself.

I passed the laughing, Spanish-speaking teenagers on the corner, not so different from me and my friends hanging out back in the day, and the young professionals waiting to get into the glossy new Thai restaurant with its smells of garlic and curry calling to me as I went by. I waved to an acquaintance, calling, "Hi, got to run, I'm late."

Summer night in a living city neighborhood.

It hit me, not for the first time, what a long way from home this neighborhood is for me. Only a few miles physically, but mentally, more of a leap than if I'd come here from North Carolina. I grew up on the other side of Brooklyn, blue collar Brooklyn, Italian, Irish, Jewish, filled with endless rows of semi-modern, identical attached brick houses, boring and charmless, though much loved by their owners. Children went to college locally, if at all, married, and moved nearby. I had happily expected to spend my life right there, where people mostly looked alike. Mostly thought alike too.

This whole odyssey across Brooklyn was financed by my young husband's life insurance. After he died I became desperate to make a fresh start in a neighborhood completely devoid of his presence. Now a small legacy from my mother was making the desperately needed work on the house a reality.

I ordered myself to push all those all thoughts away. Tonight the here and now was more than complicated enough.

In a few minutes I was sitting in the patisserie, tossing back my iced coffee, heavy on the sugar and whipped cream, and waiting for my chronically late best friend. We met at a nursery school bake sale all those years ago, and instantly clicked over the chocolate cupcakes. I have no idea why. I don't exactly understand her work—media research—what the heck is that?—and I'm a Brooklyn girl and she's a Darien girl, and she has an MBA from Wharton and I started out as a social studies teacher, but—I don't know—we turned out to be the friend we each didn't know we were looking for.

She greeted me with a hug and sat down. "You don't look well. In fact you look awful. Are you in shock?"

"Me? No, just tired. Well, maybe shock. I don't know!"

She patted my hand. "Oh, honey, you're in shock, and you have a right to be. Let's order and I'm treating to wine, too. Call it restorative. Then tell me all."

So I did. I must have needed to talk, because we were looking at the dessert menu before I suddenly stopped. I apologized for the monologue and Darcy said, "Don't be silly. Ready for an éclair? Or two?"

"You are a bad influence."

"Of course. Isn't that what friends are for?" I nodded, still scraping up the last of my Cobb salad.

"So did I get it, that the cops took everything away and now you go back to normal?"

"I don't know. They said to leave it alone so they can take another look if they want to. And I don't know about back to normal. I don't think either Chris or I will just forget about it. It was too.... it was a shock.....and you know Chris was already mad at me for making her work instead of going to camp. And the part about it being a young girl most likely..." My hand started to shake a little.

Darcy gently took the wine glass from my fingers and set it on the table. "I didn't mean that you would forget. Even I won't, and I've only heard it from you. No one who has teenagers could. Did they at least say they'd let you know what they learn? If they ever do?"

"Umm, not exactly, but I could get back to them. Badger them if I have to. She'll haunt us otherwise." I smiled at Darcy to let her know I was joking. Sort of.

"I'm sorry I can't help with that. I don't have any contacts to tap into in that world."

That made me want to smile for real. Networking is like breathing to Darcy. In our decade of friendship she has found me a pediatric ophthalmologist, a termite expert, and someone to make a flower girl dress. I had no doubt she could find me samba lessons too.

"I'll ask my dad, but I think it's out of his sphere too. Oh!" she went on. "I completely forgot. Your discovery blew it right out of my mind. Speaking of contacts, could I set up a meeting with a friend of my dad's?"

She saw my bafflement and said, "Sorry to change subjects, but just listen. He's advising on a deal involving Brooklyn development and he asked me about how to get a quick tutorial on the issues. I'm probably the only person in Brooklyn he knows. I thought, who better than you?"

"Uh, I'm not such an expert. Not yet."

She waved a dismissive hand. "Doesn't matter. Now listen, here's my thinking. Seriously. He would be a useful contact for you. He's a golf buddy of my dad and he is very connected." She added quickly, laughing, "The proper kind of connected, not the crime kind, as in Deerfield, Princeton, family names on old banks. That kind. More to the point, his family is on museum boards. You work in a museum. And he's a nice man, too. Plus, there would definitely be a consulting fee. I've already laid that down with him."

She added, "Come on, Erika. Think. People in his world support museums. He supports museums. They all know each other. They put in good words for people they like, and they put them in with the people who are at the top of the pyramid. Getting it now?"

I was, sort of. And even if I didn't entirely, like I said, my buddy is the queen of networking. Maybe my judgment was softened by the éclairs, because I said yes.

She whipped out her phone, speed dialed and said, "Steven, Darcy here. My friend Erika said yes, she'll make the time for you. Call her." She added my number and turned back to me.

"And wear something nice? And some makeup? It makes a more professional impression." I started to protest, but she said firmly, "No, not office clothes, but not those ratty gym shorts you wear at home, either." I sighed. She knows me too well.

"Erica!"

"What?"

"Your eyes are closing. Come on, let's get home." She walked me out, hugged me and said, "No nightmares tonight," and I hopped a bus home. Suddenly the walk seemed too much. All the way home, I dreaded dealing with my moody child, even with Darcy's words still in my head. "She's a teenager. She'll be grown up someday. Trust me on this."

There was a note from Chris. "Went to bed. Please don't make noise coming up! Uncle Rick called. I told him everything. He wants to change our locks and said to tell you he's coming for dinner tomorrow and he'll bring pizza. Wants a full report." Good, I thought. Rick was the very person I most wanted to see.

Before I went up, I glanced into the dining room, where the bright yellow police tape seemed to shine in the dark, and the dusty sour smell seemed to have spread through the first floor. Then I checked on Chris, who was already sound asleep, and went to bed, finally, wondering if I would dream all night about that sad little skeleton. That body had been hidden, buried carefully, it seemed, but hidden. Had there been a terrible accident?

Or—I finally had to say the ugly words I'd been trying to keep away all evening. Had someone killed her?

Chapter Three

I met Chris in the hall as she was making a middle of the night trip to the bathroom. She asked in a voice still hoarse from sleep, "They said the bones were a girl's, didn't they? Like, a teenager?"

I nodded. "Honey, is that upsetting you?"

She shook her head, mumbled, "Back to sleep," and disappeared into her room. When I came out of my room in the morning, ready to leave for work, she was sitting on her bed, laptop open, pointedly ignoring me until she gasped and said, "Come look!"

The screen had a headline proclaiming, "Real Life Mystery in South Slope?" It was followed by a couple of paragraphs beginning, "Why was NYPD removing what looked like a body bag from 2007 13th Street? Sources on this shabby block at the border of the Slope, tell us it is the home of a mother and teenaged daughter, and no one else is known to live there. Yet the body bag was seen being removed yesterday afternoon and there were cops in and out. Was there an accident during the ongoing renovation? And why is no one saying anything? Neighbors are naturally curious and even concerned." It was signed with a screen name.

"Who could possibly have written this? And what the hell is this anyway?"

"It's a bulletin board, Mom," she said defensively. She must have heard my reaction in my voice. "Brownstone Bytes. You know, neighborhood news, gossip, restaurants, star spotting. I once saw a picture of Jennifer Connelly right there on Jamie's block."

"That's not the point! This is a…an intrusion writing about us and our home."

"Yeah. I'm like…." She looked at my angry face and finished with what I suspected was a second thought. "I'm really creeped out." I had a hunch her first word might have been "excited."

"They have no right to give our address there."

"Uh, they do, mom. We had it in American history last year. First amendment?"

That's what you get when you struggle to send your child to an excellent private school. Better educated back talk.

"Nonsense. Give me that URL. I'm sending them a complaint as soon as I get to work."

"Mom!"

"What? I have to get to work."

"Could you wait maybe, until we can do it together? I'm afraid you might go too far? You seem, um, pretty upset?"

That stopped me. I was annoyed, but I should not seem out of control to my daughter.

"Ok." I dug up a smile. "You think I might embarrass you?"

She looked so relieved to be understood, I almost laughed.

"You can be a little impulsive sometimes." She managed a tiny smile of her own.

"We can work it out later. But really, Chris, don't you see why it isn't a good thing?"

She admitted she did, sort of; I reminded her to check in if she went anywhere, and that Joe would be there soon to get back to work. I had to get some real work done myself, work as in, at my job.

After a long day buried in meetings and reports I came home at last to an empty house and a note "At Melissa's—invited to dinner, watching a video. Cops here, went over the fireplace again, but said we could take down tape."

It felt like a reprieve. I would have complete silence, dinner, a glass of wine, and the paper I hadn't had time to read in the morning. Before any of that, though, I felt I had to take a look at that fireplace.

It must have been a lovely one when it was new. It had glazed green tile on the surround, plus a floral tile border and pressed metal trim. All the inside work was gone, gas jets or andirons or whatever had been there at the beginning. Perhaps it was removed when the body was put there. I flinched, unwillingly picturing it. The questions came back. Why was it put there? Buried? Hidden? Was the fireplace walled over then, to hide it all? Or had that been done years earlier, when it stopped being used, and then the wall was ripped out and put back?

My appetite was gone. I poured a glass of wine and escaped to the deck. If I lit the candles out there on the table, I could read the paper, too. I wanted to think about the impersonal world outside my house, this refuge that no longer felt so safe, where a girl my daughter's age had seemingly disappeared a long time ago. I didn't want to think about who must have been looking for her way back then, or the terrible sadness if there was no one to look.

Actually, I felt a sudden need to hear my own daughter's voice.

"Hey, Joan. It's Erica. Is my child there and available?"

"Sure." Instant relief. "They've finishing the dishes. Erica, she was so helpful tonight, and such good company. She's a sweetie."

"Are we discussing the same child? Chris, the one who only grunts at me? When I'm lucky?"

Joan laughed. "She's wonderful here."

"Oh, yeah, and Mel is wonderful at my house, too. What's she like at home?"

She sighed. "The demon seed, of course. I'll get Chris. Hold a sec."

"Mom?"

"Hi, hon. Just wondering when you'll be back. Should I wait up? How will you get home?"

"Mom, I'm fifteen, and I'm a whole six blocks from home. Both of Mel's parents and her brother are right here. What more do you want?"

"I want know how you are getting home, if it will be late."

"Don't know, but someone will walk me. Stop babying me!"

"It's a legitimate question for a mother to ask, and I don't appreciate the whining. Joan told me how wonderful you are and I asked her who she was talking about."

A long silence, then in slightly more civil tone she said, "It's all good, mom. I'll get home safe."

"All I needed to know." I banged the phone down, but I was relieved. She was exactly where she said she would be, safe and happy.

Later, I happened to look out the front window from upstairs, as she came up the block with Melissa, their two heads bent together in serious conversation. They were squeezing in as much girl time as possible before Mel went off for a month at art camp. That was the summer Chris wanted too, but there was no way I could pay for it.

Mel's parents followed a discreet distance behind, arm in arm, a couple out for an evening stroll. All of them together looked like a family. I wondered with a pang if Chris felt that way too, as if this fulfilled some idea of family for her. Was that why she spent so much time there? Would it have been different if her father were with us?

She had gotten all grown up this year, my little girl, suddenly beautiful with legs a mile long. She was turning into someone new and I didn't know how to keep up. It had happened overnight, behind my back.

When she came upstairs she went straight into a thirty-minute shower, with music blasting out over the rushing water, and then she disappeared into her room. I crawled into bed, thinking that this was yet another night when we were sharing a home, but barely. I was drifting off when I heard my door open.

"I can't sleep."

She stood in the doorway in her sleep clothes—gym shorts and camisole—arms wrapped around herself as if trying not to shiver on this hot night. She was like a shadow in the dim light from the hall, the same little girl who used to come to me when she woke up from a bad dream, only taller.

"What?" I fumbled for the bedside lamp.

"Did I wake you?"

"Uh…no…uh…." I rubbed my eyes. "What is it, honey? Is thinking about the skeleton keeping you awake?"

"That's not exactly it."

"Come on in." I patted the edge of the bed. "I'm up now." She padded in barefoot and sat down.

"OK, it is the skeleton, but not the way you think. I mean, yes, I can't get it out of my head that it was a girl, a kid. She had her favorite music, like me, and her jewelry, and even a bear. I mean—well, I sleep with mine sometimes." She gasped. "Please never, ever tell anyone that!"

"I swear it. My lips are sealed. I have to admit, this discovery is haunting me too. If it's upsetting you so much, do you want to sleep at Mel's for a few nights? Then we can get rid of that fireplace forever, or maybe restore it to something beautiful. I bet that will send any ghosts right back where they belong."

She shook her head. "No, no, no, that's not it. It's not being scared." She fidgeted. "I was, at first, but now it seems more like sad. And really weird, of course. And I feel like—this sounds dumb, I know—I feel like I found her so I owe her something. I feel like she wants me to find out about her. Like dig out who was she and why was she here?"

"Hmm. I kind of understand how you feel…." The historian in me understood perfectly, but the mother in me was fumbling. "OK, yes I do, really, but you can't. It's a police matter now. I'm pretty sure they won't tell you a thing and you can't get in their way."

"I know that! I wouldn't, be, like, trying to solve it but I want to, you know, see that she isn't forgotten. Or lonely. You know?"

"But, Chris, it's obvious something truly terrible happened here. It was a crime of some kind. You can't be involved in this."

"But it was ages and ages ago. It's not like I found a…a…a corpse. It's more like archaeology." She looked at my face and heaved a great sigh. "I'm not convincing you, am I?"

Actually, I was tempted, but not enough to let her think this was a good idea. And it wasn't. "Not in the least," I said, not quite truthfully, but quite firmly. "It's absolutely out of the question. It's not even up for discussion."

"Mom! Why don't you ever let me do anything?"

What I should have said—calmly—was "Isn't that kind of a broad statement? If you calm down maybe we can work something out." What I did say—snapping—was, "You are out of your mind. This is something ugly and scary and you stay out of it. It's not going to happen. End of story!"

"You don't understand anything."

She ran to her room, slammed the door and left me feeling like the wicked stepmother. I felt like slamming doors myself. Instead, I went back to bed and lay there, wide awake, mind and emotions racing. A very long time later there was a tiny knock on mine.

"Well, then," Chris said, "you think we could…I mean, you could…or maybe Uncle Rick!…at least nudge them to tell us when they find out? If they do?"

"Yes, that I can try. Now maybe we could both try to get some sleep?"

She sat down, "I can't. I can't get back to sleep. I'm not scared. I'm not. I'm just…wide awake." She looked deeply embarrassed.

"I can see that. What would help? Cocoa?"

"Let's see."

It didn't, quite. After the cocoa, she stalled some more and finally said, "Come with me."

"What? You don't want me to sleep with you?"

"No way!" She looked shocked. "Of course not, but, maybe, could you sort of, you know, stay with me a little?"

"Oh, honey. Yes I can." I thought a minute. "Now, don't jump on me, but do you want me to read you to sleep?"

To my surprise, she did. I turned the light as low as possible, just as I used to do in the long ago days before she could read to herself, and in my softest, most soporific voice, I began, for the first time in many years: "It was difficult, later, to think of a time when Betsy and Tacy had not been friends." She was asleep before the end of the second chapter.

However, I tossed and turned all night, half sleeping, half dreaming, half remembering. The corpse haunted my sleep, all mixed up with Chris' questions. Once I awoke suddenly, so confused I rolled over to wrap myself around my husband.

I used to be married to a boy from my old neighborhood. I met him at my best friend's Sweet Sixteen barbecue. To this day, he comes back to me with warm summer nights, the radio playing "Heaven is a Place on Earth," and the smell of grilling hot dogs. He was big and cute and so shy I had to embarrass him into dancing with me there on Shelly's patio. We never danced with anyone else, ever again. We were deaf to all concerns from my Jewish parents and his Italian ones. We knew we belonged together.

He took me to my high school prom, wearing a tux with ice blue lapels to match my satin gown. We stayed out all night and had breakfast on the beach, watching the sun come up over the Rockaways. For graduation he gave me a locket with a diamond chip in it, and said it was a promise on a ring. Two years later I went to his fire department graduation and cried because he was so handsome in his uniform, one of New York's bravest now like his dad and half our neighbors.

We had sweet, ordinary plans and dreams. He would study hard and move up the ranks. I would keep riding the bus over to Brooklyn College and become a social studies teacher. We got married a week after I graduated with my teaching degree. We had six bridesmaids in lilac ruffles and I got pregnant one margarita-fueled afternoon on our Bahamas honeymoon. The grandmothers baby-sat and I began to teach.

We planned to save our money, buy a house, have more babies while we were still young enough to enjoy them. On spring weekends, we explored different neighborhoods, pretending we were shopping for the dream house we were a long way from being able to buy.

One Sunday afternoon while he was out riding his bike a drunk driver killed him. He was twenty-six, Chrissie was three, and I became a twenty-four-year-old widow.

I keep thinking there must be lesson for our daughter in all this. I sure don't want Chris to marry that young, but I can't tell her we weren't happy.

Well, Brooklyn girls are nothing if not tough. After I emerged a little from the fog of shock and grief, I saw that I had to take care of my baby and myself. Life forcing me to find plan B. I went back to school for a master's degree so I could become a high-school history teacher and maybe a principal some day.

And then I surprised myself. I fell in love with scholarship. My professors encouraged me, I got some fellowships, I started a PhD program in history. I am finally going away to college, all the way to Manhattan, less than an hour on the subway, to the City University Graduate Center. I became a scholar in training, and fell into a life that my Jeff didn't even know existed.

He wouldn't know me if he came back now as the boy he was then. Wouldn't know how to talk to me, and wouldn't even want to. My world has turned out to be much bigger than the one I expected to live in.

Yet some days, I'd give it all up—everything I am now, everything I have—for a single summer night in the back seat of his father's Chevy, parked at the beach with the sound of the surf rushing in and out.

I turned over in bed, pulled the pillow over my head, looked at the clock a dozen times, dozed off. I knew my worries about Chris had set off all those memories. I wanted Jeff to be there so much I was bringing him back in my sleep.

I woke up exhausted, my eyes barely focusing, but those three o'clock in the morning ghosts were gone. I had my life and I had to get on with it. As I expected, there were no sounds from Chris' room. Joe had given her the day off, so like any teen she would sleep until the afternoon. Adolescence turns them all into vampires.

I got myself ready for work and out the door with my own brain still asleep. Afterwards, I couldn't remember if I'd noticed the photographer on the block that morning, or not.

Chapter Four

I did see him late that afternoon, though, getting in and out of a big black Cadillac, and snapping pictures in all directions. It barely registered until later, that he was still there and seemed to be taking pictures of my house. He was stopping people as they walked by and having little conversations too.

A street tree blocked a full view of the license places. Chastising myself for paranoia, I nevertheless jotted down the numbers I could see. I found myself drifting past the front windows. Yes, that car was still there, every time. I wondered if he was the person who had written about us online. And why would he care?

The next time I looked out, I saw Chris standing in front of the car writing something. Of all days, today Joe was on another job. It would have been nice to have a friend watching my back when I stormed out.

I was just in time to see the very large, youngish white photographer get of out of the car. He snatched the paper from Chris' hand and ripped it into confetti.

"Chris! Into the house. Right now." I stood between her and the guy, not taking my eyes off him, but I could feel her mutinous expression through my back. "No arguments! Move!" From behind me I heard her run across the street.

"What are you doing here?"

"Who the fuck are you?"

I didn't recognize him personally but I knew him as soon as he opened his mouth. He was all the playground bullies of my childhood, all the Brooklyn hitters who hung around street corners making obscene suggestions when I was in high school. The girl I used to be back then came stomping in to take over. I thought, so we're going to have to talk dirty? Yeah, I know how to do that.

"What the fuck are you doing, hanging around my block? Taking pictures of my house?"

He was unimpressed. "It's a fucking public block, bitch. I can be here, minding my own business, which is more than you're doing."

"Are you the guy who wrote about us on Brownstone Bytes?' To be honest, he didn't look like an Internet enthusiast, or sound like one either.

He looked confused. "What if I am? It's none of your business."

He had moved uncomfortably close. He wasn't a pretty sight, that close. I took two steps back, and a deep breath and said firmly, "It *is* my business. What are you up to? Nothing right, I bet."

"Like I said, bitch, mind your own business."

"There's nothing here worth photographing, so stay away from my house."

"Maybe I'm looking for some dumb young girl to take for a ride. Yours would do." He smiled. Like a snake. "She's pretty cute. She'd do fine. Why, I could…"

"Get lost!" I heard a voice shouting. It was my voice. "Move on, or you'll be discussing your business with a cop in five minutes."

His face was turning red and I realized, a little late, that I might actually be in danger. Then he looked around and saw doors being opened up and down the block. "Ahhh, fuck it. There are other ways." He got into the car and sped off, spraying gravel.

I collapsed then, right on the curb. My head was on my knees. I didn't know if I was a heroine or an idiot, if I should laugh or cry, if I should be terrified or proud. By then, neighbors who had heard the commotion were out on the street, helping me up, and even confused old Mary seemed to be hovering around the edge of the crowd. Chris was rushing back down the front steps.

"Mom? Mom! Are you all right? Are you nuts?" She turned to our neighbors. "Did you see that guy?"

"Oh, yeah. Big. Scary. Mrs. Donato, you are one crazy woman."

"I know." I shook my head. "I know." I was calming down. "I'm OK, now. I guess. Let's go in."

"You sure? Well, call if you need anything," Mr. Pastore said. "Me or the missus, we'll come right over." All the others murmured similar support, but I thanked them and waved them away

"Jeez, Mom! What were you thinking?"

"I don't know. Maybe I wasn't thinking. I got mad. He threatened, sweetie. Us. Neighborhood, block, me, you. And we've already had one bad thing lately. And just what were you thinking, young lady?"

"Well, he was there for awhile, taking lots of pictures. I felt him sort of looking at me just now. It was creeping me out so I wanted to see if I could, like, report him. I needed some information…."

"Don't you have any sense at all? You're only fifteen! Hasn't the rule always, always, been: if something seems creepy, get help?"

"Oh, yeah. Whatever." She eyed me cautiously, as if I were a strange new person. "Can I get you something? Soda?"

"That would be great. The real thing, with sugar and caffeine."

We moved inside and I flopped onto the sofa, head back, feet up. As the adrenaline ebbed away, my ability to think started to return. I had learned precisely nothing, except that Cadillac guy didn't like me one bit and he might be up to no good.

That sure was productive. I sighed and reached for the telephone. I was going to feel like a complete fool, telling this story to any member of the police department, but I knew I had to.

It turned out that some of my neighbors had also reported the loitering car.

Chris and I gave our information to an officer who called it a report of suspicious person. He wasn't extremely reassuring about what follow-up there would be. As soon as he was done with us, we locked the doors, turned on loud music, and raided the refrigerator.

"Remember Uncle Rick is coming for dinner tonight. He's bringing the pizza."

"I don't know...I might have plans..."

"Yes, you definitely do have plans. You plan to be here for dinner. Anything else can be done later."

"Oh, all right. Mom? You think I could talk to him alone for a little while?" She brightened at the thought. "I'd like to ask him about some stuff."

"I'm sure he'd be delighted."

"You should ask him for advice yourself."

"About what happened today? You think I could use some?"

She gave me that patented teenager look, that one that says, "Well, duh," without a sound.

I was too stubborn to admit it to her, or anyone, but I did need a shoulder to lean on, right about then. I couldn't wait for Rick to walk through that door.

I don't remember a part of my life when he was not there. He and my dad grew up together. Dad's bum knee kept him out of the police department, but he and Rick had a bond that even the famous blue line didn't weaken. My dad got him through two bitter divorces; he got my dad through my mother's long illness and her death.

A couple of years ago, they had helped each other accept the idea that it was time to retire, though after that they'd somehow seemed less close. There was no open quarrel, or at least not one they told me about, but a drifting, a coolness, that I barely noticed at first.

For me, he was and remained more of a favorite uncle than any of my real uncles. I didn't have much of an extended family. My mom was an only child and my hot-blooded dad and his siblings were often on the outs with each other. Rick was the one who bought expensive toys for Chris and perfume for me, did odd jobs that needed height, invited himself for dinner and often brought it with him. I think what we gave him was a family.

He was more than an adopted uncle. He stood in for a dad, during all those many times I could not talk to my own bull-headed father.

My first fight ever with Rick was when I moved to this handy-man's special in a fringe neighborhood and our second, bigger fight was when I decided to use my mother's legacy to fix it up. He had raised hell with me, dragged me to see neat, dull Cape Cods in safe, dull suburbs, and even invoked my mother's pre-sumed opinions. The words "roll over in her grave" were used.

After all that, did I really want him to know what had hap-pened in my house? No, not at all, but I did really want to know he was there in my corner. He always was.

Before he arrived, I ran out for some dessert, and there was Mary, lounging against my little iron fence.

"Hi, dearie." She slurred the words. It looked like this was one of her less lucid days. "I saw those cops the other day. That never means good news."

"It was all right, really. They came to help. I'm rushing to the store now. Can I get you anything?"

She followed me down the block. "It always means something bad is happening. Or did happen. I used to know a lot of cops, when bad things happened. I hope your sweet little girl is all right."

"Everything is fine, Mary." I was somewhat desperate to get away. "We're all fine. Please don't worry."

She nodded. "All right, if you say so. But...." She suddenly looked more alert, as if something seemed to come into her mind. Then it left again. She turned and shuffled away, and I hustled off on my errands in the opposite direction.

An hour later, back at home, I opened my front door to a cloud of enticing garlic and tomato smells, and a tall, bald man almost hidden behind two warm, damp pizza boxes.

"Here, give me that load!"

"Hey, honey!" He gave me a bear hug. "I want to see where you found this body Chris told me about."

I pointed him to the decrepit fireplace, empty now but with the last shreds of the yellow police tape trailing from above.

"What a thing. Sure is a weird story. I told you this was no place for you, didn't I?"

He looked at me, must have seen a fight in my eyes, and shifted gears right away. "They know anything? Nah, what am I saying? Way too soon and they probably wouldn't tell you anyway. Who's investigating? Anyone giving you a hard time?"

"Not really, but it seemed like they wondered, a little, if we might be involved somehow. As if I really could be someone who'd bury a body in her house! Chris gave him what for. You would have been proud."

He pocketed the detective's card I handed him. "I'll ask around. You call me, if they give you any problems. Promise?"

"Sure thing."

"OK." Then he bellowed, "Where is that beautiful daughter of yours?"

"Uncle Rick?" She stood in the doorway, smiling and self-conscious with pleasure. A year ago, she would have thrown herself into his arms.

"Christine Marie, come give me a hug. I swear you grew a foot since I saw you last."

She giggled. I handed her one of the pizza boxes, and we took our dinner to the deck to eat by candle light under the striped umbrella.

Rick passed me a beer and said, "I think Miss Christine here is old enough?"

"Certainly not! She gets a soda."

"Oh, Mom? Please!"

"Just one tiny sip, for the taste. And I mean one."

"OK. Thank you." Rick's presence seemed to be a good influence, as I noticed further when she jumped up to clear the table.

"Thanks, honey. I'll do the dishes. You two can visit out here for awhile, and then I'll bring out some ice cream."

I stacked the dishes in the pitted, stained sink, and put the leftovers away in the noisy, leaky refrigerator that barely came up to my shoulder. Other women daydream about movie stars and tropical islands and fur coats. I daydream about gleaming stainless steel sinks, refrigerators with automatic icemakers, and shiny tile countertops.

I left the kitchen window open to the deck. Over the noise of running water and rattling dishes, I could hear snatches of their conversation.

His deep voice was louder and came through more clearly. "There's a cold case unit," he said. "That's for real old cases that were never exactly closed. I don't think I know anyone there now. I could get you a number, but I'm not going to, no way."

Her high voice murmured back, too soft for me to distinguish words, and then his response cut through clearly again. "Cause it's the dumbest idea I ever heard, that's why. What is your mother thinking, to let you do this?"

I caught an incoherent protest.

"I got it. Only research, no messing with police stuff, but you have to listen up. You can't even imagine what things were like then. This was a neighborhood heading straight for the sewer. Gangs. Drug houses. Real ugly, scary stuff. And you know there's something ugly here. Honey, it's not right for a nice young girl like you to mess around in this."

I turned the water off in time to hear her say, "Grandpa would help me if he was here."

"Your grandpa? The guy who drove a cab his whole life? After the things he saw driving and the stories he heard from his cop friends? Hell, no. He'd want to protect you from everything. Of course he'd do any other any damn fool thing you asked him to. He's a real grandpa kind of guy."

"I know. I can't get used to him being away. Moving to Phoenix was so lame. I mean, Phoenix?"

"I know he misses you too, but come on, the docs said his asthma was gonna kill him if he didn't get out of the city. You know that's why he retired."

Sure, I thought, that and the new woman who also said she'd kill him—or leave him. Dear old dad.

"Not that I don't miss him too. We were the best of buddies. Did I ever tell you about the time...."

He was changing the subject, sidetracking Chris from her interest in the dead girl, and no doubt using a hilariously disreputable story, unfit for her young ears, to do it. Time to rejoin the conversation. I brought out ice cream.

Chris heaped up her bowl, excused herself, and took her dessert into the house. Rick and I lingered, companionably stretching our legs out on the extra deck chairs, savoring the garden's quiet and the scent of my neighbor's roses.

He looked at me for a long time, with an odd expression, and finally said, "Chris said something about you needing my advice?"

"She did? Must have been when I had the water running."

"I don't suppose it's about your love life."

"What love life! No, it's cop stuff. Sort of."

He raised one eyebrow but only said, "Oh?"

After I told him about the encounter, he had a lot more to say, some of it blistering. Then he calmed down enough to ask, "Who did you piss off?"

"The guy in the car, obviously."

"Yeah, but is there anyone else? Someone who might have sent him to scare you?"

"That's ridiculous. He was only taking pictures, even if he had a nasty attitude. I work in a museum, for crying out loud. I'm in grad school. I'm a mom. Could I be any more boring?"

"I don't know what this is about, but it worries me. It couldn't be a break-in in the planning stage, because, honey, you have nothing worth stealing. And do I have this right, that he didn't seem to be after Chris specifically?"

"You mean like stalking her?" I shook my head. "She was out and around on the street several times during the day, and he never made a move. If anything, she went after him."

"What did your local cops say?"

"Not much. They'll keep an eye on the block."

"You keep an eye on your daughter."

"Yes, they said that too."

Then he said, "You might live a tame little life but you don't exactly find a body in your house every day."

"Oh, come on." Somehow, I didn't want to hear this. I really didn't want to. "That body was put there a long time ago. We're all sure about that. How could it be a problem for me?"

"Let's see. Someone wrote about it, and then someone shows up, takes pictures, and acts scary. And there's no connection? You know I'm right. Like always."

"No. If I'm a historian I have to believe in connections. Kind of goes with that territory, but in my life, I don't know. The worst thing that ever happened to me, ever, was dumb, blind chance, the thing you can't look out for, the drunk driver in the park."

He held my hand and I went on.

"After that, I could have become afraid of every single thing. Easily. So I decided I never would, and I never would do that to Chris. We would be two strong women."

"Honey, I get that. I really do But it doesn't mean the existence of random drunk drivers says you stop looking both ways when you cross the street. Right?"

My grumpy silence told him I was thinking about it.

"Your daughter seems way too concerned about this. She has an itch to look into it herself."

"I told her no. Definitely, absolutely no."

"Yeah, I was extremely discouraging too. I hope she got it." He patted my shoulder. "Look, honey. Keep your eyes on her to know what she's getting up to, keep your eyes open generally, and call me right away if anything at all doesn't seem right, no matter how trivial. OK? And for god's sake, no more jumping into situations. Think first, instead of being that hothead you've always been. You know?"

"Shut up, Rick," I swatted him lightly on the arm. "I used to hear enough of that from Dad. I don't need two fathers."

"After what I heard tonight, I think you need a whole tribe of them. Strict ones."

I had no good answer for that, so, for once, I didn't say any-thing, and just let the silence unfold.

"Don't you think you ought to tell him what's happened?'

"Who? Dad?"

"Yes, dad. Your father?"

"He chose to go off to the other side of the country with that woman. It wasn't me deserting him."

"You know," he said gently, "even old guys get lonely. Your mother was one in a million, but he's only sixty-five. He still has a lot of years ahead of him. He worked real hard all his life. You know that. He had a nest egg from selling his taxi medallion, and a house free and clear. He earned his time to kick back. It's been a year. Don't you think it's time to mend fences?"

I sat there in stubborn silence, looking away from him, unconvinced by his words and afraid that if I tried to answer, my emotions would come out in my voice. Out of the corner of my eye I could see him shake his head, and then he broke the silence with another abrupt subject change. "Speaking of love life, cookie, seeing anyone?"

"None of your business."

"Yes, it is. I'm standing in for your dad."

"Did he ask you do that, before he left? Check on me? He did, didn't he? What nerve!"

"Nope." His red face contradicted his perfect composure. "Nope, I'm just looking after your welfare. I know at least a couple of likely single cops I could bring around."

"Oh, pul—eeze! If they're old enough for me, they're divorced with lots of baggage. I have quite enough of my own, thank you very much."

"We all do, honey," he said gently. "Your dad too. We work around it."

I didn't want to talk about that, not at all, so I changed subjects on him, "What happened with you and Dad? Was it that woman?"

"Ah, maybe. And he didn't like some of my friends, too." Another long silence, then he said, "Hey, I've got a good idea.

Send Chris off to that camp she wanted, with her friend. That should sidetrack her. You rip out the fireplace, put up new drywall, paint it, wallpaper. By the time she's home it will all be forgotten."

"I doubt it. She's pretty stubborn." But, I thought, it would be wonderful if he were right.

"Now there's a surprise. Your kid, and Len's grandkid? Stubborn? How could that have happened?"

"Besides, you have no idea what those camps cost. I'm barely covering her school fees, even with her scholarship. Add up my fellowship, social security, Jeff's insurance and I'm still barely hanging on. I already wake up worrying at two a.m."

"How about the Uncle Rick camp scholarship?" He halted my protests with an upraised palm. "I'll get a check in the mail tomorrow. Honey, you need to get her out of here for a while. Trust me. I've got good instincts."

When I tried to say more, he stopped me again. "She's the closest I'll ever come to a grandkid. Let me do this."

Then he went back into the house and shouted up the stairs, "Christine Marie, get your cute butt down here and say good bye!"

She came charging down the stairs, threw herself at him for a good-bye hug, but said, "I'm still mad at you."

He chucked her under the chin. "I love you too."

I walked him to the door and saw him off. Mary was out there, leaning on my fence, as if she'd been waiting for me.

"You have a gentleman caller? How very lovely that is. Now, dear, I did have something very, very important to tell you." She looked confused. "I can't quite, quite remember what it was. I believe it was about the police coming. Or maybe it was about gentlemen callers. I know it will come back to me in a minute."

"Well, you can just tell me about it whenever it does. How's that?"

She brightened up. "Wait. I do know. I have it right here." She was pulling an astonishing variety of junk from her skirt pockets—empty potato chip bags, advertising flyers, Kleenex, cigarette stubs, a half-eaten apple. "Here it is!" She handed me a scrap of paper with a dim row of numbers and letters scrawled on it.

"I don't understand. What is this?"

She looked all around, and up and down the block, then leaned over and whispered, "License plate, dear. That terrible man who was yelling at you. Thought you might like it." She smiled sweetly. "Now I'll go on about my business." Off she went, down the block, heading to who knows where. And I had the license plate number. Maybe we could nail the s.o.b. after all. Always assuming this was a day Mary was living in our world and not one of her own invention.

Chapter Five

My first thought the next morning, before I even opened my eyes, was Mary. I rolled over in bed and called the precinct with her information. The officer on the phone promised to pass it on when the right man came in, but I thought I'd better call again later, just to make sure.

My second was that stupid local gossip board. There it was, right at the top, a photo of our house and another series of questions. Even in my anger at having my very own life out there on the blogosphere, I noticed that the writing seemed a lot more literate than the person I had confronted. He had certainly been taking pictures, though. I assured myself this would stop if there were no more news, and at the same time, I thought about writing an angry post myself. I needed to think that over. I had been making promises not to be such a hothead.

When I finally went downstairs I found Joe sitting in my kitchen, drinking coffee and looking thoughtful.

"What is going on? Are you waiting for your crew?"

He only said, quietly, "I heard an interesting story about you this morning from one of your neighbors. Have you completely lost your mind?"

I had intended to tell him a highly edited version of what happened yesterday. I did want him to keep an eye open for that car. It seemed I no longer had that choice, and realistically, Chris would have blabbed anyway. When I finished telling him the whole story, he told me, still quietly, that I was a complete idiot.

"I don't know about that," I protested, without a lot of conviction.

"Whatever he was or wasn't up to, he sounds like a nut case. You should have called me. For crying out loud, Erica, what if he'd punched you? Don't you know there are people who worry about you?"

"Well, what if you were here, and he punched you?"

He gave me a don't-be-stupid look and said, "I'm not you, obviously. I could have punched him back. You weigh—what? Hundred and ten?"

"You know what? Yes, it was dumb, but I'm kind of glad I didn't let him scare me. And I did make him leave us alone, so good for me!"

He laughed and shook his head. "All right, small but fierce, good for you. And if he didn't scare you then, how about now?"

"OK. Now I am scared. Or, sort of nervous, anyway."

"I'm glad to see you still have a little sense. I'm going to get some supplies out of the truck and my crew will be here any minute." He stood up. "Try not to do anything dangerous before then. Think you can manage that?"

At that moment I knew I could lean on Joe but I didn't want to. He is older than I am, but not at all old enough to be a father figure. That's not our relationship. He's more of a big brother figure, my neighborhood buddy. We hang out, we barbecue, we kid each other. He shovels my walk, I advise him on his complex love life. That's how it has always been from the first time we met, when a cousin of my husband sent him to help me with a house repair.

His work crew began drifting in and soon they were ripping out the scary bathroom with the hole in the floor.

I sat at my computer, door shut tight, working, but the noise and chaos on the second floor soon made concentration impossible. I wasn't expected at my part-time job today, which made it the perfect day to go in and get a lot done there, while escaping from the noise and confusion here. Not everyone would be thrilled to spend a morning looking at microfilm of decades-old neighborhood newspapers, but I was. Perhaps the seed was sown in third grade, when I read the Little House books and the Betsy-Tacy books and realized there was something called "a long time ago" where little girls like me lived very different lives.

An hour later I was in my cubicle, glued to my desk, buried deep in my printouts and news clips when I heard a tentative, "Excuse me? They directed me here at the entrance. Would you be Erica Donato?"

"Uh, yes." I dragged my brain back from Brooklyn in the 1950s and I'm sure I looked as unfocused as I felt.

"I'm Steve Richmond, Darcy's friend. You look busy. I'm sorry if I'm interrupting."

Oh, crap. I'd completely forgotten we had an appointment. He was tall, slim, dark-haired, in tan pants and a striped dress shirt with rolled up sleeves, matching tan jacket slung over his shoulder. Loosely knotted silk tie. Elegant Mark Cross attaché, just like Darcy's—the reason I recognized it—in his hand. Nice enough but I was busy.

He didn't look that sorry. He sounded tentative but he looked confident.

"Yes." I almost stuttered it, I was so surprised. "I'm sorry… Darcy…she didn't say you would be…."

"Were you expecting someone different?"

"Yes, I was." I might have sounded indignant. "I was expecting a gray-haired guy in a Brooks Brother suit. She said a friend of her dad's. I've *met* her dad."

"Ah, you were expecting the traditional model. I'm sorry to disappoint you." He leaned over and whispered, "We haul those guys out of storage to meet with the major investors." And he smiled. "I do play golf with her father, but I went to business school with Darcy."

I gave up. "Come on in." I waved to the only chair in my tiny, cluttered space. "Just what is it that Darcy thinks I can do for you?"

"She says you are an expert in the history of Brooklyn neighborhoods."

"I don't know about that. I am writing a dissertation, and I am working here on an exhibit…"

"I've known Darcy since b-school and her judgment of useful sources is never wrong."

"That's exactly what I have found!"

"So there." He smiled. "She can't be wrong about you. Let me explain the problem I am working on. I have a client who is thinking about a major investment in this part of Brooklyn. I can't say more as it's entirely under the radar for now. He wants to do it right and he also wants to do it without a lot of controversy. We're just in the early stages of defining what the 'right way' would be and that means getting a lot of background." The polite tentativeness was gone. He was all business, crisp and to the point. "Could you help with that? There would certainly be a nice consulting fee. We don't expect you to give away your time and expertise."

I was flabbergasted. I really had no time. None. But I sure could use the money. And what was this mysterious project anyway?

I looked at the pile of work on my desk, the calendar on my wall with looming job and academic deadlines, and thought about how one of the deadlines was Chris' next school payment. So I held my breath and said, "Yes." Followed immediately with, "What would you expect from me?"

"Why don't we start with a conversation and see what develops?"

I nodded, keeping quiet so I would not say something dumb, or inappropriate, or unbusinesslike. Business to me was maybe a neighborhood hardware store. A construction crew. The guy who fixed my ancient plumbing. I sensed I was now in a whole different realm.

"We are starting with the basic assumptions that development is neutral. It can be positive for some and negative for others; it is possible to create new properties for profit while preserving neighborhoods and also, alternatively, to wreck them." He added, with a self-deprecating smile, "We also know that the very word 'development' is liable to raise fears and lead to—let's say, confrontations. My client really, and I mean that strongly, does not want that. So they—my client—feels that we will do a better job if we get a good sense for how these things have played out in the past."

"That's where I come in?"

"Exactly. Am I making sense so far?"

"Sure. It's way too complex an issue for a quick discussion though. There are whole academic careers built on this topic." I remembered he went to Harvard Business School with Darcy and added, "As I'm sure you know." This was not, after all, a high school student doing a social studies assignment.

"For now, we need a get-smart-quick orientation. The view from 40,000 feet, let's say. How about some case studies? That's how we like to organize information and it's a great way to focus it for the client. Can you give us examples of some situations that were done well, and some disasters?"

"Hmm. Probably. Let me give it some thought. Can I send you a list? Do you specifically want Brooklyn? That's what I know best."

"Exactly. Some very local examples would have the most impact."

"My own neighborhood is practically a case study in neighborhood change and it will probably be one of the examples in our exhibit. Where I live is on the very rough edge of a highly gentrified area..."

"Park Slope, right? Near Darcy?"

"Park Slope, yes. Near Darcy, no. Big difference. Huge. She lives in the very gentrified section. Let me see if I have some pictures that would show you the difference." I looked over my paper-covered desk and started moving things around. "Somewhere in here. Aha."

I handed him a booklet about the posh historic district, and some recent photos from other, less renovated blocks. He lined up the two sources side by side on the edge of my desk, and turned the pages with interest. "I'm seeing what you meant. Here we have the historic district, looking pretty shabby, right? And here, after what I guess is considerable restoration. And revived main street shopping too. Skyrocketing property values here?"

"See?" He smiled. "You are already earning a fee, with this material and the idea of some interviews. Let's say...."

"Well, well, well. It's Steve Richmond! I just got your message. What brings you across the river to my world?"

I looked up and it was the director of the museum, standing right there at my cubical entrance. Smiling. That had never happened before. I was sure he did not know my name.

Richmond stood up and grabbed the boss in an enthusiastic handshake. "You got my message! I had business at one of the courthouses and came over to get a little education from Ms. Donato here. She is a friend of a friend."

He looked at me, and back at Steven, "And has she been helpful?"

"Very much so. You have a good employee here."

"I'm sure of that." I wondered if he would remember my name next time he saw me. "Now I'm taking you to my club for lunch. "

Richmond gathered up his papers. "I'll hear from you then?" he said to me. "With more information? And I'd really like to have some of those photos. Here's my card with all my contacts. And you will hear from me too. Do you have a card?" I shook my head and quickly jotted down my phone and e-mail. "I'll get a proper consulting agreement sent to you." He turned to the director, "That's all right, isn't it? For her to work for me off hours?'

"Of course, of course. Give Steve any help he wants and consider it cleared with me. He is an old Deerfield roommate and if you make him happy enough, maybe we can even lure him onto the museum board." He winked.

Steven laughed. "I'm in your sights, is that it?"

"You know it." As they left, he was saying, "Now, tell me, have you heard from Buzzy? Or Dex? We're planning a reunion...."

And they were gone.

I was about to have a consulting contract. I wasn't sure what that would entail, except that it was one more responsibility. What had I done? And what did he really do on his job? The business card was on thick creamy stock, with real engraving, like a wedding invitation, discreet and elegant. The company name was discreet too and told me precisely nothing. His title was director. I tried unsuccessfully to call Darcy and get her to tell me what to expect, and to explain why she deceived me about who he was. Her dad's golf buddy? I still felt indignant about that.

But Deerfield was a fancy boarding school and he was a friend of our museum director. Just as Darcy had predicted.

And I had accomplished precisely zero for the museum today, but there was one useful thing I could still do. I called the precinct again.

"Mrs. Donato, we were about to call you. Good news, bad news. We ran the plates, but the owner reported those plates stolen awhile ago and the car doesn't match…"

I groaned.

"Yeah, well, it was long shot. Here's the good news. Since a couple of other people reported it, we're keeping our eyes open—we'd like to know what he's up to—but it doesn't look like it was directed at you. He was seen parked in other places too. We've got a few pictures we'd like you to take a look at, known neighborhood nuisances and such."

Relief flooded through me. He's a neighborhood nuisance, that's all. This was not about us. I was not going to send my daughter away. I was not going to cash Rick's check, no matter what he said. What I was going to do was get on with my life.

Right now, getting on with my life meant getting some actual work done. I headed to the museum archives where material was waiting for me.

My job is really an internship with a tiny stipend. I need the money and experience, they need the labor and it fits perfectly with my academic work. The museum is dedicated to local Brooklyn history, everything from the Dutch settlements to the building of the Brooklyn Bridge to the most recent immigrants from Afghanistan, Ghana, Russia, Yemen, Jamaica. Part of our mission is to educate the public that history is happening all the time. Eventually I will write a paper for credit about my work here.

My assignment was to research background for an upcoming exhibit about neighborhoods changing through the decades, and all the turmoil that created. No doubt that's why Darcy had hooked me up with this Steven Richmond.

Scrolling through the newspaper film, I found everyday lives laid out for me in words and pictures. There were graduations from public, private, and parochial schools. The hairstyles changed from backcombed beehives to the long, straight Joan Baez look to the curly shag and the cute Hamill wedge. Hmm. That one looked like my own graduation picture. And of course there were the mothers with beehives and the daughters with shags, too. And fathers with military-trim barbering and sons with flowing curls and drooping mustaches.

The clothing styles went from prim dresses for women and stiff suits for men to flowing bell-bottoms and daisy prints for everyone. Only the parochial school uniforms were the same from one decade to the next.

And the smiles for Halloween, graduation, First Communion, prom were the same, year after year.

New businesses opened, with proud owners holding the first lucky dollar in a photo. Most of those stores have come and gone. I miss the friendly butchers at 3 Vets Meats, but here was Park Diner, seemingly immortal, in a picture from the 1950s, and here was a corner bar that had changed names from Eagle to Flynn's to Shamrock to Oak, but never disappeared.

I looked at the street scenes with teenagers and wondered if the girl in our house was in any of them, part of the everyday crowd, living her everyday life. Until…

I mentally slapped myself and ordered my mind to focus on work.

Politicians were criticized, defended themselves, faded or were promoted out of local public life. There were letters from the early seventies, railing about the hippies who were moving in, and from the eighties, railing about the investment bankers moving in.

One of the summer interns popped in to chat and pass on the gossip that the boss was really pushing on deadlines. Great. Just what I needed to hear.

Actually, I did tend to get sidetracked, so fascinated by these tiny windows into life in the recent past that I almost forgot researching. By the end of the day, though, I had learned about some major actions way back when. Landlords were sued, and by the city, no less! There was even a small-scale riot. I made copies and notes. A tenants organization and its lawyer. A judge. A reporter who kept showing up as the author of the news reports.

That reporter, Brendan Leary, intrigued me.

He would be such a terrific source for our exhibit. He seemed to know everyone and be everywhere, and he wrote with passion. Then he seemed to disappear. I ran a Nexis search, hoping his byline would turn up at another paper.

No luck. I found a few other Brendan Learys and tracked them down. There was a fireman in the Bronx, an Aer Lingus pilot with a beautiful Irish accent who tried to get a date, a potter in Boston named Brenda Leary who was annoyed to find out she was showing up as Brendan. No reporters or ex-reporters.

I refused to believe he could not be found.

The major paper where he had worked might have some records for him but in a large organization, which department might be the most helpful with information? Dope, I said to myself. If you want information, start with the library. A couple of phone extensions later, I was talking so someone at the newspaper library's reference desk.

I explained what I wanted and the voice at the other end exclaimed, "Brendan Leary? Why, I haven't thought about that old reprobate in a decade or so! Good thing you got me today. I'm the only old-timer still here. Sure, I knew him. He retired a long time ago. No party or anything, just left, just like that. Not a clue as to what's become of him. Well, you've given me a very interesting problem."

"I'm sorry. I didn't mean…"

"We live for interesting problems. I have a few ideas. Give me your number and I'll see what I can do. I'll get back to you Monday or Tuesday."

I had accomplished a lot today and as I started to wind up, I suppose it was inevitable that I started thinking about our skeleton again, much as I had hoped to push it away with work. My work on this project was too close to my home.

I wondered again if that living girl was in any of these pictures? Had she walked these streets or spoken to these people? What was she doing in my house that caused her death? Of course that's what I really wanted to know.

I forced myself to stop thinking and to stop working, too. I closed up all my folders, stacked up my notes, and left. I stopped in at the precinct and examined an array of photos but none of them were the ugly guy in front of my house. So much for my fantasies of seeing him hauled off in cuffs. And I did have to ask myself what exactly could be the charge? Annoying me—no, scaring me—probably was not cause for an arrest.

When I got home, Joe was washing the dust from his arms in my kitchen sink, but Chrissie was nowhere in sight.

"She asked for the day off," he told me. "She said she had to do something important and it would be fine with you."

"Well, it's not fine. It would be nice if she would clear these changes with me. Or if you would. What were you thinking?"

"That she's smart and responsible? You worry too much. See you tomorrow."

Chris came home a few minutes later.

"Mom, I had the most interesting day!"

"I'm sure you did, not being at work and all."

"I asked Joe and he said it was OK." The excitement was replaced with uncertainty. "I mean, wasn't that the right thing to do?"

"It depends on what you were doing, which you did not tell him. How about telling me?"

"I—I don't want to." She saw my expression and added quickly, "I mean, not yet. It's—it's a secret. You won't mind, honest. I just—I just—I needed to do something myself." I'm sure my face was grim; hers was a mixture of uncertainty and defiance.

"This isn't all right, Chris. You can't take off for a day with nobody knowing where you are. What if...?"

"Mom!" It was the three-syllable mom, as only a teenager can say it. "I'm not going to get into any trouble. I'm smart and I'm careful. Or is that you don't trust me?"

I was staring at defeat and I knew it. Did I trust her intentions? Probably. Did I trust her good sense? Not completely. Does any parent of a teen? Nope, not really.

Was it a good idea to tell her that? I didn't know. I gave up. For now.

"OK, miss," I said. "You get a pass this time. Don't make me sorry I believe you and next time you take off for the day, I want to know. Got it?"

She heaved a great, martyred sigh, muttered yes, and stalked from the room. Wise choice. One of us had to. The old stairs shook under the angry pounding of her platform sandals and almost immediately music poured from her room at top volume. The volume was normal but the choice was odd. From way before her time, and even before mine, it was The Doors who were rocking the house, singing about lighting their fire.

I sighed and resigned myself to being unable to work as long as Chris was home. I could go up, though, and switch on my bedroom air conditioner, change into cooler clothes, check my e-mail.

My computer screen was covered with a piece of paper. A note from Chris?

It said: REMEMBER WHAT HAPPENED TO THE CURIOUS CAT. CATS AND THEIR KITTENS SHOULD NOT ASK QUESTIONS.

Chapter Six

My blood turned cold. I used to think that was a poetic figure of speech. It is not. The blood froze first, then my breathing seemed to freeze, too. Then my knees buckled and I had to sit down.

Was this a threat? It *was* a threat. My brain must have chilled too, because it took a minute to sink in, that someone had been in my house. He let himself in. Walked around here in my room. Touched my things.

Was he still there? No, I thought, no, not very likely, with Chris and me having been in almost every room of our small house. Still there was the basement and the empty downstairs apartment. There were closets and the roof, accessed by a trap door in the ceiling, at the top of a shaky internal ladder. In a closed vertical passageway. By then my heart was beating louder than Chris' music.

I tiptoed to her room and opened the door without knocking. Her indignation stopped when she saw my face, and the finger held to my lips. I motioned to her to keep quiet and come downstairs with me. I managed to snag my phone from the kitchen counter on the way out.

Out on the front stoop, with my daughter next to me trying to ask questions, I called my friendly contact at my neighborhood precinct. Again.

"This is Erica Donato." I was stammering. I couldn't help it. "We've spoken about an incident…really, a few incidents.…"

"I haven't exactly forgotten you. Must've been two whole hours since we talked. I feel like we're going steady here."

Was he being sarcastic? Or trying to lighten up?

"I have something else to report."

"Tell me." He was all business now.

When I was done he said, "Stay outside until I can send someone over to check the house, Did you touch anything in that room? No? Good, keep it that way. I'm going to come take a look myself. Oh, yeah, and is your daughter there? I'm on my way over."

Then I turned to my white-faced daughter and used as tough a voice as I could muster. "Tell me now what exactly is going on? And no more nonsense. You heard what I told him about the note on my computer. What could it possibly mean?"

"Well, I don't...I mean...it's a prank, isn't it? It must be." She couldn't look at me.

"I don't think so. Not for minute. Someone was here. In our house. And call me crazy, but this looks like a threat. There's going to be a detective here in a few minutes and I don't plan to be stupid with him, so before he gets here, I'd better know whatever you know!"

"I thought I was doing a good thing," she whispered. "That girl...I wanted to know more about her...I thought you would be proud of me..." Tears started rolling down her cheeks.

"Oh honey, stop." My anger was seeping away, as my puzzlement increased. "Just stop and tell me all about it. I'll try not to be mad, but I really need to know. Here." I handed her a tissue from my pocket.

As her tears slowed, she started talking between sobs. "It was that poor girl. I felt like I needed to do something for her. So I thought I'd try to find out about it on my own."

"You did what?" I remembered too late my promise not to get mad.

"I tried to talk to the police about it, but they treated me like a kid. Can you believe that? They were so rude! And I asked Uncle Rick for help but he turned me down too and said I was nuts. I let him think he convinced me." I was fuming but forced myself to be silent. I knew it was the only way to keep her talking.

"So I thought maybe I could find out about the house and work from there?"

"All right," I said cautiously. "What did you do? How did you even know where to start?"

"Umm, you had something from the museum, a pamphlet about researching your own house."

My daughter, who always claimed my work was boring, said that. This was getting more surprising by the second.

"So I went to the City Register office, to see if I could find out about who owned our house back then, you know, when they think whatever happened here happened. And I did it!"

The rest came out in a rush of words. "There was this guy working there, he's in college and seemed pretty bored, so you know, we got to talking and I brought him a soda, and he was really, really helpful. He even gave me his number and said to call anytime if I need more help. He made me copies for free and everything. It's all up in my room.

"Lots of people owned it. Did you know it's a hundred years old? But around then, when they think that skeleton is from, it was this guy named Rogow. It's Rogow Realty, I think, and he had it until 1980 when he sold it to a couple, and they sold it to you." She took a breath and said, "That's it."

"Rogow? No kidding. I was actually reading about him today. So they owned our house?"

"And this Mr. Rogow—I think it said he was the principal?"

"That means he's the main partner."

"He owned a lot of houses around here. I have a list. That cute guy looked up a bunch of other locations for me, they were all around here, and his name was on most of them."

"Forget cute. A college boy is too old for you." She looked indignant. "I don't know if I should be proud of your initiative or ground you for life. For crying out loud, Chris, what were you thinking? I wasn't being whimsical when I said to leave it alone! Was I speaking Russian?"

"But I told you...I was even having dreams...."

"I know. I do know." I stopped, thought, then told the truth. "Oh, hell. I had some myself. But this is not acceptable behavior, not even...."

She slid across the step and put her head on in my shoulder. I put an arm around her, but I was saved from further discussion by the arrival of Detective Russo, who had been here when we found the body, and a team of uniformed officers. They took my key and disappeared inside for an endless period of time.

When Russo came out at last he assured us that no one was hiding anywhere and that they had seen the note when they searched. The cops dusted for prints on the computer, took mine and Chris' for comparison and examined the front and back doors and all the windows. Russo finally said, "No one broke in, so either you've got a very skillful lock picker, or it's someone who has a key. I need a list of names, the people with keys and anyone who could have been here today."

I wrote out everyone I could remember, with Chris prompting me, and I was surprised at how long the list was. Joe of course. Rick. Two sets of neighbors in case we were locked out because of keys lost or left at home or work or school. A plumber who'd come for an emergency repair. I was pretty sure he'd never given them back. Our regular exterminator, who came to spray for ants and roaches when I was out. Various people who'd stayed with us for a while. Perhaps some of Chris' friends? I added a note that Joe and his work crew had been in and out much of the day.

Russo looked it over. "What are you, nuts? Any of these people could have passed it on, left it lying around, lost it. You shouldn't be giving your key out to repairmen."

"Well, sometimes it's been altogether too much. I had a job, classes, a child to get to school, a flooding sink...."

"I know, I know. But that leaves a lot of loose ends here. If you had workmen here, I want to talk to them. Give me your contractor's number and call a locksmith now, tonight. I can give you some good places that work twenty-four/seven. Your window bars are in good shape but change the door locks ASAP. And keep a good control on the keys this time. Got that?'

"I got it." I felt like a fool.

"Now let's discuss that note. You got any ideas about what it means?"

With obvious reluctance, Chris described her day.

He said softly, "This is pretty scary, isn't it? And you're already having an eventful week. I have to ask you some questions, anyway. You won't get into any trouble, but you need to think hard about the answers. And your mother can leave if you'd prefer."

She shook her head.

"First, I need everyone who might know you are asking questions about this. I gather it was all news to your mother, but who else?"

"Lots of people." Her voice was despairing. "I told everyone. All my friends. They think a skeleton is weird but in a cool way. Who knows who they might have told? Uncle Rick. Some cops. Even that cute guy at the Records department." She turned to me. "And there's a little more."

"Chris!" I swallowed the expletives on the tip of my tongue.

"There was an address on the papers for that Rogow company? Well, it isn't in the phone book now, but the papers had a phone number too, so I took a chance. And called it."

"And?"

"I got a machine and it said Rogow Incorporated so I thought, why not leave a message? You know? I told them who I am and what I wanted. And asked if they were related to this Rogow. I mean," she added quickly, "I only talked about history and didn't say anything about the girl."

"Ok, I got it, but I sure don't like it. Now, is there anyone you know who might be trying to scare you, just in case this is some kind of prank after all? Anyone who has it in for you?"

She shook her head. "I'm a regular kid at school. Not so popular that everyone hates me. Does that make sense?" She looked from him to me and back again. "And not one of the kids, well you know, there are always one or two, that everyone picks on, you know, because they just do." She saw my face and added quickly, "I don't do that, though."

He closed his notebook. "I think that's it for now. I might be back and you can call me any time you need to, or if you think of something. Ms. Donato, I expect you have my number memorized by now. After all, we don't want anything happening to Sergeant Rick's goddaughter."

He laughed at my surprise. "Yeah, I asked around. How is Rick anyway? I had him for a teacher one time at the academy."

"He's fine. Real busy."

"Give him my best, when you can. Tony Russo. Tell him I made detective."

"I'll do that."

As soon as he was gone, I made my decision, right then and there, before I even tackled the locksmith problem.

"If we can get you in this late, do you still want to go to camp with Mel?"

"Well, duh, yes, are you kidding? I—but this is crazy—I don't understand…"

"Uncle Rick offered to send you."

"You mean I'm sprung from the chain gang? I have to go call Mel!" Her expression went from joy, to confusion, to worry and back to joy in the space of two breaths. Then she stopped. "Are you trying to get rid of me?"

"Yes."

"Cause you think I've gone off the deep end?"

"You bet."

"I'll go, but only if you promise not to forget about her. Promise to bug the police."

"Let me get this straight. After completely blowing off everything I said about this, I am sending you to camp instead of locking you in the house until you're forty, and you are bargaining with me?"

"No. Well, yes, I guess you could see it that way…but I didn't mean it like that. Mom, you know…don't you…I didn't…"

I let her off the hook. "I do. Now go away. I have a locksmith to get over here tonight. No doubt it will cost an arm and a leg. Or maybe my first-born child. That would be you. Don't tempt me." I hoped he would take a credit card. That would at least give me a little time to scrape up the money.

A few phone calls early the next morning and it was done. The camp had a cancellation due to mono, and if I faxed a mountain of paperwork and my credit card information, Chris was going. I sent up a prayer that Rick's check was on the way.

After that, I hardly had time or energy to think about anything but getting Chris ready. As Joan, Mel's mom, said, "Moving Catherine the Great from the Winter Palace to the Summer Palace was nothing compared to getting a teenage girl ready for camp."

My bank account program showed Rick's check had transferred. Hooray for electronic transfers. I wanted to say thank you, to tell him Chris was really going, to give her a chance to say goodbye, but I didn't reach him in several calls. That wasn't unusual; he was living a busy life in his retirement and often took off for a few days of fishing or a gambling excursion to Atlantic City. And I didn't have time to think about it after a couple of tries. I knew he'd get back to me.

Oh, yes, and I had a fight with Joe. I meant to give him a heads up that the police would be asking him some questions about security when he was working at my house, but they got to him first. He was more than a little ticked off about this and told me so by phone at seven a.m. I had an uncomfortable feeling he was right, too, so of course I came back with a strong "I really don't have time to deal with this!" and hung up.

There was no work on my house scheduled that day, and I did not have a moment to think it over until very late that night. I reached for the phone to apologize to Joe, stopped myself, thought it over and did it again, sucking in my breath as I punched the buttons. He wasn't there. I wasn't about to leave a message for anyone who came in with him to hear. His phone would record that I had called.

Chapter Seven

Camp departure day. The sounds of Chris opening and closing drawers. I squinted at the clock—five a.m. Like any teen, she normally had to be dragged out of bed for lunch. Today she was up so early I wondered if she had gone to bed at all.

By nine, we were cramming her bags into Mel's parents' overstuffed car trunk and heading out to the bus meeting place in New Jersey. Joan had made the trip many times before, with all three of her children. Every once in awhile she'd turn from the front seat to me and say, "Don't worry. It will be fine." Did the knots in my stomach show in my face? Or was she reading my mind?

The scene at the vast mall parking lot was one of barely controlled chaos, with parents parking and unloading, small children running around, teenagers screaming in the bliss of reunion with last summer's friends, and counselors with clipboards shouting for attention. Somehow, with Joan's crisp direction, we got the gear unloaded and stacked in the correct pile. Mel, doing her share of screaming, took Chris off to make introductions, and I watched my daughter's expression change slowly from apprehension to wide-eyed excitement. I was surprised, relieved, exhausted, anxious to leave, anxious to grab her for a big, embarrassing hug. Exhausted.

Before the bus boarding started, she came back and pulled me aside, whispering, "Don't forget what you promised. About our girl."

"I did not promise. In fact…"

She cut in. "I'm counting on you. I know you won't let me down." I knew where she'd learned to say that manipulative, guilt-inducing phrase. My own words over the years were coming back to haunt me. What nerve.

One last hug and then she was gone, on the bus and on her way. I slept all the way back to Brooklyn and Joan had to wake me when we reached my house.

Though it had been a few days since that frightening note, and nothing else had happened, I still paused at the front door, looking it over to make sure it was just as I had left it, locked and untouched.

The house was empty, not the delicious, all-to-myself emptiness of coming home to find Chris temporarily out, but the complete emptiness of too many rooms that suddenly seemed too big even in my small house. It took me by surprise, that disorienting feeling, tripping me up like a cat around my ankles. I could not remember how to be in my life without Chris.

I wandered around. I put the breakfast dishes away. I fiddled with the old air conditioner. I noted that the work in the kitchen was progressing, even though I had not seen Joe in several days. I guessed he was still mad at me. I would need to do something about that, but not today.

Come to think of it, I still hadn't heard from Rick either. Sometimes his *in loco parentis* behavior annoyed me, but it wasn't like him to be out of touch for so many days.

Where was everyone? I needed to hear another human being. The Pastores next door had gone to the shore with their son. Mel's parents were celebrating the departure to camp of all three children. Darcy was packing for her Maine vacation. I don't have a lot of other social friends, hanging out friends. One, because I am too busy to make them. Two, because my too-adult responsibilities cut me off from my classmates. Three, because my academic responsibilities and changed life cut me off from my old neighborhood friends. Usually I am too busy merely getting through my days to care. This day was most definitely not the usual.

I did have cousins but we saw each other rarely, at family occasions. I did have a mother-in-law but she lived with her married daughter in Buffalo and she would never understand the whole idea of camp anyway. In her day, Italian kids didn't go away to camp. That was only one of the many things about my life she did not understand, but she was the only grandmother left. It was a tie I would never break, but no, not today.

My house was a mess, no place in it seemed comfortable, the unread Sunday paper was bound to have disturbing news, and even my garden was too hot to hold any appeal.

I finally got fed up with my own mood. Since I couldn't face housework, I headed to my desk to tackle professional work to keep my brain occupied for a few hours. My e-mail had a note from the helpful librarian at Leary's old paper.

"I did it! I found someone here who's been around as long as I have. Pete Miller. He said to call him at home any time." I thought, why not?

A friendly man's voice said, "What do you want to talk to Leary for? I'm a lot more fun."

So I explained, yet again, and he said, "I'd give a lot to hear that conversation!" I had the disconcerting impression he was laughing. "Look. Leary doesn't like talking to many people—we were drinking buddies for a couple of decades and I still never know if he'll speak to me—but, on the other hand, the guy does have an ego. Always did. There's a chance he will be flattered. What the hell. Your name and number checked out at the museum."

"You checked up on me?"

"Sure. I was a reporter. I'm paid to be suspicious. I'll give you his phone number. He never answers his phone anyway, so leave a message. And let me know how it goes." I was sure he was chuckling as he said good-bye.

In a few seconds, a cigarette-roughened voice was saying, "Leary here. If you're selling or soliciting, hang up now. If you're offering money, leave a message."

I managed to blurt out, "I'm looking for Brendan Leary, who used to be a well-known reporter in New York. I'm with the Brooklyn History Museum and I'd like to interview him. If this is the right number, please…"

The voice broke in. "This is Leary. How the hell did you find me? And what the hell do you want?"

"Uh, Mr. Leary, I'm Erica Donato. We're doing an exhibit at the History Museum on tenant-landlord issues over the years, and you covered that extensively, back then."

"So what?"

"I was hoping I could talk to you about it, use you as a source for the project?"

"Why would I want to do that?"

OK, I sighed. A curmudgeon. I answered, as sweetly as I could. "Most people enjoy sharing their expertise, and we would be so grateful if we could…."

"Grateful doesn't pay my rent. And it was a hell of a long time ago. Different life, different me. Who needs to go back?"

I could have come right back at him, but I doubted it would be productive. I smiled and hoped the smile would get into my voice. "Well, we do. That's our job. What would be an inducement for you?

"Money talks."

"Mr. Leary," I said gently, "you must know we're a nonprofit. Money is the one thing we don't have, but I could probably take you for a nice lunch to say thanks." On my deeply stressed credit card, if it had to come to that. "And wouldn't you like to have your name and picture up in the exhibit? Have people remember you?"

"Couldn't care less. My name used to be in more important places than your exhibit. And now? I made a few enemies in my time—I'd rather be forgotten. Lunch doesn't do a thing for me, either. I've got diabetes—can't eat anything I like."

He was the opposite of friendly. I could even have called him hostile, and yet he wasn't hanging up.

"Aside from cash, which I don't have, and food and fame, which you don't want, what would tempt you? I bet there's something?"

"Time was, it could have been Scotch. Or even rye. Now doc says it will kill me. My barfly days are long over. In the words of an Ellington song you probably don't even know, I don't get around much anymore. And who needs it anyway?"

I thought I heard a little something there and went with my hunch.

"Would you like an outing? I have a car. We could take in a movie, or a music club, even without drinking?"

There was a long silence, and then he said abruptly, "Tell you what. I'm sick of the sight of my own four walls. Take me for a ride out to Coney Island, buy me a hot dog at Nathan's, and we'll talk. Maybe I'll tell you something. Throw in a kasha knish and maybe I'll even tell you something useful."

"Sounds like a deal to me. When?"

"Tomorrow is good. My calendar isn't exactly crowded these days."

"It's a date."

Then the house went deeply, emptily silent again. I tried to glue myself to my work, but some other part of my mind was fixated elsewhere, becoming nearly desperate enough to consider calling my dad, or doing some house cleaning. When the phone rang at last, it was an unfamiliar Manhattan number.

"Ms. Donato? It's Steven Richmond."

Darcy's friend. The Wall Street guy. On a Sunday. This was not a phone call I wanted.

"I apologize for calling you on Sunday and if you tell me you are too busy, I'll go away until it's working hours, but if you are not...?"

"I am not too busy at the moment now. I have a few minutes." Technically, I wasn't busy at all, as I was not actually doing any of the things I should have been doing. My instinct, however, was caution. Something about our previous meeting made me think he would take favors for granted.

"Excellent. Something has come up, in connection with the project we have been discussing." That was an exaggeration. We'd only had that one brief meeting, but now I was curious. "Would you happen to have time to go over it now? It would be on the clock, of course. I could pick you up and go to a café, or whatever you would prefer?"

I'd been up since five o'clock. What I would prefer was a nap or perhaps a long soak in a tub. No, a nap. I would definitely not prefer going anywhere. Actually, I would prefer to say, go away.

"Come here. My house is a construction mess, I'm renovating, but I have a deck where we can be comfortable. Does that work?"

'I'll be there in ten. And thank you."

I looked down at the now-wrinkled and very random cut-offs and t-shirt I had put on that morning, and my bare feet, considered more professional or merely more adult attire for a split second and thought, the heck with it. He is intruding on my down time; he can take me as I am.

Eight minutes and he was ringing my doorbell, juggling two luxurious iced drinks and his computer bag, and saying, "Sorry again for barging in. I hope these help make up for it. I didn't know your favorites, so I brought one chocolate, one mango."

A bribe? Why not?

"Come on in, and excuse the mess. We can sit outdoors."

My house was certainly not at its best. Construction debris was everywhere. I was trying to hustle him past the mess, but he stopped in front of the fireplace. The construction mess around certainly was attention getting, and so, perhaps, were the remaining shreds of bright yellow police tape.

"Darcy told me what happened here."

I hoped he didn't see me flinch. I didn't want to talk about it with every random stranger. So I didn't.

Instead I led him straight out to my sunny deck. As in most of these renovated brownstones, the garden floor, with its separate entrance tucked under the high front stoop, had been turned into a rental unit, now needing major work and vacant at the moment. The deck was built out from the back of the raised parlor floor, giving access to the garden by a long flight of steps.

Of course that means we look out over our neighbors' gardens, all up and down the back of the attached houses. True, there is a loss of privacy, but I get to look at the pink climbing roses, grape arbor and gently splashing fountain on the Pastores' side and enjoy an oak tree's shade on the other. It's not a bad tradeoff.

Richmond looked around. "This is nice. You know? Cozy. My apartment is large, and, oh, very decorated, in a very good building. It's a legacy from my marriage, but it's about as homey as a hotel suite."

It seemed natural when he asked, "Do you feel differently about this house now? Maybe I'm out of line even to be asking that?"

It didn't seem out of line. It seemed perceptive.

"I don't know yet. I hope we'll get over it, if I can sidetrack my daughter from being too interested. In a few hours she went from being, as she would say, totally grossed out, to wanting to investigate it." I responded to his puzzled expression by adding glumly, "Teenagers are like that. The mood swings are faster than the speed of adult thought."

"But why would she want to do that at all?"

"There were some items buried there with her. It. The cops thought it was a young girl, like Chris, and she feels some kind of kinship. I guess."

I didn't want to talk about it any further with this stranger. "What did you want to discuss with me?"

"First, here is your consulting contract. It's very standard. Read through it and sign, please."

I glance over it. The hourly fee was satisfactory. Actually, it went way beyond satisfactory. There was a cap on how many hours they would need and the work I produced would belong to them, Hudson Investors. Had I ever seen such a contract before? No. Was I going to sign it in any case? Of course. He handed me a pen, heavy, gold, engraved but I already had a Bic from my pocket.

He had opened his notebook computer and was pointing to a familiar page. It was that annoying Brownstone Bytes blog, headlining the question: "Who is gobbling up parkside property?" The story went on to discuss the purchase of the rundown neighborhood movie theater and several nearby older apartment buildings, all around the attractive traffic circle at a park entrance. This was the less gentrified end of the neighborhood. The buyers were several nameless, faceless companies, shells within shells, all different but with a heavy implication that they were actually the same buyer. It ended with a promise that "our tireless researchers would track the companies' names back to actual people, back as far as it took."

There was nothing very disturbing about the facts, but there was a heavy undertone of suspicion, that there were nefarious doings to be uncovered. There were already some flaming reader comments, repeated references to octopus-grip developers and destructive, heartless tycoons.

"Your clients' project?"

Richmond nodded. "They wanted to stay under the radar for awhile. These writers don't seem to know who they are but they certainly know more than we wanted them to."

"I don't know what I can do for you. Or them. I mean, I—is there a reason for local people to be upset?"

Richmond looked stunned and then he laughed. "Well, our goal is to convince people that this project is going to be worthwhile, exciting, and an enormous asset to the neighborhood. But we weren't planning to have that process now. "

I thought, I bet you'd like to keep the prices depressed for a while too. Then I said it, and he replied with a terse, "Of course. It's business. The goal is to both be creative and make lots of money." For the first time, he looked unsure of himself. It was an improvement.

"It's an unusual project for my clients, and for me. We usually deal with things you can't see, financial instruments, and putting it all together is like a puzzle. Challenging and exciting, but more abstract. My client and a friend, a famous architect, hatched this idea to build something together, something big and beautiful."

"Does that make any business sense here?" It didn't to me.

He shrugged. "Only time will tell. It's an exciting change for them and for me. They are certainly people who expect to succeed at everything they do. For now, my role—one of my roles—is to try to make the process as smooth as possible. No muss, no fuss. They want me involved not because I know any-thing about this, but because they are used to me." He added quickly, "Of course we are hiring expertise all over the place."

"I don't fully understand." I was trying to sound suave. "What are you most afraid of?"

"We are not sure. To be honest, I don't comprehend the hostility in this article." He tapped the computer. "We see huge untapped potential—housing with park views on one side, views all the way to the harbor on the other, and far better shopping and dining choices. To us, it seems to be a win for the neigh-borhood. At the quality level we have in mind, merchants and buyers will be fighting to get in."

Goodness. He was making a presentation. I guessed he had a whole set of PowerPoint slides stored in that slim computer.

"Aren't you forgetting something? People live there now. And how many local merchants will be happy to have the competi-tion move into the commercial space?"

He looked at me with an assessing eye. "That's where you come in. Darcy wasn't wrong about you. You live nearby, you have the background, and you know the people. Reluctant as I am to admit it"—I saw the tiniest hint of a smile—"we might, let us say, be blinded by our own vision. What really gets people upset about this? What can we offer that would make this gener-ally accepted? You know, many people would, in fact, will, call this progress." He sounded aggrieved. "Change is what keeps a great city alive! Did you know Lincoln Center was built on the slums that are the setting of *West Side Story?*"

"Well, yes, actually I did." It took some self-control not to add, "you condescending prig."

He had the good sense to flush a bit. "Of course you must know that. Forgive me for lecturing. So, do you see what we need to do?"

"Sort of. I could get started, send you some ideas, I guess, and you can tell me if I'm pointed in the right direction?" I tapped his computer. "But isn't this guy a public relations issue?"

"Certainly. We'll have someone on that, but now I can also assure them we are going to get ahead of the substantive issues, too."

The buzz of the doorbell startled me right out of the conversation. I found Joe standing on my steps.

"How are you doing? I thought you might be lonely with Chris gone." He looked guarded, not quite his usual self. It's true; we had had a fight. Or if not a fight, at least words.

"And I thought I should check on the kitchen progress." He could see all the way from the doorway straight though to the deck.

He was already moving toward the back as he spoke. Then he stopped when Richmond stood up and walked toward us. "I guess you are not lonely."

I know Joe so well, I forget how fit and attractive and plain big he is, until I see him with someone else's eyes. This moment I was seeing him through Steven Richmond's. And Joe certainly didn't expect to see me having coffee with a well-dressed stranger. He looked like a wolf with his fur bristling.

It would have been funny if it hadn't been so annoying. No, it was funny.

"Joe, this is Steven Richmond. Steven, this is Joe Greenberg, my neighbor and also my contractor. He's the guy who's going to turn this neglected house into something beautiful. Or at least, comfortable."

Steven smiled, slightly. "You must be a busy man doing contracting in this neighborhood."

Joe nodded. "The right business in the right place even in a recession. This particular job is a labor of love, of course."

"What? My bank account says otherwise!"

"Hey, kidding. I'm kidding. But squeezing you into my schedule really was a favor."

Steven broke in. "Was it you who found the skeleton? We were talking about that earlier."

"More or less." His chilly tone telegraphed, "End of discussion." Bless him. Angry at me or not, he knew how I felt. "I'll be back soon to look at the kitchen. Give my love to the princess." And he was gone, letting himself out with his own key.

Richmond was gathering his belongings. "I've taken up enough of your time for a Sunday and I appreciate it a great deal." He shook my hand and was gone too.

I was all alone at last, and still, or again, not at all comfortable with it, but I had no desire to call anyone. The sofa beckoned insistently. I fell asleep and must have missed the phone ringing because later, it was the insistent beeping of my answering machine that pierced right through the fog.

Ohmigod, Chris! I fumbled for a light, and punched the play button, eyes wide open now and holding my breath.

An elderly but firm voice said, "This is Nettie Rogow. I am calling for Miss Christina Donato. She left a message at my daughter's office number and said she had questions about my late husband's business. I'd be happy to talk to her, no matter what my daughter…well, never mind that. Please feel free to call back."

It wasn't a call from Chris. Or about her. I got that, and that was all that mattered. All the rest could wait. I would call sometime tomorrow, or even the next day, to thank this Mrs. Rogow, tell her that Chris was away for the rest of the summer and she need not concern herself further. That's what I would do. As I walked up my creaky old stairs, hand on the banister for balance, eyes not quite focused, I did wonder what she meant by "no matter what."

Chapter Eight

The morning sun sent a knife into my brain. I pulled the pillow back over my head again, but it was useless. There were loud male voices coming from downstairs, and the sounds of furniture being moved, hammering, tools being dropped. Joe's voice. Did they have to be so loud? I gave in to the inevitable, fumbled for a robe, and carefully negotiated the stairs, squinting again at the sun and trying to keep my head motionless.

Joe was in my kitchen setting out his tools.

"You look like hell."

"Thanks, Joe. Good morning to you too."

"Were you out tying one on last night? I can see it in your face. Lucky girl! Was it that preppy-looking guy? I didn't think he looked like much fun." He didn't say it with his usual good nature. Oh, yes, we'd had a fight.

"He's a friend of Darcy. He hired me for some work. And I was up late cause it was weird with Chris not being home. So there." I squinted at him. "You're awfully noisy this morning."

"Oh, we're just getting started. It will get worse." He sounded happy about it. "We're going to rip out your kitchen today. Hey, you are supposed to be happy about our progress."

I managed to mumble, as I turned back toward the stairs, "Guess I'd better get out of here." Then I turned back.

"Joe."

"Yes?"

"I'm sorry I didn't give you a heads up about the cops calling."

"Yeah, well, it would have been nice." He didn't look at me, but he sounded less chilly. I was going toward the stairs when he said, "Hey. I'll keep the noise down until you leave." Now he was laughing at me. What nerve.

I guess that meant we were friends again.

An hour later, showered, dressed, hydrated, medicated, I was in a coffee shop, inhaling a large, heavily sugared iced coffee. I was almost back to normal, and ready for my interview with Brendan Leary, former reporter, Brooklyn expert, curmudgeon. I found my way to his neighborhood, one that had seen better days. The address was a grimy brick apartment building, with cracked front steps and overflowing garbage cans. It too had seen better days. I rang the bell labeled Leary and he buzzed me in.

When I emerged from the creaky elevator he was waiting in the hall, a fat, unshaven man wearing a stained t-shirt, sitting in a wheelchair. I was startled to see he had only one leg. I hoped I hid my surprise.

"Ms. Donato? You're early. Guess you found your way. Welcome to my palace." He turned the chair deftly, and preceded me into the apartment.

Newspapers and magazines were stacked in piles on the floor. Dirty dishes were stacked on every surface. An odor made me wonder when the garbage had last been taken out. It was dark. On this bright summer day, all the blinds were drawn.

He shrugged. "A housekeeping aide comes once a week. I don't bother much in between." His smile was sarcastic. "Of course if you hadn't showed up early, I would have had time to make it all nice for company and bake a cake."

"No traffic," I said absently. This mess was certainly beyond the abilities of a once a week aide.

"Let's hit the road. I'll grab a shirt." He lifted a gaudy Hawaiian pattern from a pile of clothes on a chair. "Hand me my sunglasses on that table—light hurts my eyes —and my crutches are there by the door."

He wheeled himself into the elevator and out again. When we got to my car, he used the crutches to maneuver himself into the front seat and explained how to fold up the chair.

"I hope you know how get from here to there. It's way past my lunchtime, but I'm saving myself for Nathan's. I can't put up with getting lost and eating late."

Mmm, I thought. Mr. Charm. I responded with false calmness, "I've lived here all my life. I kind of think I can find my way out to the beach."

"That so? Turn left up here, then right, and we'll be on Ocean Parkway. It'll take us right out." He opened a car window without asking, turned on my radio, changed the station, and closed his eyes.

Exactly as I'd planned to do without his advice, I turned onto Ocean Parkway, the tree-shaded boulevard connecting Prospect Park to the ocean. We'd be able to zip there in twenty minutes, barring traffic problems, as I knew very well.

He woke up with a start when I parked, barked commands to me about getting his wheelchair set up, and led the way down the paved path to Nathan's vast snack stand.

Gigantic signs shouted the availability of every fairground food known in the northeast. After Leary had put away two of the famous foot-long hot dogs, with mustard and sauerkraut, a couple of knishes, and a large order of French fries, he seemed marginally more cheerful. However, when I tried to ask him some questions, he said, "Put the damn notebook away. Can't you see I'm eating?" One frozen custard later he said, "Take me for a walk. Maybe I'll feel up to questions then. Maybe not."

We meandered along the boardwalk, where he could use his wheelchair. I knew the surrounding neighborhood had become tough over the years, and even dangerous, but on this bright summer day the amusement park itself didn't look so different from what I remembered.

In the kiddie section, tiny screaming children rode the miniature rides and begged in Chinese or Russian or Spanish, as well as English, to please, please go again. Groups of tourists—or were they recent immigrants?—in saris or Muslim scarves or bright African head wraps took photos in front of the famous roller coaster, holding up souvenirs gaudily decorated with feathers and sequins. Groups of teenage boys challenged each other to win a teddy bear while their girls giggled and egged them on. Didn't I have one of those bears stashed away somewhere? Now probably moth-eaten and moldy.

I was jerked out of my reverie when Leary snapped, "Stop now. I'm tired of moving the chair." We parked it at the end of a bench and sat silently, taking in the waves, breeze, and sun.

I was surprised when he said softly, "I grew up not far from here. I watched them build the Aquarium, when they moved it out from Manhattan." He sighed. "I always loved the beach. Nothing like it to calm you down. I'd be running all over the city, chasing stories, drinking too much—getting crazy—sometimes I'd get home about dawn and come out and…ah, well, it was a long time ago."

After another quiet few moments, he said, "We had a deal. Whadda you want to know?"

"You knew Park Slope really well back when. I've pulled all your old stories that I could find, but I don't know if I found all of them, and then I bet there were stories you never wrote, too."

"Well, you're a smart little one, aren't you? Oh, yes, there were plenty. Of course my specialty was landlords and tenants and the G word. "

"What?"

"Gentrification, of course."

"I should have known."

"Yeah, you should have. Obvious. So you already know, I would hope, that in the fifties and sixties everyone who had even a prayer of being middle class wanted a nice new ranch house? Modern kitchen, air conditioning, patch of lawn?"

"Suburbia called and they listened. Mostly the people still there were ones who couldn't figure out a way to go, or didn't care."

"Oh, sure. Pardon me for forgetting you are a historian. So, in the seventies, some young families wanted more space than they could get, or afford, in Manhattan, but they were the ones who grew up in the suburbs—they'd slit their wrists before moving back to conformityville."

"And that's when things changed again. They looked at those old brownstones and saw the potential for life in the city, but with space and a garden. And cheap, back then."

"You got it. Lots of those old houses had been chopped into apartments, or even rooming houses, pretty crummy, and landlords were making a nice, nice living owning slum housing, more or less."

"Wait! I know what happened then. I found it in old news stories. The landlords wanted to sell out, now that there were buyers, so they were harassing tenants to get them to move."

"Yep. That's the one that ended up in court. A couple of them went to jail and my stories helped put them there. At least I liked to think so, and they sure did, too. Hated my guts, I'm proud to say. Yeah. Rogow, Lensky, Donnelly, couple others I can't remember. Equal opportunity slumlords."

"That Rogow name keeps coming up in my life. I got a call from a Nelly Rogow—it's not worth explaining why—and I'm going to go talk to her." I decided to do it at that moment, as the words came out of my mouth.

"Yeah? Could be same family, his wife, or maybe his daughter. That old s.o.b. died years ago, but I have an idea his daughter went into the family business. Ahh, it was so long ago, I don't remember anything else about those crooks. Read what I wrote back then."

He turned his chair and started rolling. "Come on! All this strolling down memory lane has been swell, but I need a beer and then I want to go home."

He suddenly speeded up, rolling headlong into a flock of gulls, laughing when they rose into the air in feathery, squawking panic.

He watched them and shrugged. "Got to get my excitement where I can."

Later, he dozed off in the car. He didn't look well. His color was off and when I woke him, he was sweaty and disoriented. He finally shook his head and mumbled, "I need a shot. Get me up into my apartment, and damn quick!"

I tried to hurry, fumbling with the chair. When we got upstairs he angrily refused my offer of help and disappeared into the bathroom for a very long few minutes. I paced back and forth, unwilling to sit on his filthy furniture and not sure what to do.

He looked somewhat better when he emerged. "You've used up all my sociability for today and the whole rest of the week too. I'm going to take a nap and I don't care for company, so go on."

"Do I need to call for help? Are you OK?" He fixed me with a hostile stare and I added quickly, "Yes, yes, of course you are. May I call to ask some more questions? And come again?"

"You're almost as bad as a reporter. Annoying little mosquito." Then he sighed. "What the hell. Come again but not too soon. Tell you what…"

"Yes?"

"I've got some files you might like to have. Make a deal? Come take me out again next week and you can have them."

"You have files? From the period I need?'

He turned the chair into a back room. I was astonished to see it was lined with meticulously labeled cabinets. A clean desk and a computer table stood at one end of the room.

"I guess you still write."

"If you'd call it that. It sure isn't reporting. Yeah, yeah, I can see you're dying to ask, so I'll tell you. I quit reporting when diabetes took my leg. Doctors seemed to think a few decades of smoking and drinking did some damage, too. Imagine my surprise. So now I write men's adventure novels. I can turn one out in six weeks. Crap, but it pays the rent. Satisfied now?"

"But I didn't ask…I…"

"Nah, but you were wondering." True. "Can't kid a kidder or something like that. And don't think about looking for any of them, either. I sure don't use my real name." He turned to the file cabinets. "Try the fourth in, third down."

The drawer was perfectly organized, files color-coded, meticulously labeled by topic and date. Not a speck of dust on the surfaces.

I wondered if he knew how much this told me about him. Then again, would he care?

"They'd be just a loan. And no quoting without permission and credit!"

"Well, of course not." I could hardly contain my excitement. "And I'll take good care of them. You won't regret this."

"Yeah, I might. I already do. I just had an unusual moment of weakness." He slammed the drawer shut. "After our next outing."

The thought crossed my mind that he was lonely.

"Now you answer a question for me. I'm tired but I'm not dead and I want to know. You never said why you're so stuck on all this old stuff."

That stopped me. "I don't know, exactly. Because it's news again? Haven't you seen the stories? The same issues keep coming back. And because I live there myself and—I don't know—I don't quite fit in—but my daughter does—and I guess I'm trying to understand it. Sometimes it seems like a foreign country to me, too."

"Yeah? Whereabouts do you live?"

I told him and he gave a short, raspy laugh. "I could tell you some stories about that end of the neighborhood, back in the day. Wild old times back then. Next time."

I took a deep breath. "There was a skeleton hidden behind the wall in my house. We just found it."

His whole face lit up. "Jesus H. Christ, what a story! If only I was still who I used to be."

He yawned. "But I'm not that guy anymore. Get going. I've had enough visiting for today."

I headed out, mulling over what he had told me and knowing that I would call Mrs. Rogow as soon as I had a chance. I could ask her all kinds of questions about her husband's business. It might give me a wealth of interesting details to play with, and I thought I ought to get the landlord's point of view on all this. I was skeptical that I would be persuaded by it, but I had to admit that it was a missing piece. It was now obvious I should not mention Leary in that conversation and I understood Steven Richmond's work was confidential, but I knew I might learn something he could use. Or at least, I hoped so.

And in the back of my mind, I wondered if she could tell me something about my own house, and who had lived there. The fact that I had ordered Chris to leave it alone, and sent her away to make sure she didn't ignore me, certainly did not mean I could not ask some questions myself. I am a mature, careful and sensible adult, unlike my daughter. It was different for me. Of course it was.

And I was a historian, living in a house with some real history. I couldn't be expected to walk away from that.

Back at my car, I reflexively checked my phone for messages. Nothing from Chris. Not that I was expecting anything. Nothing from work. And still nothing from Rick. With no child at home now—and wouldn't she be insulted to hear me call her a child!—and this not being a workday, I was completely free. I made a snap decision to drive over to Rick's house in Queens and lean on his doorbell. Or leave him a note, at least. With traffic it could take awhile, but what the heck? I was already in the car, and I was fed up with his disappearing act. And underneath it all, I thought that if he was in some alcoholic or other trouble, then he needed me.

I hadn't been out there in a long time. He usually came to visit me, or took me out, wanting to see Chris or perhaps, as I often suspected, checking up on me. Queens streets confuse me. Avenues, drives and streets could all have the same number, but some of the old landmarks were still there. Turn right at the supermarket, I told myself, then left at the community center, right at the white brick apartment tower.

I turned onto Rick's street of modest homes on tiny lawns, and saw a whole flock of police cars. They were roosting right in front of his house.

Chapter Nine

Something was wrong. This wasn't a social scene, not in patrol cars. I proceeded slowly down the block until an officer stopped me. Rick's door was open and people were going in and out.

"What's going on?"

"Police business, miss. Sorry. You'll have to go around the block if you need access to the other end of the street."

"No. No, I was going here, to that house. The owner is a close friend."

Something shifted in his expression, away from his official mask mode to an expression I couldn't read. It scared me, and I was already scared. He only said, "Wait right here," and disappeared. He was back in a second with a plainclothes officer.

She leaned into my car window. "Name, please."

"Erica Donato. I was coming to see Rick Malone, who lives here." It took a huge effort of will, but I was keeping my voice firm and my gaze steady. "He's a long time family friend, for my whole life, and I'd like to know…"

She cut me off. "ID please." I showed her.

"Ah, Ms. Donato. I believe we've been looking for you. When was the last time you called here?"

"This morning. I wanted to see him."

"I thought so. Yes, we heard your message on his phone. OK, we need to talk. May I get in your car?"

Could I say no? I nodded, turned off the ignition, kept my hands glued to the wheel so they wouldn't shake.

"Do you have any idea who his next of kin is?"

My heart, that big lump in my throat, sank like a stone.

"What's wrong? I know it's something terrible."

"You need to answer my questions first. Next of kin?"

"I don't know that there is any. He's divorced, no kids. He was an only child. He used to joke about how weird that was for an Irish kid." I could hardly get the words out. "No, wait, he had some cousins at the Jersey shore he sometimes visited. Red Bank, maybe? Or Seaside?" I shook my head. "I don't even know their names."

"He lists Len Shapiro as an emergency contact, but we're not getting any response at that number."

There were tears on my cheeks now. I could feel them. "That's my father. They were old, old friends. But Dad moved to Arizona last year."

"That explains it. It's a Brooklyn number. You have the current one?"

"I'm not telling you anything else until you tell me what's going on. You know Rick is a retired detective? And I saw him, just a few days ago…"

Her face softened slightly. "I guess we could tell you a little. I'm sorry to break this to you, but we got a call last night. He was found, he was identified, and he is deceased. It must have happened a few days back."

The tears fell harder but I only brushed them away impatiently until the detective handed me a handkerchief. I refused to start sobbing; I needed to know everything.

"An accident? A heart attack?

"I'm sorry. It definitely was not either of those. He was shot."

"What? Was it a robbery? In the house? Or on the street?"

She shook his head. "Can't tell anyone anything yet. You could tell us some things though, like when was the last time you saw him? Or heard from him?"

Somewhere in there another cop joined us. I told them. I told them about the phone calls not returned, too. I told them Rick hadn't said a thing about problems, but then he never did.

I told them I knew next to nothing about his personal life. He always said with a sly smile that the details were not fit for my young ears.

She nodded, wrote, didn't say much.

"I might be the closest thing he has to family. I've known him my whole life. He and my dad were friends since they were in second grade." I had stopped crying, for the moment anyway, and could say firmly, "You should be treating me as family."

She smiled sadly. "He was one of our own. You know? Trust that we'll do our best for him. We need to contact your father. Write out his number for me."

She went on to explain that they still had to contact kin. There would be an autopsy. No funeral until that was done and the entire department brass was satisfied his body had no more to tell them. Then the kin they found could bury him. I wondered if that would end up being me. That was enough information. At least, it was all I could take in for now.

I wanted to go home.

I was never sure, after, just how I found my way there. I pointed the car west, toward the city, and somehow ended up at my house.

The phone was beeping at me as I walked in and there was a message from the cops, the call they had made before I arrived at Rick's. I started crying again.

I should be calling my father. I knew I should. He was about to hear shocking news from total strangers. No matter what the coolness was between them the last few years, they had been lifelong friends. And no matter how I felt about my old man myself, I had some responsibility here. But my mind and body both were be shutting down. I would suck it up and call after I rested a little.

I sleepwalked up to my room and curled on my bed, fetal position, under my old comforter on this hot summer day, and cried until I couldn't cry any more. I got up with an aching head and raw eyes, fumbled my way to what used to be my kitchen, looking for who knew what, found a bottle of wine in the cartons in the dining room, could not remember where I had packed the corkscrew, and instead poured vodka into a plastic cup I found.

It didn't help the headache and it didn't stop the tears when they started again, thinking about how I would have to tell Chris. Thinking about how, when I stopped crying, I would have to think, really think, about what had happened to him and why. Was I crying for everyone else I missed too, my mother, my young husband, even my father? The father he used to be?

I woke up to bright sun pouring in. My first thought was yesterday, and everything that had happened. And that I had never called my father.

My stomach tied itself into knots. I would have to tell Chris too. Somehow. I would have to somehow take in that Rick was dead. Rick was dead. How was that possible?

Oh, and there was something wrong in my house. It was too quiet. It was after ten and there were no workmen creating a head-splitting racket. Oh, yes, they were getting supplies today. I could walk around in my pajamas.

Where to start? Cold water on my face and a hot shower. Wrapped in a beach towel, I went downstairs, gulped down the room temperature Greek coffee left from the night before last, wandered to the computer to look for mail. There was one in the New Mail folder:

HEARD ABOUT RICK. I AM IN REHAB
CENTER WITH A BROKEN HIP (YOU
OUGHT TO SEE THE OTHER GUY). I'LL
BE IN NEW YORK AS SOON AS THE DOCS
SPRING ME, DAD

He'd written it late last night.
I wrote back:

YOU HAVE E-MAIL THERE? WHERE ARE
YOU? WHAT HAPPENED?

The phone rang, shockingly loud in the silent house.

"Yah, they have all the modern conveniences out here on the frontier," he said without a greeting. "Tell me everything."

It was his gravelly voice and Brooklyn accent for the first time in six months. And last time, the last few times, we had nothing good to say to each other. It was so good to hear his voice I had to remind myself I was still mad at him.

"First you tell me."

"I see you still think you're in charge? Well, I had a little car accident, I broke a few bones and I'm going to be fine evenually. That's it."

"A car accident? And you didn't tell me?"

"Yeah, well, seems like you were not too happy with me last time we talked."

"But that was…"

"If my memory isn't failing, you hung up on me."

I did, much as I would have liked to deny it. Or to remind him of what he said that caused me to do it. Or…no, this was not the time. For once, I swore, I would not engage.

"Besides," he said, almost inaudibly, "it was a little embarrassing for a man who drove a car for a living." Then he added quickly, "It was the jerk other guy's fault, his insurance paid for everything, his license should've been lifted when he turned about a hundred, but still. Now. You want to fight, or are you going to tell me what the hell is going on?"

Of course I wasn't going to tell him everything about my life, but I could feel him listening hard, across the wires, from halfway across the country while I told him what I could about Rick. It wasn't much.

He was silent for so long, I thought the line had gone dead. Then he said, "I should tell you some things. Are you up to dealing with some business?"

"I can be, if I have to. I'm a tough girl. Remember?"

"How could I forget? So. Years ago, when he got divorced for the second time and he was still with the department, he made me executor of his will. It was supposed to be me dealing with the paperwork, the insurance, everything. He figured, on the job you never know. I've got no idea if he ever changed that. There might be no one to step up. Or maybe it would be you, until I can get home. What a mess." He used a few choice expletives. My dad, who never even said hell in front of me.

"Remember, when I rented out my house, I brought over a file cabinet, stuck it in your basement?"

I did. I balked at having the responsibility, angry as I was about his move.

"All my old papers are in there, and I have a file for Rick too. Top drawer, a file with a green stripe at the top. Copies of his will, insurance, funeral arrangements, everything. Get it and follow up. Call the numbers on those papers, find out what to do. You'll need a death certificate. There should be some lawyer to call."

"Dad..."

"If I was there I would be doing it all so you wouldn't have to."

"Dad. I know what to do. I've done it before."

There was a long, long silence, and then he said softly, "I know, baby. I haven't forgotten. I should be there, and I will, soon as I can."

"Dad, I..."

"One other thing..."

"Dad!" I finally got it out. "You don't have to come home. It's too far. I'll deal." If he was here, he'd try to turn me into his kid, helpfully telling me what to do at every turn, remaking my life for me when I didn't want it remade. And he might bring that woman, too.

"Honey, I never doubted you'd deal. I just wish you didn't have to. And there's something else. You sitting down? If he never changed it, he left his life insurance to you."

"You're kidding."

"Nope. He figured he would never have kids, his parents were gone, he felt like you were the family he wanted to take care of."

"That's crazy. I can hardly believe it." I was too shocked even to start crying again.

"I think it meant something to him, to do that. Ya know? I don't know but it might make you sort of in place of 'next of kin.' So when you make these business calls say that. OK?"

I had to say OK, but none of this was OK, none of it, and he heard it in my voice. "Are you all right?"

"No, I'm not all right. Of course not. But I'll manage. I'm home, I have friends."

"Tell you the truth, I don't think I even believe it yet. Know what I mean?"

"Do I ever."

"Sending Chris to camp must have been one of the last things he did. Yeah, we talk, Chrissie and me. You think she doesn't stay in touch?" Another expletive. "Talk to me about something else, something good. Tell me about my only grandbaby."

"Oh, Dad, she's beautiful. She got so grown up this year. You'll be shocked when you see her. I'm shocked."

"Yeah, tell me about it. Now you know about the trick kids play on us They grow up when we aren't looking. Oh, nurses are here. Looks like I've got to get off now. Keep me up to date, and don't let any of those paper pushers push you around. Got to go." His voice faded, as if he turned to someone else. "Hold on, can't you?" Then he was back to me. "Last thing. I've done some thinking, these last months…we'll talk more."

And he was gone.

I could barely force myself to put the phone down; I wanted so badly to hold onto the connection. I guess I missed him after all.

I told myself that he had given me a job to do, and I'd better get to it. I dug out a flashlight and headed down to the damp, musty, badly lit basement, one level below the garden floor. There were spider webs, and it was so far below street level it flooded when there was rain. I never knew what puddles and mud I might find when I ventured down there. Joe had said something about installing a pump for that. Oh, sure, I thought, as I cautiously navigated the old stairway. Someday when I had some spare cash lying around. That would be never. But why, I asked myself for the hundredth time, didn't I ever remember to at least put in brighter light bulbs? Oh, yeah, because I never wanted to go down there for any reason, even to do that.

The file cabinet was shoved into a corner, covered in a layer of dust and looking somewhat more rusted than I remembered. I wrestled the drawer open, struggled with propping up the flashlight so the beam gave me light while I used both hands to flip through the files. They were neatly labeled and arranged, so like my dad, and yes, there was Rick's.

I could see I would be spending this day dealing with papers I didn't want to look at, making business calls that were sure to become more painful with each conversation, and the one I dreaded most, contacting Chris somehow. I should start with a call to my museum job, telling them that I would not be in for the rest of the week. And a call to Steven Richmond, too, that I would not be available. That there had been a death in the family.

Chapter Ten

I looked at the folder with the green stripe. Drummed my fingers on it. Put it on the table next to the phone and got a pad and pen. Carefully placed them next to it. Then I decided I could focus on this difficult business better if had some breakfast. Heartened by that thought, I threw on some clothes and went out in search of pancakes. Or bacon and eggs. And definitely, hot coffee.

I stepped out into sunshine so bright it hurt my eyes and a light breeze to make it a perfect summer day. That seemed all wrong to me.

Mr. Pastore was out pruning his roses and Mrs. Pastore was vigorously sweeping the sidewalk. She gave me a friendly wave. I had to stop, even though the need to make small talk made me want to run away.

"Hey, Erica. How ya doin'?"

"I'm fine." I forced out the ghost of a smile. "How was the shore?"

"Sandy and hot. Give me the city streets any time. But the grandkids enjoyed it and we enjoyed them." She squinted at me. "Are you really all right?"

"I…yes…really…it's been…a family friend…" My eyes began to sting and I blinked hard to stop the tears.

"Hey, you don't have to talk, but I see something's wrong. Don't you forget, we're here, Sal and me? Come for dinner any time, and bring Chris too."

Then I had to smile for real. "She's at camp, but I do appreciate the offer. I'm on my way out for breakfast now. Contractor's torn up my kitchen."

"Joe and his guys? They made an awful racket yesterday, but they did a good clean up, no mess on the street." She nodded emphatically. "Good workers. Well, listen, I'm always up and dressed and got a pot of coffee going by seven. Plenty for you." She turned back to her sweeping but something struck me as I walked past.

"Mrs. Pastore, I never thought to ask before—I know you've been in this house forever, but exactly when did you move in?"

"1980. Yes, a long time now."

"Sure is, but I was hoping it was even a little more, back to the early seventies."

"How old do you think we are?" Mr. Pastore finally looked up from his roses. "We were still a young couple then, living with my mother. Actually, my uncle lived here." He shook his head. "You think I can garden? I learned it all from him. He grew everything. All kinds of tomatoes, herbs, roses that make mine look like weeds. Even had a grape arbor and made his own wine from the grapes."

"He isn't, by some chance, still alive? I'd like to know more about this block back then."

"Nah. He would never have left his house while he was still drawing breath in this life. He'd be about a hunnert and five, too. Matter of fact, he died under his arbor drinking a glass of his wine, like he would have wanted. When he passed on we bought the house from my aunt. She passed a long time ago now, too."

Mrs. Pastore said thoughtfully, "I might have some pictures, if you'd like to see them. Sal, you know, from your mother's albums. If I can find them, I'll be happy to show you."

"I'll hold you to that, and soon. See you later."

At my favorite coffee shop, the kind with Formica tables and sticky plastic-covered menus, I ran into Joe coming out of the hardware store.

"Hey, Erica. What do you think of our progress? Some of the guys are picking up your appliances today. We build tomorrow."

He was looking at me oddly and said, "Let me buy you breakfast."

We took a booth and a waitress brought us coffee without asking. It was that kind of place. We ordered without even looking at the menu.

"All right. What's the matter? Tell buddy Joe."

I told him about Rick. They had met a few times. He put his big, calloused hand over mine, and held tight for a minute. Strangely, it seemed to be just what I needed.

"How can I help?"

I shook my head. "I have to go home and face everything. All of it." I looked at the plate where bacon and eggs had been piled a few minutes ago and added, "At least now I'm fueled."

He picked up the check. "Come on. I'll walk you home. I have a thought."

"Really, I'm…"

He was already steering me out of the door. "You need to tell Chris. Do you want to go get her? I'll drive you there. You only have to say the word."

I came to a dead stop, right in the middle of the crowded morning sidewalk. "You would do that? That is so—oh Joe, that is so kind. I don't know yet. I don't know what to do, but it helps just to know you would."

"Hey." He smiled. "She was part of my crew this summer. I take care of my own."

We were at my corner. "Thank you. You don't need to come to the house now. I'm going to go do what I have to." I added, "About Chris. I'm thinking that I'll wait a little, until maybe I know what's what. You know her. She'll have questions and I don't have any answers. Not yet."

"Are you sure that's the best way to go?"

"Oh, hell no, I'm not sure about anything. But for now…"

"I got it. I'll see you at the house early tomorrow to work. Call me if you need anything. Don't be a dope about it."

I trudged on up the block, turned into my gate and saw him still standing on the corner, watching me.

I finally forced myself to read through the file. There was the will, with my father as executor. In case of inability to serve, it was me. I guess Dad being in the hospital qualified as inability to serve. Geez, Rick, I thought, what made you think that was a good idea? Did you never think Dad might not be here? You knew he went away. Did you never think something could happen before he came back? Obviously not.

His pension papers and his life insurance with my name on it. Power of attorney, with dad's name and then mine. A funeral home form that seemed to say it was all pre-paid and that they had instructions about what he wanted. I sure wouldn't have known but I now owed it to him to carry out his wishes.

And here was the next of kin, someone in New Jersey, with Malone in between Eileen and what must be her married name. The cousin I half remembered existed. I dug out the card for the detective at Rick's house. Sergeant Simms. She remembered me.

"My father is his executor but he's in a hospital in Arizona and I'm the back up. I have all the papers. Can you tell me if his family was notified? He didn't have any living siblings, but I have a cousin…."

'Yes," she said. "We found a name. She knows. A cousin."

"Donovan? Eileen Donovan in Seaside Heights? So I can contact her? I need to talk to her about the funeral and things like that."

"Yes, go ahead."

I had resolved to keep this call businesslike but I was weakening swiftly. "But what can I possibly say to her? She'll want to know what happened, I'm sure."

"We don't know yet, beyond that it was certainly a crime, and you already know that. Besides," she said, not unkindly, "if we did know more, we couldn't tell you."

There was a long silence, so long a silence that I felt it was telling me something, but what?

"I'm going to tell you a little, and only because maybe it will help you think of something useful to us. It will get out anyway sooner or later. Cops gossip, and no doubt it will be on the news soon and everywhere." She sighed. "He was killed and it wasn't an accident and it wasn't a robbery. I'm not telling you where we found him. There are some details we need to keep quiet."

"What are you saying?" It seemed important but I couldn't seem to understand it. Maybe I didn't want to.

"Someone shot him, probably in a fight, and tried to get rid of the body."

"That's crazy. I don't believe...that is so not possible...you must...." I stopped myself from babbling more.

The was another long silence, and then she said, "Look, Ms. Donato, we understand this must be painful for the people who were close to him, family or not, and that includes some still in the department who knew him, but I cannot discuss an investigation with you any further. We are..." She paused. "We are concerned about some aspects of what we found and we need to move ahead very carefully. And along those lines, anything *you* can tell us about his associates, friends, hangouts, might be helpful. I know you said you don't know much, but if anything at all comes to mind, please call."

"Sure," I said, automatically, my mind caught by something else. "But what did you mean, you are 'concerned?' Does that mean you found something? I'm sure I could be more helpful, if you would just explain more. What do you want?" It was worth a shot.

She sighed. "It's up to us to decide what is helpful, not you. You can keep thinking about what you might know. Asking me questions I can't possibly answer is not helping. We do the asking. Call if you think of something to tell me."

"But..."

"There are no 'buts.'"

And she was gone. I hated everything she said. She wasn't exactly wrong, but I still hated it.

What did I really know about Rick? He liked to go fishing off Long Island and in the Caribbean too. He liked to go to Atlantic City so I guess that meant he had a taste for gambling. Sure he did, because I knew he liked the track too. He liked live music clubs in New York, the older places that still played straight ahead jazz. I don't suppose he did any of those things alone, but who he went with and where he stayed, I had no idea.

He was retired, but he never seemed old. He never even seemed older. He was always the unencumbered bachelor who seemed immune from the everyday cares of life that kept my parents busy. He always seemed to be having fun.

I worked my way through a couple of business calls about insurance and pension, filing the necessary information, finding out what my responsibilities were.

Then there were only two items left on my to-do list: call Rick's recorded next of kin, and call the funeral home named in Rick's papers.

I'd run out of excuses.

"Is this Eileen Malone Donovan? This is Erica Donato. I'm so sorry to be introducing myself in these circumstances, but I was a friend of Rick Malone, your cousin, and it seems I'm his executor, too, at least until my father is able to come back to New York. He was Rick's old friend...."

She cut me off. "I've had a flood of calls from some New York detectives." It was an old woman's voice. "First call was about Rick. Such a shock. And then all these questions and questions. What is going on here?"

"Trust me, I wish I knew. The police haven't told me anything at all except that he was killed. And I want to express my sorrow for your loss."

"Ha. Not much of a loss. We weren't a close family, miss, not at all and I never liked Rick that much, with his swagger. A show off, he was."

I had no idea how to respond to that.

"Even if I'm the closest one left—our mothers were sisters—but they ought to be talking to his good time buddies if they want to know what he was up to. I'm sure I have no idea."

That got my attention.

"What he was up to? What in the world are you talking about?"

"I don't know! They had a lot of insulting questions for me, as if he might have been some kind of low life. Why would they ask me about things like that? As if I would even know. I saw Ricky maybe once or twice a year, at someone's wedding or funeral. He was a lot younger than me and my late husband didn't get on with him at all." The indignant voice started to quaver. "Another funeral now, and somehow it's my job?" She stopped, seemed to gulp, then said, "You're the executor? It's your job," and hung up.

I was speechless. I didn't know if I should laugh or cry but knew both impulses were shock. I needed to calm down but I wasn't there yet when the phone rang.

"This is Eileen Donovan calling back."

She went on, "Please explain again why you called. We probably need to talk more."

I did.

"I should not have hung up like that. It was very rude." She said it stiffly. "I was shocked by all the calls, and I'm not young and not well. If you are Rick's executor you don't need me, I wouldn't think, but yes, I do have some family responsibilities here. There are blood ties, no matter what."

I thanked her then for calling back, and did my best to have a real conversation. "I thought you might know who else should be called and maybe you have some requests about the funeral."

"Yes, there are some other cousins. I'll tell them. I don't have anything to say about funeral plans. You tell me where and when and I'll show up. Is there anything else?

"Nothing I can think of, right now."

She made an exasperated sound and said, "I just realized who you must be. You're Len's daughter."

"Yes, exactly. I guess you know him?'

"Met him a few times, years ago, when Rick was married to—oh, one of his wives—and entertained some. I should have picked up on it sooner." She sounded a tiny bit warmer.

"You said you weren't close, but you know, Rick was good to me and my daughter too, and I'd like to understand what is going on." I need to, I thought.

"We were far from close. My late husband and me, we thought Rick was way too much of a good time Charlie. Family, yes, but he just wasn't our kind of person, BUT—and it matters—I was offended by the questions those cops were asking. I don't care if he fell away from church and all but I know what his upbringing was." She came down hard on the last two words. "He knew right from wrong."

I took a deep breath. "Just what were they asking?"

"They thought he was involved with some no good stuff. Never exactly came out and said it, but I could tell. Did he use drugs himself? Did he ever associate with questionable characters? Why would he have a lot of cash in his house? How should I know? Maybe he didn't trust banks! The nerve of that woman."

I couldn't believe what I was hearing. Did they think Rick's death had something to do with Rick's life? Something that was all wrong in his life? Rick, who behaved like a protective father toward me? A cop, on the right side of the law? Not possible. Not for a moment. That cool detective was going to get a sizzling earful from me, too.

Eileen went on. "Even if we were never friends, we were family. He was my baby cousin and I was fond of his mother." Her voice shook. "I'm going back on what I've been saying. When you get to emptying his house, if you find some pictures or keepsakes, some of his mother's things, could I have them? I'm hardly a sentimental woman, but still and all." She stopped. "I remember the day he was born."

"Absolutely. Of course I don't know when I will be in the house again. I suppose it's still a crime scene."

Chapter Eleven

A huge headache was forming right behind my eyes. Again. Maybe I could go beg a cup of coffee from Mrs. Pastore in awhile. For now, it was back to work. I called the funeral home.

The answering voice was warm and even soothing. Perhaps it was an act, straight from the funeral directors' training program, but I was happy to take it.

He had Rick's file in a moment, and told me they would take care of everything. Rick had made all the arrangements. Did I want to come and see where it would take place? He said it was certainly not necessary but that many people found it reassuring.

Strangely, I did want to. I was having trouble comprehending the reality we were discussing. Perhaps seeing the location would help me get some focus. We made an appointment for early the next day.

I would call the camp tomorrow, after that visit, when I would at least have something concrete to tell Chris. Was I trying to put it off? Definitely.

I couldn't do that without more coffee. I went to knock on Mrs. Pastore's door. She was home, and I was surrounded by a cloud of sweet baking odors and garlicky tomato sauce as soon as she opened the door. It was so much like my mother-in-law's kitchen I felt a pang of longing for my old life with Jeff and his big family.

Mrs. Pastore saw me looking around and shrugged. "I'm cooking, I don't know for who. Guess I miss the grandchildren.

Your timing is perfect. You'll have a piece of coffee cake." It wasn't a question. "And come back for dinner?" She looked at my face, and quickly added, "Or if you are tired, I'll fix you a plate of ziti with sausage to take home."

"You are a life saver."

"Honey, you're doing me a favor. Who's gonna eat it? Sal and me?" She put out a generous slice of cake. "Raspberry and pecan. Sal grew the berries himself." She added a small mountain of whipped cream and put down a mug of coffee as big as a soup bowl. "You eat, we chat, get your mind off your troubles."

My mouth full of cake, I managed to mumble, "Thank you. I…we lost a family friend…and I've been dealing with things…."

"I'm so sorry." She patted my hand. "I tell you what. You stay right here and I'm going to get that old photo album from Sal's mother. Sal would laugh at me, he says no one cares about old times, but you do. Give you something different to think about."

I let the cake and whipped cream and coffee work its spell, and she returned with two books. "The pictures are mostly her own kids and grandkids, but see, right here, Christmas dinner in this very house. Aunt Philomena with the ham, right over in that corner." She pointed in her own kitchen. "Of course that stove is new. And the food processor. That skinny kid is my Sal. Cute, isn't he? He looked like that when I met him. And that's Uncle Sal there, hanging the lights on the tree." A short, broad man, perched on a ladder and waving at the camera. "And there's some party pictures right here in this house, too, when cousin Marco got back from Viet Nam. So you see what you can make of this." She shook her head, smiling. "He would sure get a kick out of his house being some kind of research project, you can bet on that."

She made up a plate of dinner for me, and walked me to her door. There on the stoop was Mary, looking more cheerful than the last time I saw her. She made a grand gesture toward the garden. "Roses are looking good, Mrs. P."

"I'll tell Sal you said so. Can I interest you in some baked ziti?"

"You betcha. I smelled it from way out here. And how are you, honey?" she said to me. "And your little girl? I keep forgetting to tell you. You should get that Egyptian necklace away from her. I saw it before she went away. That's real bad luck." She put her hand on mine and looked deeply into my eyes. "Real bad. You've got to get it away from her."

I had no idea what she meant, but I humored her. "I will, Mary, next time I see her. Sure I will. And how are you?"

"I'm good. Nice weather we're having, isn't it? And I do like a nice plate of ziti. My lucky day. That's cause I wouldn't never wear an Egyptian necklace."

Mary accepted Mrs. Pastore's paper plate with thanks and left, to go on about her mysterious business.

"She hasn't been around lately." Mrs. Pastore said. "Poor old soul. I don't think she's always had this life, but I can never get her to tell me anything that makes sense."

I went home balancing my own plate of ziti and my house keys. My plan was dinner and really loud rock and roll to power-chord every grim thought out of my brain, at least for an hour or two.

It did cross my mind that I needed to talk to someone, but I couldn't even focus on who to call.

Darcy called me. Girlfriend ESP. "I haven't heard from you," she said, "even e-mail, so I thought I should check in."

I burst into tears. She waited patiently, and when I was done, I told her about Rick.

"Oh, Erica. Oh, how awful. He was a nice man. What can I do for you? I'm so far away, I can't come over and give you a hug. Can I send you anything? Do you want to come here for a change of scene and some mothering from me?"

I teared up again at that but said, "No, thank you, but no. I have too much to do, I can't walk out on my job, which I'm neglecting as it is. I'll muddle through."

"Well, of course you will. That was never in question. Ummm." There was a long pause. "I'm thinking of ideas. Now, how is Chris?"

I was half aware she was trying to move my mind into other directions, and, truthfully, I appreciated it. We went on to have a normal conversation about the ups and downs of large family gatherings, Maine's beautiful coast and vicious mosquitoes, her sailing mishaps, my house renovation progress. She was fascinated and amused by my meeting with Leary. The ordinary stuff of life. At the end, she said, "Don't forget for a second that I am only a phone call away. Call anytime. And there is a bed for you here anytime you need one. You get that?"

I went to bed, somewhat cheered, and slept through the night.

The next morning, I battled truck traffic on the Brooklyn-Queens Expressway all the way to the funeral home. A battle suited my mood perfectly. I was ready to cut off large trucks ruthlessly and outrun showoff kids in sports cars.

The funeral home looked reassuringly like a bank. I was relieved to see that it did not at all resemble the church where Jeff's funeral had been. The last Catholic funeral of my experience. This would be nothing like Jeff's, I assured myself.

In the hushed, carpeted, oak paneled lobby Mr. O'Hanlon was already waiting for me. He was a middle-aged, middle-sized man in a discreet suit and he shook my hand warmly, expressing his sympathy in a soft voice. We went on to a comfortable office, vaguely cozy in a neutral way, where he offered coffee or juice and we went over the plans.

He quickly realized I had no context for the discussion and explained that Rick, though raised religiously as Catholic and socially as Irish, had specified no traditional wake or visiting hours. He wanted an immediate businesslike cremation without a service, and a large memorial later, a real celebration, nothing sad. He had left a page of details.

"Sinatra and Ellington are unusual music choices, but of course we are happy to carry out his wishes. He has a message to be read at the event and a list of people he wanted to speak."

One of them was my dad. One of them, I thought, seemed familiar. A cop friend I met sometime, perhaps. I said I would contact him and fill in for Dad myself and the director said he could handle the rest.

He walked me to another room with rows of comfortable chairs and a podium. This is where the speeches would take place, with a reception in the adjoining room. Here was an easel for a photograph of the departed. They could blow one up to portrait size if I had one to give them. I told him I would hunt one down.

With no funeral, there would not be an open coffin. Raised in the Jewish tradition of a closed coffin, I must have looked as relieved as I felt, because he said quickly, "It would have been, if he had wanted it. We make them look perfect."

The last time I had been to a funeral with an open coffin was Jeff's. And he did not look perfect. He looked dead.

Then we were done. There were keys to Rick's house in the fat envelope of papers I had with me. If I could get in, I would look for a picture to display at his funeral, a picture of the Rick we knew, not the Rick who would be in the coffin. And if it was still a crime scene and I could not go in, I could talk to the cops on duty. With luck I would get an inexperienced, bored one who would want to talk to me. I was sure I had a right to be in the house. Pretty sure.

Now I had to go do battle on the Long Island Expressway. I had a date with Nettie Rogow, widow of a Brooklyn real estate millionaire.

The first twenty miles of the Expressway, not so fondly known as the world's longest parking lot, took an excruciating hour, but once I had escaped the tentacles of city traffic I barreled along, rock and roll blasting from the radio. I had fulfilled my immediate responsibilities, I would force Rick out of my mind for a few hours, and reclaim a piece of the rest of my life. At least that was my plan. My interest in Mrs. Rogow was what she could tell me for my project. And if I should learn something further, about my own house or my own block, that would be an interesting bonus to share with Chris.

That's what I told myself.

When I responded to her call, I had told her Chris had to go away. Well, she did have to, because I said so. As I explained what my work project was, and that I would love to meet her myself, she said "Of course, dear. I'm happy to have a chance to set the record straight about my Harry, may he rest in peace. I don't drive anymore. Would you like to come out here? I'm free tomorrow morning. Let's make it noon. We'll have lunch. Now, you'll need directions. Do you have a pen? Yes? Listen carefully."

That quavering old voice gave exhaustive information, down to landmarks at every turn and distances in half miles. I had a feeling that this would be an interesting meeting.

Here was the exit. I held her directions in one driving hand, looking nervously from the road to the paper and back again, and had my Mapquest directions on the passenger seat next to me. I always get lost in suburbia's gracefully curving parkways. Give me a city grid any time.

It was immediately apparent that this was not the Long Island I knew, the land of neat bungalows and split levels, with above-ground pools and quarter-acre plots. That's the Long Island where my cousins and my parents' friends lived. I drove down a landscaped parkway, then roads that wound their elegant way past stone and brick houses with spacious lawns, manicured gardens, and many shiny cars in each driveway.

After a few wrong turns I arrived at last at the address I had been given. I could see the tennis court from the road. I didn't see the pool—in-ground and landscaped, of course—until later. Chez Rogow.

I expected a butler, or at least a maid—yes, I watch Master-piece Theater—but the door was opened by a plump old lady with perfectly coifed white hair and penetrating blue eyes. She wore a smart silk pants suit in bright turquoise and a lot of rings and necklaces. Some matched; some didn't. I suppressed a smile when I saw she was wearing bedroom slippers on her feet.

"Mrs. Donato? Come right in! What a treat to have a young visitor. I am Nettie Rogow. Come in, come in, don't stand on ceremony."

I hoped my startled double take was invisible. Coming from the mouth of this expensively dressed woman was the famous Brooklyn accent mocked throughout the English-speaking world. On the phone, she had used a phony, oh-so-genteel "telephone answering voice," learned from secretaries in old movies, I guessed, but here was the real Nettie Rogow. I knew who she was from the moment she opened her mouth—a stranger in a strange land, an immigrant all the way from the tenements of Brownsville to the land of five-acre zoning. And she had never had elocution lessons to hide it, either.

"I've set up lunch in the sun room, so lovely this time of year."

She led us through some heavily knick-knacked rooms to a glassed-in porch overlooking a perfect garden.

"Do you see?" She pointed to the bird feeders. "We might get a visitor or two. Look out for cardinals—they're the bright red ones. I love to sit out here and watch them flit around. And we have deer! Such a nuisance. My daughter rages about how much they cost us, when they eat the shrubbery, but I kind of like them. We didn't have too many deer, or cardinals either, when I was growing up."

"Now young lady, you take that chair. It has the best view." She waved her hand over the table. "It's only a light meal."

Her idea of a light meal seemed to be going to the nearest delicacy emporium—what we New Yorkers call an "appetizing store"—and ordering half a pound of everything. The table was covered.

I couldn't resist smoked salmon and whitefish, flavored cream cheeses, blintzes. Fresh bagels and fragrant soft onion rolls. Fancy cookies and two kinds of coffee cake. Why even try? Mrs. Rogow kept adding more to my plate, refilling my coffee cup and generally urging me not to hold back.

"You're young yet," she said. "Dieting is for old people. The food is here to enjoy. Would you like some more cookies?"

Finally I paused for breath. She beamed at me and said, "What can I do for you?"

I offered up a well rehearsed, heavily edited version of my museum project and assured her we would ask her permission if we wanted to quote her directly.

She patted my hand and said, "I have waited a long time for this, a chance tell our true story. Those lousy newspaper reporters always got it wrong."

She jumped up and cleared a space on the table. "I pulled out my albums to show you." She came back with an enormous stack and said, "Now don't be frightened. We don't have to look at all of them. I thought it would help my memory, which is definitely not what it used to be."

She proceeded to prove just the opposite. As she opened album after album, she walked and talked me through her life: the girlhood, as I had guessed, in the Brooklyn of cold water walk-up flats and phone messages taken at the candy store on the corner, because no one could afford a phone at home. Going to work in a neighborhood store at sixteen because her family needed what little she earned.

"But I did graduate first," she said, displaying the page with her diploma. With honors, I noted. "And we sewed our own graduation dresses in home economics, too," she added, turning to the photo of her class, all in ruffled white.

"And your husband?" I prompted. I was actually charmed by her stories, but they were not unique. I needed to get us back on track.

"Well, there he is. And wasn't he handsome?" she said, pointing to a stiffly posed, sepia-colored wedding picture. "Of course it was a modest little wedding, in my parents' apartment. I was only eighteen. No one had money for a big party, but there was a real wedding cake, and schnapps, and the relatives brought food. I wore my cousin's gown, but my Harry bought me lovely flowers."

"You have to understand," she said earnestly. "He wasn't any neighborhood boy, not one of the no-goodniks from the streets, even though he started with nothing, just like me. But he was one with plans. I could see that even then, and that's how he swept me off my feet." She made a gesture that encompassed the whole house. Her whole life, I thought. "Was I smart?"

"And how did he get started?"

"The local bank foreclosed on a crummy little building with a store and a few apartments. He saw his chance and he took it, my smart Harry.

"It wasn't easy at first, I can tell you. I went without a new dress two years to pay off that first building. But bit-by-bit, he added to his holdings. After the children came, we moved out of that Brownsville walk-up to a nice new apartment building on Ocean Parkway—with elevators!—and then, in time, we came out here. Look at what he was able to do for us—lovely home, the best schools, a country club. He gave me the life of a queen."

"It sounds like he was a good husband."

"The best. I was a lucky woman. He was a doting father too."

I took a deep breath.

"Weren't there some tenant organization issues right around that time, too? Were you—I mean—your company—ever affected by that?'

She looked away, and when she looked back there were tears in her eyes. "My Harry, may he rest in peace, he was a wonderful man. He worked so hard to make something of himself. He did not deserve what they did to him, those crooked politicians and those lousy, lying reporters."

She struggled to regain her composure, and then said abruptly, "Have you had enough? Another slice of lox? Or more coffee cake?

"So, you're interested in Park Slope, where you live? Hand me that book over there—not the green one, that's the family pictures—that black one—these are our buildings. We started picking up cheap buildings there in the early sixties, I suppose. Maybe even late fifties. People who used to live there were dying to sell and move out to the suburbs then."

She flipped through the pages as she talked. "Well, of course they were. Drugs, gangs, oh, Brooklyn got bad then. And they wanted green grass, too. Ah, here they are, see what you recognize."

I was having trouble stemming her flood of talk so I could learn more about her husband and his questionable business practices, but I could get back to it. I could not pass up a chance to learn more about my own personal information quest. And Chris would never forgive me if I did.

"I know that one. There's a dance school now, and Slope Books."

"Bookstore? Dance school? Well! They do tell me the neighborhood has changed a lot. This was a locksmith, I believe, and that was a bar. And I'm not talking about a nice club, either, where nice young people go to meet and hear music. I'm talking about the kind of place where there were fights every Saturday night. My Harry wouldn't let me go near the place. Still and all, those bars paid good rent, like any other business."

I kept turning the pages and then stopped. "That's our block. Did you own all these houses?"

"No, dear, of course not, but we did own several. Which one is yours? Can you tell?"

"The first of the row of little houses. Right there." I put my finger on a photo of the familiar block, with very unfamiliar cars in the street.

"Why, yes, I believe that one was ours. The whole row was."

"Mrs. Rogow, when was this? And what was it like on our block then? That's what I really want to know." It wasn't close to being all I wanted to know, but it was a start.

"Let me see." She slipped the large photo out of its plastic sleeve and looked at the back. "This is from around 1970. What was it like? A lot of the buildings were chopped up into tiny apartments before we ever bought them. Low rents and very unreliable, low-class tenants. And sometimes we tried renting out the whole house to groups of young people. We figured they couldn't be worse. And we were in business, after all—a large group could pay more than one family. Were we ever wrong about them!"

"They couldn't pay more?" That didn't sound right to me.

"No, dear, of course they could. My Harry was never wrong about something like that. But they were terrible tenants, even the ones from nice families. They always said they were students.

Dropouts, that's what they were, lazy hippies and draft-dodgers. Filthy habits, skipped out on the rent, had all kinds of friends staying there with them. And who knew what they were doing? Wild parties, we heard, and selling dope, no doubt. The other people on the block hated them and the police—don't ask. They were there again and again.

"Sometimes they just disappeared in the middle of the night." She paused. "Goodness, it's been years since I thought about this, but it is coming back to me.

"Of course they owed us money when they did that, and if that wasn't bad enough, one time at least, they left garbage piled up in all the rooms. We didn't find out for weeks. Why did they have to do a thing like that? And what a mess it was! Smart aleck little spoiled…well, I don't use the kind of language they deserve. And then they called Harry names. Those s.o.b.'s."

Was the genteel mask cracking? I saw my chance to get back to the hard questions. "The tenants? Or is that the reporters again? Or the courts? Forgive me, but there is evidence that it was not all lies."

"To call him such names! A man who worked so hard all his life! There was no reason, no reason at all." She was turning pink. "Aren't you listening to what I have been telling you? He was a good man, and those momzers, you should excuse the language, in Yiddish it means someone whose parents weren't married, the lawyers and the reporters, even worse—they tormented him."

I was very quiet. I nibbled a bit of cake, took a sip from my cup, and waited.

She looked away, not meeting my eyes, and finally said, "Ah, well, I suppose you know all about it already." She sighed. "All right, Harry was, I must admit, a stubborn man. So maybe there were a few violations. Heat that didn't always come on. Cranky old plumbing. So maybe he should have cleaned them up. But his tenants, those low lifes, demanding changes? Demanding? Taking him to court?" She shook her head. "He couldn't stand it, and then he couldn't give in. It was so long ago now, but I remember the day they took him off to jail. Contempt of court, they said it was. It was such a public humiliation, and of course there was plenty of talk." Her eyes filled with tears. "My poor Harry. And it was hard here too, to hold my head up high at PTA and the club."

"Mother?" A thin blonde in a black pants suit stood in the doorway. I had a quick impression of diamond pin, lacquered hair, red mouth, spike heels. "What is going on here? Is this a reporter?"

Mrs. Rogow said with a tight smile, "Please allow me to introduce my daughter, Brenda Rogow Petry. Brenda, this is Erika Donato, a historian." She emphasized the last word.

"Your mother is kindly sharing stories with me about Brooklyn in the 1970s for a museum project. Would you like to join us?"

"Oh, Brooklyn. All those old nickel-and-dime holdings." She waved a dismissive hand, her bright red nails glistening. "There's nothing to tell." She gave me a bright, confiding smile and sat down. "Now the real story is the way we have grown from my dad's day to being true players in real estate development. We have even had a cover story in *New York* magazine. Why don't you write about that?"

"I'm a historian, so it was your dad's day that is relevant to my work. Maybe you could fill in some details?"

"Dad's day? I never paid any attention to his older business, barely even knew where it was. I had a bigger vision and I unloaded those low-end properties as soon as I went into the company."

By then she was looking over my shoulder at the notes on my laptop screen. Some of the color seemed to leave her brightly made-up face as she looked at her mother.

"Mother, may I speak to you in the kitchen?"

"Of course, dear." Mrs. Rogow turned to me, said, "Please give us a moment for family business," and walked away.

I heard a door close, but perhaps not all the way. As their voices rose, I could hear them clearly. And I admit it, I was listening.

"What are you doing? You promised not to talk about dad's convictions. Not now of all times, now, when I am about to make our name mean something completely different."

"But, dear, it was all such a long time ago. Who cares?"

"I have to make sure nobody does. I cannot have negative publicity fouling thing up. Do you think I've been playing around all these years, making sure his reputation is buried?"

"I remember." Mrs. Rogow ground out the words. "You wanted to take his name right off the company he built. A second death, that's what it would have been. He was a wonderful man, your father—hard-working, devoted to us, ambitious. Look how well he provided for us."

"Yes, mother, he was a very successful slumlord. Have you forgotten the police at our door, where everyone could see them?"

"I know, dear. At the club…"

"The club! Spare me. I had to go to school every single day and listen to them whisper, 'Jailbird.' You don't get it. You never did."

"Don't I get it? That slumlord provided you with a very nice life. And whose money got you into your first Manhattan project, the one that put you on that map? And I might remind you, whose money still controls a large chunk of that company you refer to so carelessly as yours? Mine, last time I checked. Let's have a little respect, please."

There was silence, and then the sound of high heels clicking away in the opposite direction.

Mrs. Rogow emerged again with only a slight flush to give away there had been an emotional conversation.

"Well! Well." She smiled, shakily. "I suppose you and your daughter have the occasional heated words?"

Shaking her head, Mrs. Rogow passed the cookies again and said, "So you've found the skeleton my dear daughter wishes to put back in the closet, but really, it's never been a secret. You found it yourself in the old papers." She sighed. "No one cares any more, no matter what my daughter says. Only she cares."

She looked directly into my eyes, unsmiling and intense. "So, young lady, when you write your report, I hope you will be kind to my Harry." She had tears in her eyes when she added, "A man's whole life doesn't boil down to one bad period, or one bad decision either."

Then she smiled suddenly. "And don't forget to say that his loving widow puts out one fabulous lunch! In fact," she added, "why don't I wrap some of this for you to take home? I'll whisk a few of these platters to the kitchen and be right back."

She rode right over my protests with a firm, "It's a shame for it to go to waste. You'll take some of the cookies, of course, and the cake. I certainly don't need it. And some fish too?"

Mrs. Rogow returned with her eye liner repaired and cheeks all rosy, carrying two large shopping bags. She walked me to the door. "So you'll have what to eat when you come home from work or school. My pleasure! Now, young lady." She patted my shoulder. "You keep in touch. I'd like to know what you do with all this."

I walked to my car thinking about my house in those days. My take was a little different from Mrs. Rogow's. In my imagination I was seeing a house full of life, full of young people, trying on new selves and new ideas. They wore hippie clothes, big striped bell-bottoms and those wild flowery shirts. And long print dresses. And music playing all the time. Jefferson Airplane and the Rolling Stones? Smoke and incense.

Just as I reached the car I was accosted by Ms. Petry, walking the only unfriendly Labrador I've ever seen. It snarled, she pulled it to a hard stop and said, "Don't come back. Don't call. And don't write about my father."

I slammed the car door and peeled out of the driveway, not stopping or slowing down until I was almost at the expressway entrance. Then I pulled over and sat in the car until I could stop shaking. When I did, I started laughing. Ms. Petry might be scary, but she also reminded me of a soap opera villainess. Any soap opera villainess. I couldn't tell them apart but Chris sometimes watched. I wondered if Ms. Petry did too, and then I started laughing.

I needed to tell this story to someone who would both appreciate the absurdity and help me sort out the drama from the facts. I was on my way to Rick's house to look for a photo, having done my duty to both my professional research and my personal mystery.

Now I was back to thinking about my lost friend. I so wanted him to be there at his house. We could have laughed about the absurdity and who better than a retired detective to sort things out?

Chapter Twelve

There were no cops in sight. The yellow police tape was gone. It had never really been a crime scene anyway. They had told me it—that event, Rick's death—did not happen here. I could pull right into his driveway. Nothing was stopping me except my own second thoughts. Rick's house without Rick.

I sat in the car wishing I had a partner in this, but I had insisted to my dad I could handle things, so now it was time to prove it. I gathered my purse, slammed the car door, squared my shoulders and marched right up to the house. I had a perfect right to be here.

I let myself into the kitchen and hit all the light switches at once. It didn't add any cheer, it only made it easier to see how old-fashioned, shabby, and sad it was. I suspected Rick never used it for anything but a place to mix drinks.

I went on to the small dining room, crowded with a massive, darkly varnished dining room set, including a sideboard filled with rose-patterned china. The drawers below held ecru lace doilies and tablecloths. Surely none of this was Rick's? Perhaps his mother's?

Across the hall, a small living room was furnished with what looked like Sears Early American, 1955. Plaid upholstery and lamps with ducks on the shades. Bookcase shelves were packed with the distinctive jackets of Reader's Digest Condensed Books. Had Rick never changed a thing?

Rick had lived in a few places of his own, over the years, but at some point, as his mother aged and he was divorced, he moved back into his childhood home. He never invited us here. He always came to us, or we went out. Now I knew why.

I don't believe in ghosts, not for a moment, but if I did, this place had a few, and they weren't Rick.

Upstairs, I expected to find a rusty claw-footed tub in the one bathroom, but no, it was slickly tiled in black, with a big glass-doored shower and shiny chrome fittings. Ah, someone had gone for something like luxury here. Two of the small bedrooms were barely furnished and dusty, but a third had a desk, a computer, and a shredder. All the file drawers were open and empty. Oh, yes, the cops must have taken everything.

The biggest bedroom had a black and chrome, king-size bed with a down comforter and a lot of matching pillows. Track lighting. There was not a single photo on the dresser, or anywhere else, but there was a massive TV/VCR, and a sound system, with discs stacked in a special cabinet. It was very comfortable, in a bachelor pad sort of way. It was a little creepy to think of Rick like this, and yet comforting too, to see that he did take care of himself in the ways that mattered to him, in this dreary house. But there was no sense of him here, only a less chilly emptiness.

I opened some dresser drawers, by then not knowing what I was looking for anymore or even if I was only snooping. They held clothes, of course, in considerable disarray. Rick was a rather dapper dresser; I couldn't see him treating his clothes so carelessly. The drawers had been searched too. Of course they had.

Rick, dammit, I thought. Why isn't there anything of your life here? I thought of my own cheerfully cluttered house, and my parents. Darcy's home, higher-style, but filled with art purchased on trips and vacation photos. My advisor's, stacked with books and journals. This place was as personal as a hotel room.

Did the cops take it all? And why? Dammit again, Rick, what did you get into, and what have you gotten me into?

I was so lost in my thoughts I almost forgot that I was there to try to find a photo. Perhaps in the living room bookcases? It seemed he did not keep photos, but perhaps his mother did?

I finally found it way in the back of the empty hall closet, a dusty carton filled with pictures. There were tiny Kodaks of the New York World's Fair of 1939; wedding portraits from the 1940s, with grooms in military uniform and brides in satin dresses; this very house looking brand new on a bare lot, and here, from perhaps 1970, was Rick in a blue uniform, handsome and spiffy. It looked like a graduation portrait and was exactly what I needed. And here were framed newspaper clippings, too, stories about Rick getting awards. No doubt about who collected them. Some had notes in perfect, Catholic-schoolgirl penmanship: "Ricky" and a date.

I left the house after making sure all the doors were locked. Outside I saw two teenaged boys across the street, hanging around with no apparent purpose, but looking furtive. They wore shorts hanging off their hips. One had no shirt at all, and blond dreadlocks. The other wore a sleeveless undershirt and a bright red Mohawk. Even from across the street I could see a dramatic tattoo crawling up his neck. Their whole style was meant to be intimidating, and it certainly worked on me. I knew they were up to mayhem when one shouted up the street, "Wait! Someone's coming!"

Then, when I turned to prudently go back in the house he yelled, "Come on!" and a third boy came speeding around the corner on a skateboard.

I gasped in surprise but then I had an idea. I walked across the street, and said to the lookouts, "Nice moves! My daughter has tried it but she's not as good as that. Is this a good street to practice? Maybe I should tell her."

"Yeah, we'd show her moves," the red Mohawk said. He actually sounded quite normal. "It's not much of a challenge but there's hardly any traffic so we practice here. You live around here?"

"No, I was only visiting." By then his friend had come back up the street. "Do you?"

"Yeah," blond dreads said, "Up there, last house. They just hang here."

"Hmm. I wonder, did you ever know my friend, the man who lived in the house?"

"Rick?" They all laughed. "Sure we did. Great guy, drove a way cool car. Very cool friends too." They laughed again and exchanged knowing glances.

I smiled at them. "He was like a member of my family."

"Cool family, then." They stopped grinning and one said, "We heard something real bad? Like he's dead? The cops came to ask questions all up and down the block."

"That's interesting," I said, trying not to sound too curious. That's the end of learning anything from teenagers. "Did they tell you anything?"

"Not really." He shrugged. "He was shot, they said, and they wanted to know if we knew anything suspicious, but about his life, not like for crime witnessing. It didn't happen here, I guess."

He went on, "My dad, he lived on this block his whole life. He always said the old lady who was there before was scary, she was Rick's mother, but Rick, he was friendly, talked to everyone, came to the block parties and all."

"And he was—you know—not boring, like everyone else around here is."

"Like our parents!"

They laughed again, as if they had a shared secret.

"What about Rick's cool friends?"

"Yeah, well, lots of time we were here, there were cars in the driveway, really bad sports cars, and sometime parties at night."

Very warily, I asked, "Did he ever invite you in join the parties?"

They looked shocked.

"Hell no. We're just kids, you know?" red Mohawk said. "Our parents would have killed us."

"We saw his girlfriend a few times," the boarder said.

Blond dreads looked around, as if about to share a secret and whispered, "I saw her leaving sometimes in the early morning!"

They really were very young. I tried not to smile. And they say girls are gossips.

"She was..." The speaker turned red and then his friend elbowed him.

"Yes, she was...?"

"Um. She was hot."

"Yeah, way hot, for an older chick."

"How old would that be?"

They looked at each other, baffled, and didn't answer.

"But she can still wear those wild outfits."

"She really *wears* them, if you know what I mean."

"And her car? Red Miata convertible. I mean...." Words seemed to fail him.

I didn't want to write anything down, and maybe scare them into silence, but the tape in my head was rolling.

"It says fox on it, her plate, I mean. Like in caps with an extra X—FOXX."

They both nodded with what looked like reverence, and then one suddenly said, "We gotta roll!" and roll away they did.

As I walked back to the car, I was smiling at the encounter with boys who were probably in junior high. And I was wondering how hard it could be, to track down the owner of a license plate that said FOXX?

So Rick had a girlfriend he never wanted me to meet? I certainly wanted to meet her.

Before I could go home, I had to make one last stop. It was about time— no, it was way past time—to check in with Elliot, my boss at the museum. I had called in about bereavement leave, but I felt I was pushing my luck here. Part-time internship though it was, they were giving me a small paycheck and I needed to get academic credit for the work. I had to compose my face and my mind, and simultaneously find a parking space in impossibly crowded Brooklyn Heights. Calm in the face of stress.

It took twenty minutes of circling the crowded streets before I found a parking space. I sat in the car for another ten, waving away hopeful parking-space seekers, while I thought through what I needed to say and how I needed to say it. Apologetic yet firm, reassuring, and responsible.

Elliot is a laid-back former professor, but I'd had a message from him that THE boss wanted to talk to me. It's a small museum so I'd sat in on meetings with the boss and she knew my name, but I didn't really know her. She was older than I am but she was neither old enough to be motherly nor so inclined. She was new on the job and very determined to raise our museum's profile, raise attendance, and, of course, raise money. I found her smart and somewhat scary.

I knocked on her door.

"Erica! Come in, and tell me what is going on. Elliot had some distressing information for me."

"Yes, I had a family crisis, a death…"

"So he said. Please accept my sympathies. Now, what I really need to know is, how will that affect your work here? We do have a schedule for our upcoming exhibits and deadlines we need to meet."

"I am unexpectedly involved in a funeral. I mean, it is usually unexpected but in this case…"

She stopped me with a raised hand. "The details don't really matter and you have no obligation to tell me. What I need is to know that you will manage to fulfill your responsibilities in a timely fashion, or—if you cannot—then we will need to reassign your projects. Normally I would leave this to Elliot to manage but this fall will be a busy time here, and I need to be more hands-on. So?"

I gulped. This was even harder than I had expected. "I may need to take some extra days off to manage these personal responsibilities but I'm sure Elliot and I can work this out." I was afraid my voice shook. "I can complete work at home, at odd hours, writing up research and so on, so we do not fall behind in anything. Absolutely."

She smiled, a very small, very tight smile. "I'm glad to hear that. Of course you know we will be unable to give you a favorable report for your academic program if you cannot complete the research assigned to you? I'm sure you will keep that in mind, that if you let us down, you will also let yourself down."

"Thanks. I promise you have nothing to worry about. Nothing."

I walked out with a firm step, head held high, and then sagged against the wall in the hallway. I knew I would have to make good on that promise, even if I had to steal the time from sleeping. I could not afford to throw away a whole summer of work.

When I finally got home Joe's crew was gone, but as evidence of their presence, I had shiny new appliances in their assigned places in the kitchen and the frames of my new cabinets were up all around them. It was the one bright spot in my day but I had no time to check them out in detail. And nothing was hooked up yet, so I had no food to cook and no access to cooking equipment anyway. I was too exhausted to go out and did not want any of Mrs. Rogow's care package. One meal like that in a day was enough. Too much.

Then I found a shopping bag on the coffee table with my name in bold black marker.

It was full of containers: Greek salad with salty feta cheese and delicious olives; lemony chicken kebabs and rice; a platter of Middle Eastern dips with fresh pita bread wrapped in napkins. A bottle of water, a bottle of my favorite beer, a large Styrofoam cup of high-test Greek coffee and two slices of baklava oozing honey syrup. And a note in more marker:

> Thought you might need dinner, now that we've
> packed up your kitchen. My treat, and have a
> relaxing evening at home.
>
> J.

Joe. What a good friend he was. A Middle Eastern feast, so appealing on a hot night; a sinful dessert; a cold beer.

I had excellent intentions to get to work, but I could not focus. My whole life right now was about researching, asking questions, finding answers. Of course that's what my professional life always was, but that work took place in libraries, whether they were stone and brick or virtual. It felt less compelling right now than the real world questions about Rick and the girl in my house and recent events in my life, all tumbling around in my mind like clothes in a dryer. Of course I couldn't focus.

What I wanted to do most, this minute, today, was find Rick's girlfriend. That was the one concrete thing I could do. Maybe she was the key I needed. Maybe, I hoped faintly, she could lay all my doubts about him to rest. She could tell me he was a fun loving guy—well, he must have been, if he had a girlfriend called FOXX!—but that he was the straight arrow cop I always thought he was. She could tell me that those detectives with questions had it all wrong.

A quick Internet search turned up several offers to get this type of information fast and cheap. I hit the right keys, sent in my request, paid for it electronically, and crossed my fingers.

I had one more task I could not continue to duck. I punched in the numbers for the camp office and asked for the camp director.

She was sympathetic and understanding and assured me it was not the first time they had to cope with a situation like this. We worked it out that Chris would call me soon, when she came to the dining hall for dinner. We could arrange to have her leave camp if she wanted to, or to come home for the service and go back, or perhaps it would be better for her to hold tight to her routine and stay there. I would have to feel her out.

Finally, she offered all the support Chris might need, and volunteered that I had a lovely daughter who had instantly fit into camp life.

It was all I could do to keep from telling her the whole story of my life and pour out everything that was on my mind. She was that good.

In a few minutes Chris would call. I paced the floor; thought about what to say, having no idea what to say. Noted that I already had an e-mail answer to my query about the license plate. The FOXX was named Wanda Beauvoir and she lived in Bay Ridge. In Brooklyn. Not far. I was working out my next move when the phone rang.

"Mommy?" She hadn't called me mommy in years except for the day we found the body. "Why am I calling you? What is wrong?"

"Oh, honey." I flashed on her face, so far away from me. "Something…happened. Do you have someone there with you?"

"Yes, yes, Katherine, the director. And Mel came with me. What IS it?" Her voice shook. "Not grandpa?"

"No, no, it isn't that. In fact I talked to him yesterday. No, it's Rick.'

"He's in the hospital? It's his awful smoking, isn't it? We told him and told him…."

"No, honey, it's worse than that." I swallowed hard. "Chris, I'm so sorry to say this. He passed away. It was several days ago. I didn't…no one knew…for awhile."

There was an endless silence, then a flat, "That's impossible."

"If only, but it's the truth."

Another long silence, then sobbing, then Mel came on, "Mrs. Donato, what's wrong? What should I do?"

I gave her an extremely edited version of the facts, then said, "Give Chris a big hug and put her back on with me, please."

"Look, Chris," I said. "Are you listening?"

She whispered, "Yes."

"If you want to come home right now, we'll find a way. OK? Talk to Katherine there, and think about it, and call me later. She said that because of this, you could call me any time. I would so love to see you, but you don't have to come home. It's your choice. You could wait and come back for the memorial service when we finally get it planned. You got that? Or stay there in your camp routine and come home when camp is done.

"And Katherine knows everything and will help you with everything. Including feelings. She said you can sleep in her cabin tonight if you don't want to be in yours. Oh, honey…"

She started sobbing again, and so did I. She was the one who stopped first, I am ashamed to say, and said, "Tell me what happened to him. I have to know."

So I gave her the same edited version I had given Mel. I thought I knew my daughter. I thought she would have plenty of questions, once the shock wore off, but it didn't even take that long.

"I don't believe it, not a word of it. He died, just like that, and no one knew for a while? That's ridiculous. What are you not telling me? You have to stop treating me like a baby!"

"Honey, I don't know the details myself."

"You know something. I can tell."

I crumbled. She would learn the facts eventually, and they would hurt no matter when.

"He was shot, Chris, and it was not an accident. His body was found—somewhere, I don't know where, *and* it's a police investigation."

"Someone killed him? I don't…that's…." Her voice faded and I was afraid she might faint, but she came back strongly with, "And what are they doing to find this…this murderer?"

I assured her they were working very hard, and when she tried to ask more, I maintained I had nothing else to tell her. There was no way she needed to know about the ugly suspicions.

"Mom?" she finally said. "I don't want to hang up yet. Could you, like, just talk to me? About anything? For a minute more?"

So I told her about the Pastores' albums, and turned my meeting with Leary into an adventure, and about the progress on the house. I told her the entertaining parts of my visit with Mrs. Rogow and expressed pride that she had made the contact all on her own.

I talked until I could hear in her voice that she would not fall apart when I said good-bye.

"Did you do anything more about our skeleton?"

"I've had a couple of other things to think about! I still have a job, you know, which I haven't been doing, and responsibilities about Rick and I have the house. Joe misses you, he says. And I have…"

"I know, I know, but you did promise not to forget about her."

"I know I did, sweetheart, and I haven't, but I've been pretty distracted. I won't forget. Really."

She sighed. "I feel a little better now. Oh, Katherine had someone bring our supper in to her office, she says so I can have a little privacy and quiet. And then I think I'll go for a walk, you know? To to think about things."

"Do I ever know. Let's talk tomorrow, same time? And sooner, if you need to? Love you."

"Love you, too, mom. Don't worry. I'll be fine. And YOU call ME if you need me, too. Or call Darcy or someone!"

I was so touched by her concern for me, the tears prickled in my eyes again. "I'm not alone," I told myself. "I have plenty of friends but I've been too busy to talk to them. And I have neighbors. Plenty of people to call on if needed."

Then I swore to myself I would not cry or even mope, I would do something useful. My fingers pushed the phone number still up on my screen, Rick's girlfriend with the provocative license plate.

Chapter Thirteen

The answering machine told me I'd reached Wanda. Good. Her voice told me she was a Brooklyn girl. Good again. I didn't leave a message. I already knew I was going to see her first thing tomorrow and didn't need or want an invitation.

The phone rang with an unknown local number. Not work, not Chris' cell, not Darcy from Maine, not my dad from Phoenix. It was no one I wanted to talk to and I was done talking, or doing anything productive whatever, for this too-full day. I let it go to the machine.

I was astonished to hear Steven Richmond, responding to my message about being unavailable for work this week. He didn't sound angry so I picked up.

"You are there after all. Excellent. I was hoping to say it in person. I'm sorry to hear of your loss and don't worry about getting your information to us."

"Well, uh, thank you. I'm happy to know it won't be a problem." Right. His project was the least of my current worries, even with the generous fee.

"Not at all. We are working on other aspects of the project and have plenty to keep us busy for now. Too busy, in fact. However..."

There was a pause, and then he continued.

"However, I am giving myself an evening off for a Central Park concert. Any chance you would like to come along? I thought—well, I happened to talk to Darcy—maybe you could use a night off too?"

I was too tired to go anywhere. I was too tired to talk. Or even think.

"I…it's late…too late…dinner…"

"I have a picnic." He sounded amused. "And I'm not far. I could pick you up in a few minutes. If you'd like to play hooky for an evening?"

Suddenly I saw myself under the stars, with nothing to do but let the music wash over me. An evening of respite from my entire life looked like a wonderful idea.

"Ten minutes?"

"I'll see you then."

Energized, I jumped into a one-minute shower and subjected my pathetic wardrobe to an increasingly frenzied search mission. I pretty much wear the same clothes, casual pants and tops, for school, for work, for daily life. I hardly ever need anything else and my limited time and budget for fashion is dedicated to Chris. But tonight, I was going out. To an event. I didn't want to be a slob.

Finally I settled on an old print sundress that—maybe— didn't look old, and sandals with heels to dress it up. No, not heels for walking on the park lawn. Espadrilles. Chris had a nice pair. I raided her jewelry collection for earrings. A necklace? Yes, no, maybe. I was out of practice with this girl stuff and wished she were here to help me with my hair. I looked for her curling iron and then remembered she had packed it. A curling iron for camp? Not like my Girl Scout days, that's for sure.

I fumbled with my mascara and was wiping it off my cheek when the doorbell rang. I flew downstairs still barefoot.

"Two more minutes. That's all I need. And I have something for you, for my assignment, right there on the coffee table. I have old photo albums of this very block. Take a look." I flew back upstairs, wincing at how unsmooth I had been.

I took a deep breath before I went down again, now with make up on my face, shoes on my feet, purse in hand, calm and composed.

He was so absorbed in the albums he didn't look up until I was in front of him. Then he stood up quickly, refocused and smiled at me. "Let's go."

He looked great. Why had I not noticed that before? I had an impression of a crisp haircut, highly polished shoes, and a blue shirt that went way too well with his blue eyes. It was unnerving and I was already a little unnerved.

"Thank you for helping me turn my life off for tonight." We were walking down my stoop. "It was strange enough to have Chris away and now....I'm barely functioning."

"I know. Maybe a pleasant night out will be just what the doctor ordered." He helped me into his car, a pale beige convertible of some kind. I sank into pale beige soft leather seats and air conditioning. Not much like my decrepit Civic.

Even on the rough local streets, the car glided smoothly ahead. With the radio pouring out even smoother classical music, and the top down, I started to feel a bit like Cinderella in her coach.

We went over the magnificent arch of the Brooklyn Bridge, with all of New York harbor, the Statue of Liberty and the whole ocean beyond, spread out below to the left; the East River, dotted with sailboats and barges, stretching north to our right; and the downtown skyline straight ahead, beginning to turn pale gold from the low sun. I never got tired of that view.

Traffic was light and we chatted about nothing much. He thanked me for the look at the album and asked me to have copies made, at his cost of course. I told him about my eccentric new source, Leary, and what I had been learning from him. He laughed at my description, and I assured him if anything came up that was relevant to his project, I would include it. He asked me about my house. "Being a historian, have you ever been tempted to find the story of your own house?"

"Funny that you should ask. I'm toying with the idea now." I wasn't going to tell him why I was tempted, though. I still wasn't about to turn that lost young girl into a social anecdote for this suave stranger.

"I suppose it could be risky. You never know if you will like what you learn."

I changed the subject, asking him where he lived. "A big, old apartment building, no place special. It's near here."

We were on the upper East Side by then, where the avenues are lined with massive apartment buildings; the side streets with elegant Edith Wharton-era town houses, many of them now sporting diplomatic flags; and the shop windows held shoes that cost more than I earn in a month.

I did not know what to say next to someone who lived this life so I was glad we had arrived at Central Park. He drove right in, handed a note to the first park officer who stopped us, and parked where there was no parking.

"What? How can you?"

"Ah. I have friends in the right places."

We strolled toward the Sheep Meadow where the concert would be. He carried nifty collapsible chairs that folded into their own canvas carriers and an elegant tote bag from a caterer.

He walked with purpose and soon settled us on a slight hill, with a view of the stage, and plenty of grass.

"Did you know this was the perfect place?"

"Pretty much. The whole park seems like my own backyard. I grew up right across the street, a bit uptown."

I was a long way from home now.

His bag produced two bottles of wine with glasses, dips with vegetables, sliced beef filet, with cutlery and china, French bread, French mustard, French cheese. Oh, and English horseradish sauce.

For a little while, conversation stopped as we ate and watched the sky turn to gold, then pink, then deep blue, and the surrounding park grew dark and mysterious.

Steven said, "Better than a movie, isn't it? One of the finest shows in the city."

Then, perhaps it was the wine, but we were telling each other little pieces about our lives, like any first date. Was I, Erica Donato, hard-working mother of a teen, on a first date tonight? For the first time in a long time? I wasn't sure. I wasn't even sure I liked him.

I barely knew him, but I was telling him why I am a Mets fan and a little about growing up in the far reaches of Brooklyn. I kind of skipped over my father, though, and I wasn't at all ready to talk about Jeff.

He told me about his sailing camp summers and skiing winters, the father who faded out of this life, and his uncle, James Hoyt, a mover and shaker and a front page name in New York even I recognized.

"He taught me everything a boy needs to know, like how to tie a tie, how to survive boarding school, how to drive a stick shift, how to dress for an interview."

"How to ask a girl to dance?"

He laughed. "No, they sent me to dancing school for that, but he did teach me how to mix a martini."

"I so get it because that's who Rick was to me. He taught me to how to play poker and how to turn down a pushy guy. And I filled in for him as the kid he never had. Chris too, like you did with James."

Steven looked away. "Not exactly. James did have one of his own, my cousin JJ. James, Jr. of course. He was much older, and, well, I idolized him, at least for a time. His life didn't turn out so well. So in essence, I'm all James has to follow in his footsteps. Not that I ever could."

Across the park the tall buildings were slowly disappearing into the night sky, and then reappearing, outlined by the changing patterns on the lit-up windows. Bands of lights lit up, went dark, lit up again somewhere else.

The orchestra was tuning up by then, and so we stopped talking and lost ourselves to the Philharmonic. I don't know much about classical music but the conductor told us it was Beethoven. It worked for me.

At intermission we stood and stretched and he pointed to some of the buildings just visible on both park perimeters.

"Did you know, over there on the west, it was once considered the edge of civilization, the frontier?"

"Of course I do. That's why there's a famous apartment building named the Dakota. It was considered as far away as the Wild West."

Soon we were talking and laughing again about what it takes these days to get anything built in the city. He was contending, not very seriously, that payoffs and graft were more efficient than proper channels.

"Now Uncle James is someone who knows how to get things done. He lives right over there." He turned me away from the park, out toward the Fifth Avenue, and pointed to one of the grand buildings that loomed up above the trees.

The warming up for the second half of the concert began, and we settled down for something I did not know by Strauss and ended with familiar music by Tchaikovsky and fireworks, and a nightcap from a bottle of cognac. I pretended to like it.

We flowed with the crowd along the park paths, found the car, and park officers motioned us out to an exit. The car was smooth and silent, the cognac was unfamiliar and strong, and I was exhausted from a hard week. I embarrassed myself by falling asleep.

Steven woke me with a gentle tap on my shoulder. I was startled awake, apologized incoherently, straightened my clothes, hoped I wasn't a mess, blamed it on the wine and brandy.

He put a gentle hand over my mouth and said "Shh. Shh. It's fine. You looked cute."

Cute? Chris is cute. I am too grown-up to be cute. He helped me out of the car, walked me to my door, helped me unlock it. He was smiling. "You still look pretty foggy. Will you be all right?"

"Yes, of course." I was not so sure but too confused to know what I wanted to say. "It was lovely evening. Thank you."

"I'm glad Darcy introduced us, Ms. Donato. We'll do it again." He leaned in for what turned out to be a friendly kiss, and then he was gone.

Apparently it was a date.

◇◇◇

I was wide-awake as soon as the first light came through my window. Eye-makeup smears were on my pillow, my dress was on the floor. Had I collapsed the moment I saw my bed? My first thought was of Chris, wondering how she was dealing with yesterday's heartbreaking news. Was she was tossing and turning, or crying, and was it too early to call her? I told myself sternly that I should not hover.

My second thought was of my evening with Steven. I didn't know what it meant, or if it meant anything or nothing at all. I didn't even know what I wanted it to mean. When I sorted it all out, I might call Darcy, but for now I decided the solution was to think about something else. The problem of Ms. FOXX was right there at the top of the list. I could be in Bay Ridge in fifteen minutes.

Bay Ridge is a big neighborhood, sprawled out at one end of the gigantic Verrazano Bridge, with a mix of spacious old homes with harbor views, aging apartment buildings, and cramped rows of attached houses. How odd that Rick had never mentioned he knew someone there, a much different Brooklyn from mine but not far as the pigeon flies. I wondered what I was going to find there.

It turned out to be a small house on a street of ugly attached brick homes with garages squeezed under a raised first floor and chain link fences around the minute front garden. I thought I could linger, double-parked, letting people think I was waiting for a parking spot. I slumped down in the car seat and moved the window visor to make me harder to be seen.

There was a red Miata in the driveway but the license plate was the ordinary mix of numbers and letters, nothing special. I jotted it down. No one came in or out, and the house revealed nothing except that someone was home. There were lights on and an enormous set of matching flowered luggage was piled up on the front steps. It looked like my impulsive visit was in the nick of time.

Would she open her door to a complete stranger? Probably not. As harmless as this street seemed, this is the big city after all. I called from the car. I was answered by the voice from the message on the machine.

"Miss Wanda Beauvoir?"

"Who wants to know?"

I put on my friendliest voice. "I understand you were a friend of Rick Malone?"

She gasped.

"This is a terrible time for all of us. Maybe he mentioned me, Erica Donato? I'd love to talk to you."

"What do you want?"

"I'd just like to talk to you," I repeated. "He was like a member of my family, my father's best friend, and I am supposed to speak at his service. Could I come by and ask you a few questions? He was such a special person."

"No! Don't come here, don't call me."

The phone slammed down so hard it hurt my ear. I pulled into her driveway behind that flashy car, and went to ring her doorbell. I almost heard Rick's voice, telling me once again I had to be less impulsive. I responded that he got me into this and he should blame himself.

I leaned hard on the doorbell and added an assertive fist on her door. She was home; she was damn well going to respond. She finally looked through the door panes and shouted from behind the closed door, "Who the hell are you?"

"Erica Donato, and I'm not going away," I shouted back. "If you don't want your neighbors noticing, you better open the door."

The locks clicked and the door opened. She was a voluptuous brunette with a lot of curls, tight jeans, high-heeled sandals, and a glittery crocheted top. The boys in Queens were right about everything, but she was not actually as young as she wanted people to think.

"Why won't you talk to me?" I said quickly. "I loved Rick. I'm not trying to harm you."

She did not ask me in. She kept me in the doorway, asking, "How the hell did you find me?"

I was baffled by her reaction. "Someone told me about Rick's visitor with the catchy license plate. It wasn't that hard."

"I don't know what you're talking about." Her words were tough, but her eyes were nervously straying to her car in the driveway. "You bitch, you blocked me in. I've got to leave!"

"I'll move my car right after you tell me about Rick." Anger made it easier for me to stand firm. "He was practically family. I knew him all my life. Now he's gone and I'm wondering if I knew him at all. I never even met you, and I only live a few miles from here."

She shrugged. "I never met you either. So what? But he did mention you a couple times. You're like a goddaughter? We were together a few years. More than a few. We had a lot of laughs. It was good times all the way. Then he disappeared for some days, not for the first time, mind you. Then he was found." She shivered.

"Who told you? Did detectives talk to you?"

"They tried. Me and cops aren't the best of friends." My astonished look stopped her in her tracks. "Rick was an exception and," she added with heat, "I would have never given him the time of day if I'd have known he was a cop in the beginning."

"Did you tell them anything useful? Did they tell you anything? I really want to know."

"Can't help you, honey, any more than I helped them, and now if you'll get out of my way, I have a plane to catch."

"You're running out? Don't you care what happened to him? Don't you want to help?"

She flushed, but stared back at me without another word. I held my ground.

"You do know something. I can see it. What was going on? My car stays right where it is until you talk to me, dammit."

She suddenly looked smaller, older, not as pretty. She sighed. "I actually do not know. And yes, I care. So what? He never told me anything, and I never saw anything, either. Yeah, he was a gambler but it never seemed like he was in too deep. He, maybe, had friends who were, maybe, not quite what they should be. Maybe, but I dunno. They were only his buddies, played poker, went out on a boat. It never seemed like he was in business with them, if you know what I mean."

She nervously licked her lips and then added, "Until now."

She darted a glance out the window. "But if it was those guys—if!— I don't want to be around. Listen, honey, you must know someone is real mad at him. I want to be as far away as possible."

"Where are you going?"

"What, do I look dumb? You think I'm telling anyone, even a cupcake like you?"

"You changed the plates on your car." It wasn't a question

She shrugged again. "Hang out with a cop for awhile, you pick up a few tricks. Now step out of my way, and go get your damn car out of my driveway. You could lend a hand with these bags, too, having held me up like you did."

She opened the door, and said, "Ah, shit." No one was going anywhere. There was another car parked across the end of her driveway and two burly men were getting out. My quick glance took in one oldish, one youngish. Windbreakers, sneakers. They looked ordinary enough, except for the guns at their waists.

Chapter Fourteen

We ducked back inside but they were at her door before we had time to lock it, go out the back, call 911 or any of the other possibilities that occurred to me.

Instead, Wanda abruptly screamed, "Peter! Down here right now!" Thundering footsteps sounded on the floor upstairs and then pounded down the stairs, followed by the appearance of a very young, tousled looking man in a sweat suit. A very large young man.

He eyed the two men who had forced their way in past Wanda and they eyed him. Wanda and I, terrified, eyed each other, and backed a few steps into the hallway.

"What the fuck are you doing in my house?" the young man said, ignoring the guns and moving right into the other men's space, chest to chest.

"We came to discuss something with her. None of your business."

"She's my sister, and you're in MY house with weapons and your car is in MY driveway and you think it's not MY business?" He stepped in close.

"My sister needs to leave for a trip." He said it very slowly, as if talking to the mentally impaired. "You car happens to be in the way. You need to move it so she can leave as planned. She has no interest in talking to you. Understood?"

"We're cops, you idiot. Step back and I'll get my shield."

"Wanda," he said without moving. "Get over here and see if there's a shield."

There was, and he let them go.

"Uh, no hard feelings? You should have said."

"Yeah, yeah. We could have but Ms. Beauvoir here hasn't been exactly making herself available to talk to us."

I was trying to disappear into the background as quickly and quietly as I could. I hoped they would forget I was there. I wanted to see and hear everything. This had to be about Rick.

Wanda and Peter mirrored each other now, arms crossed, faces grim.

"I got a plane to catch!"

"You noticed our car is in your driveway. You're not going anywhere right now."

"Sis," Peter said, "want me to call a cab?"

The detective shook his head. "Don't bother. No driver is going to pick her up if we say no with a shield in hand. So come on, why don't we talk?"

"I don't have to say one freakin' word to you," she said, belligerent words in a shaky voice.

"Yes, she doesn't," Peter echoed.

"Actually," one of the detectives said politely, "she does. You know perfectly well we are investigating the murder of a cop. She talks here, or she can talk at the station."

The other added, "We could arrest her."

"Arrest me? You're crazy. I had nothing to do with…you have absolutely no reason…"

"Think we couldn't find one? Don't underestimate us."

The first cop added, "Wouldn't you rather talk here, in the comfort of your own home, than in an interrogation room?"

She turned pale.

"But my plane…"

"Well now, lady, if you hadn't been giving us the runaround we could have been done with this days ago." That was the second cop. I could see there was a tag team going on here. "We've been surveilling this house and your job, calling all your numbers. Where have you been?" When she didn't answer, he said, "Seems to me you'd want to help us. Someone killed Rick Malone. Don't you care?"

Peter turned red and stepped forward as if he was ready to argue up close and personal, but Wanda just looked ten years older. "Yeah, I've been making myself scarce. Not just to you, to everyone. I had my reasons. Let's get this over." She dropped abruptly onto the bottom step of the hall stairway. "What do you want to know? And nothing about me—I know my rights."

One of them glanced around at Peter and me. "Would you prefer to have some privacy?"

I tried to appear harmless and dumb, even as both cops and Peter looked me up and down.

Wanda looked alarmed, "No way. I want Peter right here with me. Her, too. The more witnesses the better, just in case you try something."

The older cop sighed. "Lady, we just we want to talk. And shouldn't we move someplace where we can be more comfortable?"

"This isn't a social visit. I'm fine here on the step. You can stand."

While they asked questions I listened hard, making mental notes and hoping to finally have some answers, but she hardly told them anything she had not told me. She acknowledged Rick liked to live on the wild side from time to time, that maybe he knew questionable persons. She parted, under pressure, with a couple of names that had the detectives raising their eyebrows and looking at each other.

A voice said, "I don't believe any of this." It was my own voice. I could not play the silent, invisible mouse any more. "I've known him my whole life. He was a great cop all those years. I saw citations, for God's sake! And he never really got hurt and then he got involved in whatever it is you think got him killed? Not Rick." I glared at Wanda. "How come you don't know better?"

"Who the hell are you anyway?" Peter said.

"Peter, she's a friend of Rick's. She came to talk to me, that's all."

"Rick's friend, huh? He was a good enough guy but seems like he got sis here involved in some trouble. I don't want her involved, and that includes involved with you."

"But I don't understand anything about this!"

"Big deal. I don't. Wanda doesn't, either, but we don't like it and no offense, but that means we don't like you."

Wanda put a gentle hand on his arm, turned to me, her eyes full of tears and said, "Because I got a phone call. That's why."

Three voices said "What?" Loudly. Peter silently moved in to hold her hand.

"Someone called," she whispered. "A few nights ago. They said Rick's body would be found, soon, at the park near his house. And they suggested I get out of town, like yesterday, cause they didn't want me to ask questions, or answer any, or whatever. Like, they said I shouldn't be a loose end. I'm not stupid. Ya know? I drew my own conclusions and started packing."

The detectives were asking a torrent of questions. Did she know the voices? No. Had she used her phone to identify the caller? She said, "Do I look like an idiot? I know how to work a modern phone. Or you think the guy was stupid enough to make it that easy? It was an unknown cell number. You wanna bet he didn't toss it right after?"

They didn't say anything, but their faces told me they agreed.

A few more unanswerable questions and they stood up saying, "This is useful, Ms. Beauvoir. Thank you. Tell us how to reach you later, and you can go."

She jumped up. "If I wanted to be reachable, do you think I'd be leaving now? And don't talk to me about confidential! There are people who love to run their mouths, including plenty in the high and mighty NYPD. Not to mention the ones who can be bought with this or that. Peter, get my bags, would you? While I hit the toilet?"

"Have you forgotten our car is in the way?"

Peter, trapped, said, "She's going to Montréal. Outside, up in the country. We got family there." He stood up. "That's all you get. You're getting the car out of the way right now, right?"

They left to move their car while Wanda came out clutching a coat in one hand and purse in the other, and Peter picked up her bags. I was still numb.

"You, whatever your name is," Peter snapped. "You got to move your car too."

I obeyed, and watched them tear down the street. One of the cops stayed in the car, now at the curb, writing madly in a notebook, but the other got out and knocked on my window.

"If you were such an old friend, we need to talk to you too. Who are you?"

"Erica Donato. And I've been interviewed already. Detective, um, Simms, I think. I have her card somewhere." I scrambled through my purse.

"Wait right here." He made a brief call. "Good. Simms is the boss. We don't need to do it again. But be careful yourself," he added. "Doesn't look like this has anything to do with you, but call us if anything at all happens. Simms, me, my partner, whoever. Got it?"

I got it.

I drove home with my hands glued to the steering wheel, my eyes glued to my rearview mirror, my mind in a whirlwind of emotions mixed with a jumble of questions.

My kitchen was reassuringly full of large men at work but I only waved and retreated upstairs to my room, so I could try think things through in private.

I wanted to tell someone what I had learned, talk it over, try to get a handle on it all. I could call that detective, Simms, but she must know all about it if these men worked for her. And probably she would not be inclined to talk it over with me.

I could call dad. Did he know Wanda? I bet he did. That didn't mean I actually wanted to talk to him. And what if I did, and told him everything? Middle-aged and out of shape as he was, he still thought of himself as a tough product of Brooklyn's tough streets. He might get on a plane, cast and all, and come home to protect me. I shuddered at the thought.

And yet, at this point in my life, I could understand why he would. There is no such thing as being an overprotective parent. Well, of course there is. I stopped walking my daughter to school a long time ago, only about a year after she begged me to, but yes, my overriding thought right now was that I was glad she was away, distant and protected from all of this.

I called Detective Simms, as I had known all along I would have to.

I tried to convince her that I had a right to know more.

"And why is that?" Her voice dripped icicles.

"Because. Because he has no family to speak of, and I am the closest to that he had. He left me everything. I owe it to him to…"

"To what? Supervise us? I'm sorry, but it does not work like that." She didn't sound at all sorry. "We are busy investigating a murder. That's our job. We are good at it. Even if you were his daughter or his wife we would not discuss our progress with you."

"But I…."

"See that you don't get in the way." She hung up.

I had learned precisely nothing from her. I felt as if I were standing in front of a large wall, high and thick, with no gates. Whatever strange turns Rick's life might have taken, I would not be able to untangle them on my own. They had become far too strange for my abilities. And far too scary.

My reason for even trying—at least the one I could use as a reason—was that I needed to know who he really was to write that eulogy. The truth is that I needed to keep in my memory the Rick I knew. I could not lose him a second time.

I might not have official answers for many months. Maybe I would never have the answers. That was a bleak prospect. Maybe the NYPD would never tell me everything. Maybe they would never know themselves. I had grown up around cops in my neighborhood, Rick, some of dad's old friends. I knew that always solving cases was television, not real life.

I knew what Darcy would say to me, if she were not off on vacation. Stick to the everyday. Go have a brownie. Take a bubble bath. Go for a run.

Deep down, I knew I needed to let the pros look for the answers for now. Detective Simms was right, I admitted to myself with great resentment. It was their job, and they knew how to do it better than I did. The same voice said that forcing my attention back to everyday life for a while was not abandoning Rick. It was sanity. It did not mean I was done asking questions.

I would anchor myself by diving into the everyday. Trying to focus on the most everyday thing I could think of, I went downstairs to look at the work in the kitchen. Today there were plumbers connecting my new appliances. They were two strapping young men who spoke pure Brooklyn, in contrast to the Mexican carpenters, the Polish electrician, and Joe's secretary, whose English had a Dublin lilt. They told me I'd have an ice-maker by evening and the stove could be used for dinner. My one good piece of news for the day. Of course I had no counter tops to use for workspace yet and no cabinets to store groceries.

I reminded myself that I had things to do, productive things. I had a project to work on or risk losing course credit. I had a stack of files from Brendan Leary. He had surprised me by mailing a fat envelope of photocopies with no notes or explanation. And I had not done anything with the Pastores' pictures, which might be useful and fun as part of my exhibit. I had not even put my notes from library research into anything like a plan. I wrote on my list: memo for my boss with progress by end of today.

It would be a note, outlining what I was doing and what I had found. Oh, yes, and maybe some ideas about what we could do with it all, to let him know I was actually thinking about what I was discovering.

When Leary's package had come I had called him to ask about it. In fact I had called him twice, but he'd never returned the calls and I had barely noticed. I was too busy and distracted then. Now I began working my way through the files.

He was a good writer and a good reporter too. He covered landlord/tenant issues, as I already knew, and here were his detailed notes, all the additional information that didn't make it into a story. There was a whole folder on the Rogow scandal, with a take on it quite different from old Mrs. Rogow's, of course. There were stories on the changing demographics of the neighborhood, the first conversion of a brownstone from a rooming house back to a private home, the hopeful energy of newcomers and the discomfort and fear of old-timers. He had an uncanny ability to tap into major shifts just as they were beginning. All this in a neighborhood weekly. No wonder he soon moved on to a major paper.

I selected article after article that we could use to illustrate points we might want to make, tabbed them with bright Post-Its for later copying, and began a computer document outlining what I had and how we could use it. I was moving in the right direction.

At last I had worked my way down to the bottom, a mystery folder with none of his usual careful labeling. On top there was a barely legible note saying, "Here's one more file. Who knows why I kept this—I keep everything—but I think you'll find it interesting."

It was filled with blurry, yellowing photocopies. There were dates stamped on top. When the copies were made? When they were added to Leary's files? All of them were about thirty years ago, give or take.

No notes. No explanations. That certainly seemed like Leary. He knew what it all meant and he didn't feel obligated to tell me. I would have to figure out what they were and why they mattered, so I started reading.

I stopped when I found myself completely confused. They were a jumble of dates and different handwritings. I tried to group the same handwritings together, and then sorted again by date wherever I could. I began again.

Dear Mom and Dad

I'm sorry but I'll die if I stay in this town one more minute. I know there's real life somewhere else. I guess you'll be upset but please don't worry. This is so you know I left on my own and haven't been kidnapped or anything. Please feed Fluffy for me and pet her sometimes. She will miss me." Written in a round, careful teen-ager's penmanship, with XXX's for kisses and OOO's for hugs.

The next page, in a hasty-looking, pencil scrawl, said simply, *"I'm outta this hick nowheresville forever. Don't look for me."* One in purple ink, said, *"Kids are mean here. I'm with Jason. They're mean to him too. We're looking for someplace nicer. We'll watch out for each other."* The next, printed in block letters, said only. *"Done with being smacked around. Go to hell."*

How had Leary ever come to have these? And why were they in such a mess, unlike his usual meticulous filing?

I worked my way through a few more. My eyes began to sting and my heartbeat seemed to speed up as I read the ones with headings that said, "mom and dad" or "mommy" or "Grandma" or "sis." What if I came down one morning and found a note like this on my kitchen table?

I took a deep, shaky breath and kept reading. Some seemed to be diary pages, all telling similar stories of hometown unhap-piness and the compulsion to be anywhere but here. I had a pretty good idea of what they must have found elsewhere. I hoped some of them found their way home.

This file was all about lost children. Who were they? Why did Leary have these notes? And what was he trying to tell me? He had a whole lot of explaining to do. It was time to try again, but I only got his grumpy message on his answering machine. This time I left a grumpy message back.

After awhile I saw that there were a few with the same rounded handwriting and hearts dotting the i's. Not runaway notes but a runaway's correspondence? Blocky messages, pho-tocopied from post cards?

Dear mommy

Please don't worry. I'm fine. I'm not where I mailed this, you'd come looking I know it, but it's a good place. People are really friendly.

Love, me

Dear mommy

I have a place to stay, I know you are wondering, and yes I'm eating enough too. Stopped taking my vitamins, too expensive. Sorry.

Hi to daddy. Don't worry.

And in the same hand, a note on paper decorated with a kitten:

Hi, Debbie

How's everything in high school? I'm done with that shit. Met some kids who are starting a band (you bet, interesting substances around, as I know you are wondering), and they live together like a commune. Does that just blow your mind, your little hick friend in a commune? Picture this—it's not like a movie with tall buildings, it's a funny, falling down house with lots of stairs, and most of the rooms are painted PURPLE. With swirly glow—in—the dark designs. Too beautiful and strange. I stay with them and clean up instead of paying rent. Think of me when you're waving those pom-poms. Ha-ha.

Love from your sis in crime.

On another kitten page:

Dear mom and dad

Getting cold here. Could use some of my winter clothes. I'm in New York, but don't try to find me. You won't be able to, and you'd hate it, it's a big, busy place, not much like home. That's why I like it. Send my stuff to GPO-Times Square. Having so much fun and my eyes are opening up to the whole magic of the universe. Love, me

There was a sketched yin/yang symbol next to her signature, and no more hearts in the text.

I saw that the handwriting was changing, too, wandering across the page, shaky and sloppy. Was she really having so much fun? Was she really eating well? I imagined her growing thin and waif-like, her eyes wide with the visions her new life was giving.

I could not bear to look at this sad material any longer. This was supposed to distract me from obsessing about Rick, but it had only substituted a different heartache. I needed to stop, right then and there.

I needed lunch too, but before that I needed something else. I called camp, reaching out to my own child. I wasn't worried about her. This was for me.

The camp secretary said she had seen Chris leaving the dining room, chattering away in a gang of girls. Did I want her pulled out of oil-painting class to talk to me? They normally did not allow that, but the director had put Chris on a list of exceptions. No, I said, that's fine. I said it wasn't important enough to alarm her. And it wasn't.

Chapter Fifteen

It wasn't as comforting as hearing her voice, but I could picture Chris in a smock covered with smears of paint, concentrating fiercely on her work in class, or giggling with Mel and other friends. Their faces were a blur, because I did not know them, but I could imagine their voices, and I was comforted.

I headed out to the nearest coffee shop and took the Pastores' albums along for lunchtime company. I had talked to the Pastores because I still I had some vague ideas about clues to the mystery in my own house, but the albums of unsophisticated snap shots turned out to be a time machine, bringing me a time and a place with touching immediacy. Someone in the family must have loved that simple camera.

Here was the older Mr. Pastore, Uncle Sal, stopped at work and posing with a smile. In a series of pictures, he seemed to be updating the house, covering the pressed tin ceilings with 1970s-modern dropped ceiling acoustic tile, re-facing the wood kitchen cabinets with Formica, laying wall-to-wall carpeting over the parquet floors. I flinched at the aesthetic choices, but could not miss how proud he looked.

Here were holidays, like the Christmas pictures Mrs. Pastore had shown me. Easter with lilies on the table, Thanksgiving with turkey and lasagna, and lots of people squeezed around the table. Older men and little boys in suits and ties, women in prim dresses covered with frilly aprons, little girls in crinolines and hair bows, teenage girls in tiny miniskirts and heavy mascara, with crosses around their necks.

Here were block parties, too. One of them had a tiny carousel and another had pony rides. And here was my house on a few occasions, with a group of intensely scruffy young people sitting on the steps. Masses of hair obscured faces, both male and female. T-shirts and cut off jeans. Bare feet. Perhaps they were not scruffy, they were being fashionable.

I was attaching tabs to page after page. This was a living block preserved in amber at a moment in time. I started to imagine a display with questions: what does this tell you?

I went back to the pages Mrs. Pastore had shown me first, the party for cousin Marco's return from Viet Nam. First, there were pre-party pictures: a careful photo of the refreshment table, with its carved watermelon cornucopia spilling fruit salad out on onto a tray; the Virgin Mary shrine in the corner, with a bouquet of flowers in front of it; the grape arbor festooned with balloons.

Then it looked as if the whole street turned out for the party. There seemed to be guests of all ages, even a few firemen in gear. Oh, right, there used to be a fire station on the corner, long since turned into an elegant private home. I imagined Uncle Sal as the kind of man who stopped to say hello to firemen, petted their dogs, and brought over pastry from Mrs. Sal. He would have said, "Stop in at the party. Everyone's invited!"

The roaming photographer caught some small girls hiding under a table with a large bowl of candy and a collection of dolls set up in a circle, and a lively argument among some old men under the arbor. What were they arguing about? The Yankees? The war? Frank Sinatra? I did not see the hippies from my house in any of the party pictures in the album, but here were some more, loose photos stuck into the album binding but not mounted.

Here was the front of the house again, with the banner welcoming PFC Pastore back home, but this one included part of my house too. There was a large anti-war poster in the window. It seemed to show men in uniform with blood dripping from their hands but it was hard to be sure, as it was X-ed out with black marker in the photo. Next to it, someone had written "What nerve!" So all was not neighborly good will on the block after all. I definitely wanted that one for my display.

On the next page, we were back in the garden. There were some young cops in uniform, burgers in one hand, drinks in the other. One was hoisting a bottle to salute the cameraman. There were some young couples with a familiar look. Those little boys they were feeding, were they occasional visitors back to the block, people I had met, now with children of their own?

Everything in the albums looked familiar, known yet different, as if in a dream. I wanted more detail and wondered if I had a magnifying glass somewhere. Slogans on t-shirts, writing on posters, what were the flowers in front of the Virgin, what kind of dolls were the little girls feeding? I wanted to know it all.

I had finished my lunch and the coffee shop was crowded. I needed to give up my booth and move on. This had been a pleasant break from Leary's files but I had not forgotten about them. I checked for my phone messages when I left the coffee shop. No Leary. I was going right over to his apartment to pound on his door until he let me in.

Mary accosted me on my way to my car. I hadn't seen her in awhile.

"Well, Mrs. Um-um —um. Where have you been, and how is your lovely daughter these days?"

"She's fine. She's still away at camp, having a good time." I edged away as I spoke, anxious to go on about my business. Anxious not to get trapped in one of Mary's meandering conversations.

"Ya, camp is good. Best to be away from here. Glad to see you. I was thinking about you the other day. You and something else. No, someone else. It was…it was…Aha, I got it. The man who brings you pizza? The tall guy?"

Who was she talking about? It took me a minute to realize it must be Rick. She was out on the block that night, when he came with two big pizza boxes. The last time at my house. I didn't think I'd tell her the rest.

"He's been on my mind, but I couldn't think why. Nice looking fella, he was, but too young for me and too old for you." She winked, then shook her head. "I dunno. The rest will come to me sometime. You know what I mean?"

Then she shuffled off on her mysterious business and I hustled off on mine.

I got into Leary's building by doing a convincing imitation of a resident who had misplaced her keys. Someone else unlocked the door and held it open for me without a second glance. It helps to be small, mature, white, and female.

I switched off leaning on his doorbell and pounding on his door, until I finally heard sounds of movement inside.

"It's Erica Donato. I've been trying to reach you." I took a deep breath and added, "Let me in. I'll stand here shouting until you do."

"You've been trying to reach me?" There was no mistaking that slurred surly voice. "All right, all right, hold your horses."

I heard multiple locks clicking and the door finally opened. He looked even worse than last time I saw him, if that was possible. "Welcome to my palace. What do you want?"

I went in before he could change his mind. "I have questions."

"Yeah?"

"You bet. You send me material you don't explain and then you don't answer my calls."

"You're not the only one." He shook his head. "I can't understand it but I've spent the last few days fighting off people with questions. Where am I now? What am I doing these days? No one I need to talk to. They're all insects crawling out of the woodwork."

"Thanks a lot."

"Oh, did I offend you?" He chuckled. I guess it was a chuckle. With him, it was hard to tell.

"You sent me all that material and I didn't have a chance to look at it until today. It was great, and thank you, but it only raised more questions. I can't use it for my work without getting some answers."

"Make it worth my while."

"Money? You know we talked about that before."

"Ah, what the hell? I haven't been out of here in…" He shrugged. "It's been some days." He chuckled. "If you're chauffeuring, you can run me over to Prospect Park. I haven't seen that zoo in a couple of lifetimes. You up for that?"

"If you'll answer my questions I'll even take you for a ride on the carousel."

"Damn. I didn't know that was up and running again." His voice changed. "I remember that from…ah, forget about that. Get me out of here. I need that bag, over there, with my gear, and we can blow this dump."

He lived diagonally across the vast park from my neighborhood, only a few blocks off the end of the park I seldom got to. I could have walked there in the time it took us to get him out of the building, into the car, and then out again.

His behavior hadn't changed any, and neither had he. He didn't look well. His complexion was even pastier than last time and there were dark circles under his eyes. When I asked him about it, he dismissed my questions with an irritable wave of his hand.

He complained about how slow I was getting him out of the apartment and into the car, criticized my driving, argued about which path to follow into the park. I bought him some popcorn and ignored every annoying thing he said.

We never did get to the zoo. The tinkling music of the carousel called to us. It is a brilliantly painted confection of Victorian art and today there was an ecstatically shrieking group of day campers, all in yellow t-shirts, riding around and around.

I settled myself on a bench with Leary's chair braked next to me, and we both enjoyed the cheerful scene for a few minutes. At least I did. Though cheerfulness never seemed an acceptable approach for Leary, he did say, "I haven't seen this since…hell, must be decades. A bunch of decades."

"I can't imagine you riding a carousel,"

"Humph. You don't know much about me. Don't know anything, really."

I took a deep breath. "I know you sent me some very interesting and very old papers."

"You call thirty years or so very old? Ha. Shows you're just a kid yourself. Well, all right. A deal's a deal and here we are in the park. What do you want to know?'

"Everything. And I'm sure you know it, too! What do you mean by being so mysterious?"

I could swear he was grinning, ever slightly, but he just said wearily, "Not mysterious. Tired. Once I'd found that stuff, I wasn't up to writing anything about it. And I wasn't up to another visit from you either—all that talking!—so I just shipped it off. My home aide did it. Figured you'd find me if you wanted more."

"I did, and I do. So give. Where did it come from? And what does it mean?"

"You wanted to know about what it was like back then, when the neighborhoods and everything else seemed to be cracking apart like an earthquake? That would be the early '70s."

"Go on."

"There was kind of an epidemic of kids running away. Part of that whole turn on, tune in, drop out deal. Some of them ended up in New York. Some of them had parents looking for them. So I sent that stuff for you to get a look at was going on."

"Leary! Not good enough. You know I can't use this in an exhibit, not without some back up info, some kind of verification. Sheesh. I'm supposed to be a scholar, ya know? Where did you get them? Did you know the kids? Or wait —wait! Did you know the *parents*?"

"Yes, sometimes, to both." He nodded. "I knew cops, and the cops knew I knew neighborhoods, so when some of these parents showed up, looking for the kids, looking for help, sometimes I got to talk to them. The cops called me. And you know, some of those parents were stone hard s.o.b.s. You could see why the kids flew. But some were kind of sad. They'd have pictures—kids in braces, in Little League outfits, in ballet clothes—and these notes the kids wrote, the only clues they had for trying to find them. Plain, desperate, hick kind of people—you know, like midwesterners or from upstate little towns—who had no clue what happened to their kids at home and even less about what might have happened here."

"Nothing good, I bet."

He nodded again. "The ones that stuck around and kept looking, they started to figure out what might have happened to them. Then they were really scared. There's a few of those parents I never forgot, even with all the garbage I've seen. Some things get stuck in your head for no special reason."

I cringed at the picture he was drawing for me. "Did any of them ever find their kids?"

"Yeah, sometimes. And there were special phone lines by then, you know, that offered to call the parents for the kids, gauging if they'd be welcome home. And if the kids even wanted to go back. Course sometimes they found the kids in other ways." He shook his head. "Dead. Addicts. In the prostitute life. And not even wanting out any more, sometimes. Some never did find them. Most gave up and went home after awhile. I'd hear from them every so often. Or hear about them. Still looking, years later."

I was speechless. There were tears in my throat. Then I had to make myself stop being a mom and go back to being a scholar asking questions. "I thought it was mostly in places like the East Village? Or Times Square, heaven help them, in the sleazy old days?"

"Yep. But like I told you before, there were some little hippy enclaves in Brooklyn neighborhoods too. And I always figured some of those houses had runaways. I saw kids way too young to be on their own, going in and out. Or they might have been buying drugs. Could have been both. Couple of times I even walked distraught midwesterners around, watched while they rang doorbells carrying pictures of their lost children."

"Why didn't you write that story?"

"I did write pieces of it. Other people were covering it too, and after awhile it stopped being news. I moved on."

He had his head back as he spoke, eyes closed, as if he was too weary to keep talking. Or was he avoiding looking at me?

I said, slowly, "Are you telling me that's who our skeleton might be? One of those kids?"

He shrugged. "Add up the evidence. You're smart enough to do that."

I had an idea. "I have some photos from about that time. Would you want to take a look, see if they jump-start any memories? They're in my bag. I didn't want to leave them in the car."

"Why not? Nothing to lose."

He began to leaf through the albums, making little noises to himself and chuckling at times. He stopped at the photo of my house with a gang of youngsters on the steps.

"This is your house? It looks kind of familiar. There were a bunch of group rentals on that block, students or hippies or drug dealers. Whatever. Run-down crummy places and a landlord who'd rent to anyone. It didn't exactly generate a lot of good will with the other folks on the block. That was Rogow. That s.o.b. Did you read those clips?" He shook his head. "I've got some memories there, all right. He hated my guts."

"You knew him? In person? Not just as a subject?"

"I'm proud to say I was one of the people who helped send him to jail. You didn't know that?"

"I knew you wrote about him."

"He could have written the how-to book on being a criminal landlord. Every building he owned was a danger to life or health. He didn't care. He was getting rich. That daughter of his followed in his footsteps later."

"Wait," I said. "You don't mean she was a slumlord too? I've met her, and that seems pretty unlikely to me."

"Well, these days, yes. Then? Different story."

"But she claimed not to know anything about the Brooklyn business."

He looked at me as if I had "gullible" written on my forehead. Maybe I did.

"She and I had a few run-ins over the years. Actually," he said with some satisfaction, "she hates my guts too."

He squinted at the photos some more and said, "Hand me my bag. I want my magnifying glass."

"You carry a magnifying glass?" I thought, how useful. Exactly what I had wanted earlier.

"You didn't know diabetes screws up your eyesight? I carry it with my insulin and needles." His expression became just a shade more sarcastic. "You never know when I might be in the middle of a big story and have to read some documents."

"Yeah," he said, peering at the photo. "I thought so. That girl…" He jabbed at the page, "She might be young Miss Rogow herself." He passed it to me and said, "Take a look at the female with the hair and long dress on the end."

I looked and looked. It was interesting to see the faces come into focus. They had expressions now, and they were all so young, but no, I did not see the hard blond I had met in the baby-faced brunette with bangs down to her eyebrows.

"She told me herself she was never even in the neighborhood."

"Yeah? I knew her face from seeing her make the rounds with her father a few times." He gave me an impatient look.

"Use your head! With all those wild young kids in the neighborhood? Think she could stay away? Like bees to honey. Or flies to garbage, in this case. Cops were watching some of those houses, very suspicious, but I don't recall if they ever got the goods on any of them."

"Did you dislike all of them? Landlords and tenants?"

He looked surprised. "Not my job to dislike them, or like them either. It was my job to question all of them all the time."

"Like a cop."

"Nope, like a reporter. The truth is I did not like *this* landlord or *these* tenants. They deserved each other. So I had an opinion. So sue me."

I didn't really want to pursue the issue of unbiased reporting. I had other things on my mind. "She was lying to me." I added, recalling the scene, "Lying to her mother too, I think."

"Put it like this. One time I saw her, before the father died, and she was hanging out on the street corner, smoking—and not cigarettes—and dressed in crazy looking clothes, like some gypsy. Next time, a few years later, there she was in a press conference, talking up a company project, dressed in a tough business suit and slick as her nail polish."

A few yards away, a different group of tiny day campers, this time in red t-shirts, had boarded the carousel. It spun in a brilliant blur of color, music, and delighted screams.

I sat for a minute trying to take in Leary's opinions and wondering if they even added up to anything. Then something else he said kicked in.

"Cops. You said cops watched these houses and you said you worked with them on some of the missing children cases? Do you remember any of them?"

He shook his head. "Street cops? After thirty years? No way. The captain I do remember, he's long gone."

"I have a couple of cops in photos. How about we use the glass on them too?"

I flipped pages until I found the party and the officers clowning around.

He looked but finally said, "Young cops all look the same to me. Like babies. And I'm tired." He went on. "I haven't been sleeping much. Those calls I get? They come at night, making threats."

"What do you mean, threats?" I looked at him and he did look exhausted. "That's not right. What are you doing about this? Have you reported it to the police?"

He shrugged. "Naah. I don't pay attention to what they say. Idiots. There's not much to do anyway. Probably some smartass kids in my building. I don't like them and they don't like me."

I tried to argue, to tell him to be careful, but he said, "Not your concern, and don't even think about trying to baby me.

I'm old but I'm not stupid. I've been harassed by scarier people than those idiots!"

His words were fierce, but his voice was slurring again, and the shadow under his eyes seemed to be going from bluish to purple. It was time to get him home.

After he was settled back in his place, and had a snack, he seemed a little better, and insisted he didn't need any help from me. I asked if I could take one last look at the photos with his powerful glass, and he waved a yes. He seemed to be falling asleep.

So I finally saw that the dolls were bigger than Barbies and had long hair, and the teenage boys were wearing shirts that said Bishop Loughran Wrestling. That is, the ones that were not wearing shirts that said "Amazing Mets." I saw that the Virgin Mary had pink roses. The cops were clowning, and the drinks were Miller's while they were on duty! Then I almost dropped both the book and the glass.

One of the cops was Rick. There could be no doubt about it. It was the same face I had seen a few days ago in his graduation picture. My mind stopped and then a thought slowly rose to the surface. I could not leave the questions alone after all, no matter what the detectives said. They kept coming back to find me.

Chapter Sixteen

My startled exclamation did not wake Leary, and I could not bring myself to shake that ill old man awake and ask him any of the questions that flooded into my mind. I gathered up my things as quietly as possible and fled. Then I collapsed in the privacy of my car, unable to move, trying to make some sense of what I had learned. And I couldn't.

How could it be that Rick once worked in my neighborhood? That he knew my street, my block, and my house? Well, at least, the house next door. And he never said one word to me about it. When he had tried arguing me out of buying the house, he hadn't said a word. His arguments were exactly the same as my parents, my in-laws, and my friends. It was too old, needed too much work, the neighborhood was questionable, why didn't I want a nice suburban ranch. His never said, "I know what I'm talking about."

Maybe it was merely chance that he was there the day of the party, I told myself. It was a temporary assignment and he had forgotten it over all the years since. Oh, sure. Even I couldn't believe that, much as I would have liked to. Was it a tough period in his own life, or an unhappy assignment, and he never wanted to talk about it? Or even remember it? That seemed somewhat more possible.

Actually, I wanted to call him and yell at him until he came up with an explanation. He could not give me one now, but I owed it to him and to myself to find it anyway, to figure out what happened.

I needed to remember the real Rick, whoever that was. I felt like I haven't known my dad for the last few years. Chris was changing by the day. I was never sure who the real Chris was anymore, and that made me feel I didn't know how to be the real me with her. I could not accept that Rick, too, was a stranger.

I sat there, immobilized both physically and mentally, until an impatient motorist seeking a parking space started honking his horn at me. He saw I was in the driver's seat and was saying, "Get a move on."

I couldn't wait to get home. My own life felt completely off-center, more senseless by the moment, but my block, my place, looked reassuringly, almost bizarrely normal. There was the regular UPS man, ringing my neighbor's doorbell. Down the block, there was the flower lady, watering her exquisite patch of front garden. There was a plumber's van, double-parked. A mom walked up the street pushing a stroller and singing with her toddler. Sesame Street.

Between my too-early, too-exciting visit to Wanda in the morning, and my visit to Leary just now, I felt as if I had been running all over creation and learning too much, and it had all begun way too early. All I wanted now was to get out of the car and into my own house, ripped up though it was. All I wanted was to stop thinking and stop moving. How quickly could I lose myself in a nap?

When I entered my house, I heard a faint hum coming from my kitchen. I had a working refrigerator. I opened its door and a delightful blast of cool air hit me. Someone had kindly added a few beers and iced tea. I suspected Joe, with gratitude. I fell asleep on the sofa, not waking until the phone rang.

"How come I only hear about your life from Chris?"

"Dad?"

"Yeah, it's your old man. You doing all right?"

"Sure I am." Not really. "Taking care of Rick's business." Also not really.

"Dad. I want to know more about Rick. Did he ever work where I live now? Way back when?"

"I've got no idea. Ideas. Idee." His words were slurred. "He worked lots of places. I probly only 'member the long time ones."

"Oh, dad, would you please try?"

"Yeah, yeah, I'll try. Give me a little time, OK?"

"And Rick and you? What's the history there?"

"Yah, Rick and me. Lifelong friends."

"Dad!"

"Oh, all right. So we moved in other directions later in our lives. You could say we didn't like each other's friends so mush. Much! That's all I've got for you. It didn't mean we stopped being friends. You let me know when the funeral will be and I'll be home, if they let me out of here. Ah, cancel that. I'll come, no matter what. Sign myself out if need be."

That caught my half-awake mind. "Dad, how are you doing?"

"So-so. Ya know, I don't get much rest here. They've got me up going to physical therapy and tests and what not all day long."

"Bet you can't smoke, either."

"Can't smoke." He almost shouted it. "Can't drink." He sounded mentally off, he was mumbling. And he wasn't bossing me around.

"Dad, are you on painkillers?"

"You betcha. Got a nice legal buzz on. Let's see. I had a thought about Rick. He had a kind of girlfriend name of Wanda. Maybe you should give her a call."

"I did. I even met her."

"You know her too? What a small world, isn't it?" Oh, yes, he was definitely on painkillers.

"But now I've got someone young here. She's pretty cute too. She says I have to go do something. Oh yeah, there's another little procedure today, toots, got to run. Yeah, talk to Wanda. She's smarter than she looks. Gotta go."

Why had he called? Even considering the fact that he was high as a kite, he didn't have anything to say. I had the uncomfortable idea that maybe it was for the same reason I had tried to call Chris yesterday. He needed me. He needed to hear my voice and know I was all right. Even if I wasn't.

It didn't sound like my tough-guy father.

He got me thinking again about Wanda. He knew Wanda? That needed some discussion, when he was able to really talk to me. Maybe I should follow his advice. I still had her cell phone number. Could she be in Montreal already, or was she still traveling and out of reach? Of course if she was thinking clearly she would not be answering, or would even have discarded the phone but she was pretty distracted when I met her. It was worth a try.

She answered on the second ring and then swore. She let loose with so many curses the air around the phone seemed to turn blue.

"I was supposed to get rid of this damn thing. I know better and Peter told me to but I was so flustered I forgot."

She could still do it and then I would lose her. Could I keep her too distracted to do it right now?

"How was your trip?" I said in the friendliest of tones. "Is the weather pleasanter there than here in the city?"

"Trip wasn't bad, all things considered. It's Canada, nice and cool now. Freeze your ass in a few months." She stopped. "Ah, shoot, now that you have me—I mean, now that I'm here — where I can breathe—nope, not saying where—you know, I'm thinking about Rick." There was a long silence, when I thought she was gone, and then she said softly, "It hurts. Ya know?"

"I know. I can't get my mind around it. I feel like maybe I never even knew him."

"Sucks, don't it?" she said. "Tell you what. Maybe last thing I ever do for that old bastard. There were some guys whose names I know. His cop friends, not his high rolling friends. Maybe you wanna to talk to them?"

"Maybe? Maybe???"

"Meaning yes, you do? I just know names so you'll have to find them yourself. And honey? When we're done, I'm doing what I was supposed to do this morning. This phone goes into the river. All my tracks will be gone so this is it."

I wrote down the names, and she clicked off. I imagined her on a bridge somewhere, saying good-bye to Brooklyn with a toss into the dark water.

I opened the NYPD website, crossing my fingers, that maybe, just maybe, one of Wanda's names was still on active duty and was doing something that would get him mentioned there.

The first two names drew a blank, but I hit lucky with the third. There he was, Danny Monahan, a sergeant in another Brooklyn precinct. No time like right now. If he wasn't there, I would leave a message. And if he didn't call back, I swore I would keep calling.

He was there. A little flustered, I introduced myself, told him how close Rick was to my family. He said, "What took you so long?"

I was so surprised, I couldn't say a word for a moment, and when I could, all that came out was "What?"

"I said," he repeated, patiently, "what took you so long? I've been wondering if you would get around to me." He took pity on me. "I heard about Rick. Terrible thing, that is, and I found out who was listed in his papers. Talked to your father couple of days ago."

"My father? He didn't tell me anything about it."

"Yeah, we know each other a little, through Rick, back when. I got the feeling he wasn't well. Could that be why he didn't tell you? Like, it slipped his mind? I told him you could call."

"Does this mean you would talk to me?" I couldn't believe he meant that.

"Sure. If you wanted to talk enough to come looking for me, I'm not going to turn my back."

I took a deep breath. First things first.

"Tell me how you knew him."

"Academy. Over the years we crossed paths a bunch of times, stayed in touch. You could say we were buddies but only in a way. We were living different lives, after awhile, but there was always some kind of—uh, guess you could say a connection."

He stopped and he added in a softer voice, "It was pretty shocking, what happened to him. You're wondering what the hell is going on, right?"

"Oh, yes."

"You got a right to know, I'd say. Rick used to talk about you, like he was an uncle or something. Yeah, you've got a right to know." He stopped, and then said, "I don't want to talk here. Where are you? Can I swing by before I head home?"

I gave him my address, and he gave me a time. I wanted to ask questions right now. I didn't want to wait. I wanted to go straight to the Pastores and say, "Tell me everything about the people in the party pictures, and especially those two young cops," but I knew they did not live in the house then and probably didn't know anything. And no one else on the block went back that far.

What to do for now? It looked like I might finally get some answers. I tried to work but my thoughts were too scattered to be productive. I suppose I finally gave up, but there I was, pouring coffee and speed dialing Darcy's cell phone. I asked about her vacation, and she gave a deep, long sigh.

"Picture this. I am sitting in an Adirondack chair that must be a hundred years old, looking out over a sparkling lake. Everyone else is waterskiing and I am all alone, sipping a margarita and reading a stack of *New Yorkers*."

"Is that as heavenly as it sounds?"

"What do you think? And how is life in the big, bad city?"

"Oh, Darcy. My life gets crazier by the minute. So much has happened I don't even know where to start."

"Tell all. Start at the beginning." She was all business now. I imagined her sitting up straight, drink down, memo pad in hand.

Some of it she knew; some of it she loved, especially Mrs. Rogow; some of it she found disturbing. I knew that because she was commenting very, very carefully.

"Oh, yes, and I think I might have, sort of, maybe had a kind of date with your friend Steven. It was a kind of impulsive, friendly, concert in the park kind of thing."

"Hmmm."

'What the hell does that mean? Hmm?"

"Ah. You think real hard."

The light bulb finally went on. "Did you plan this?"

"Well. Plan? Define plan?"

"I hear the laughter in your voice. Dammit, Darcy. You might have told me."

I could wring her neck. Or I could say thank you. Of course I could do both.

"Why didn't you warn me?"

"To what purpose? What would you have done?"

"I don't know. Dressed nicer when I met him, maybe."

"Or?"

"Or I would have said no way. I admit it."

"Like you've done every other time."

"Darcy, it isn't as though I haven't tried; you know I have."

She did know. She'd been the sounding board when I'd had a couple of not very deep relationships. In the end, none of them were Jeff and it all seemed pretty pointless.

"Well, my dear, he's recently single, and he is an interesting person, an intelligent, charming man with diverse interests and good manners. Where's the problem?"

"Oh, please. One, I have too much going on in my life to be interested in dating anyone right now. Two, I have to think about Chris and dating. That's weird. Three, I'm not even so sure if I like him. He's kind of too…I don't know. Too the world is his oyster. I don't even know if he likes me, either. Four, we have nothing whatever in common. I mean, it's obvious we are from different worlds." I paused for breath. "I don't even understand what he does for a living."

"He helps very rich people figure out ways to become richer. He's good at it, too." She sounded slightly amused.

"You see? That proves we have nothing in common. I don't even know any very rich people. Maybe you and Carl."

"Not us. We are not in Steven's world. Not even close."

"See! So what world am I in? From a different galaxy altogether? I can't talk about prep school friends or golf or whatever people like that talk about. I don't even know what they talk about. He's too…he's very suave for me."

"Consider this. His ex-wife is a golf-playing debutante with an MBA. Maybe he likes you because you aren't?"

"Assuming he does like me."

"I say this with the greatest possible affection: you are a dope. You underestimate how interesting and fun you are, and you know something else? I admit his surface is very smooth, and a little stiff, but there's more to him. He can be fun when he relaxes but there is loneliness, too, I think. But of course if you're sure he's a waste of your precious time…"

The sarcasm floated right through the phone wires, loud and clear.

"Ok, mom, I get the point. Maybe."

"Do you like him? Isn't that the question?"

"I don't know! I didn't, at first. Then, now, maybe, sort of, he's growing on me. He's kind of…I guess, kind of nice. And, he's not hard on the eyes though he's not really my type. I don't think."

She laughed. "Just so you keep an open mind and let yourself have a little fun. Keep in touch, honey."

I watched the block, hoping my visitor could find parking. I noted that the double-parked plumber's van from earlier was still here and was now parked at the curb, right in front of my house. Some part of my brain wished he would move the damn van and give me the spot. When my visitor arrived, he double-parked without hesitation. Cops can get away with that.

"Nice to meet you in person, Ms. Erica Donato." He offered his hand. "You look just like the photo on Rick's desk, only without the black cap and gown."

"High school? I can't believe he still had that one. Well, I'm surely a little older looking now."

He looked at me with squint and a smile. "Not that much." He came in, and we settled into the living room.

"How well did you really know him?" He was not looking at me while he waited for my answer.

"That is the question, isn't it, the one that's keeping me up at night. I thought I knew him as well, at least almost as well, as I know my own father. I don't think that anymore. It's shaken me."

"Let's say," he said, still not looking at me, "let's say he had a few sides to his personality and he didn't show them all to everyone."

I nodded. That made sense. I don't really know everything about my dad, and Chris certainly doesn't know everything about me. And that's a good thing too.

Why should it be different with Rick?

"He was a good friend, as I'm sure you know from your dad, and yeah, he was always as good a cop as he was a friend, citations, promotions, well thought of. He did like to have a hell-raising good time though, all through the years. That's what busted up his marriages."

I thought about Wanda, and his house, so neglected except in the places where his comfort was the issue, and I nodded again. "He never showed that side to me, but I can sort of see it now."

"Even the years he was on the job, we all knew there was some betting. He liked trips to Atlantic City and Vegas, he liked more than a few drinks, but he kept it to his off time. You couldn't ask for a better cop, better back-up, better friend, altogether."

"So how can they even think that? Those detectives…"

He shook his head. "He was doing something that made someone angry enough to kill him. Come on. It doesn't look like some juiced up kid with more testosterone than brains."

"So you're saying no questions can be off the table for the detectives?"

"Rick always said you were smart."

He held up a hand to stop my next indignant questions. "There's more. What I hear—and my sources are good—they found a gym bag stuffed with cash in his closet. So first, what's a recently retired cop running a small private security business doing with that? And second, they found pictures in a desk drawer." He responded to my shocked look. "No, not that kind. The fully dressed but wrong people kind. In his retirement, yeah, Rick was hanging out with some extremely questionable associates. The kind the FBI takes an interest in."

"Someone else sort of told me that," I said slowly, "but I haven't wanted to think it could be true. It makes him someone else, not the good man I knew." And loved, I thought.

"Understandable, but that cash isn't imaginary, and neither are the pictures. We don't know what they mean. That is, not yet. And there's no physical evidence. Not YET." He stopped. "I should clarify that 'we' means 'we, the department.' I'm not personally involved in the investigation."

"What if someone wanted the pictures…"

"To be found? Could be. Nevertheless, he was associating with, let us say, known felons and persons of interest. And don't say 'what if they were faked?' We've got experts for that."

"But these little pieces are all only pointing to things. What do they *know*? Really know?"

"They know the names of a lot of people in the pictures. They know a woman he was seeing pretty steadily has fled to Montreal."

"Wanda?"

"You met her?" He looked surprised.

"No, I found her."

"Nice work. I hear they've got some Canadian cops checking on her exact whereabouts, so they can bring her back if they need to."

I thought about how scared she had been, and had a fleeting hope that they would not find her.

He looked at me with a somewhat sympathetic expression. "I can't help thinking I've given you more questions than answers."

"I don't know. Dammit, yes. I feel like I know Rick less than ever. I wanted to know why they're asking so many off the wall questions. Now I kind of wish I hadn't asked."

He gave me a sympathetic smile. "He was a good cop and a good guy for a lot of years. I'd bet my shield on that. We don't know exactly what happened in his life the last few. We, meaning all of us this time, you, me, his friends and the detective team.

Whatever, it doesn't take away from all the years before. Me, I'm sticking with that thought. You should too. And whatever deep waters he got into, bottom line, someone killed him and left him there to be found and that person will get his. Count on it. It's not your job, but it is going to get done."

"Is that supposed to cheer me up?"

"I was hoping."

"It isn't working that well."

I had one more important question to be answered. At least it was important to me.

"I have a reason to think he worked in my neighborhood, right here where I live now, when he was young. I saw a photo. And I don't get it. He never told me that, not after visiting me here a million times. Is there anything you know about that? It's here, Park Slope, the 78 precinct."

He looked at me oddly.

"Wow. That goes back a real long way. Real long, before I was married. I was just a kid then and he was too."

He shook his head. "As best as I recall, Rick wasn't there very long, and he wasn't very happy. He didn't seem like his old self, and every once in a while he'd say something about getting out of there."

"And didn't he ever…?"

"Nope, never said why. Young cops in those days, we didn't exactly have these soulful talks. I figured he had a screw-up partner or a hardass sergeant. Like that, you know? Then, he got a transfer and was back to being his old self again." He looked puzzled for a moment. "I always felt like something happened to him there. A girl? Something? Man, this takes me back a long way!"

He shook his head again. "He wasn't like scarred or anything like that. If anything, he was even more like his old self? I don't know how to say it better than that. He was harder in some way. Still a joker but not a goofy kid at all. Harder, like he learned something and didn't like it."

He made a dismissive gesture. "Ahh, we all probably did. A few years on the job and you stop being a clueless rookie. You'd better. I don't remember any more and probably never knew any more even back then."

I had to be satisfied with that, though of course I wasn't at all satisfied. His words, that it was not my job, rattled around in my mind. It wasn't but it was. Perhaps I would have to settle for frequent phone calls to Sergeant Simms. How could I let it go entirely? I knew I couldn't.

Chapter Seventeen

I wrote up everything about the meeting and then forced myself to put the pages, and Rick, away for now. I had to get some work done. Maybe I could pursue it later. Work would be a challenge, because hammering had begun downstairs. Someone was building something in my house. Or perhaps tearing something down. I went to investigate.

The workmen looked up, waved, went back to the job. They were building vertical structures around the appliances.

"Yes, you'll have your new cabinets tomorrow," a voice behind me said. "Tell me I'm your hero."

I turned around to face Joe. My smile told him that he was my hero.

"Sorry it's taking so long." He looked a little sheepish. "You know I'm fitting you in around other jobs. That's why we're here so late today."

"I know. It's finally starting to seem real now!"

"Amazing, isn't it, how it's a mess and then it's still a mess, and then it all comes together? Best part of the job, seeing that. Those bleached cabinets will be nice in here, nice and bright. We've got the counter tops. We'll get them in as soon as we can, I promise."

"Bathroom next? Please?"

"Lady, you are getting pushy."

"Of course. That's my Brooklyn attitude coming through. But seriously, I'd love to have it all done when Chris comes home."

"Chris? Now that's upping the pressure."

I stopped smiling, though, remembering the event that would probably bring her home for a visit, well before the end of camp.

"She seems to like camp, except for worrying about you."

"What?"

'Yeah, she wrote to me."

"She's never mentioned that to me." I could hear my own grumpy voice. "What could she possibly have to write to you about?"

"We got close when she was working for me. We talked. She's a great kid and I think maybe she likes having a man's point of view." He patted me on the shoulder. "I can be that man, and even better, not come on as anyone's parent. I'm an independent adult friend. No need to be miffed."

"I'm not miffed!"

"Oh, sure. I can see that you're not." He had a perfectly straight face when he said it. "How are you otherwise? Life settling back down? Any new information about Rick?"

Suddenly my eyes stung. "It would take all evening to tell you, so much has happened."

"Remember I'm my own boss?" he said gently. "I can take all evening if I want to."

"But I can't." I blinked the tears away. "I have things to do. And I bet you're lying, anyway. It's your busy season. You probably have a whole list of stops to make after me…"

He nodded. "True. Only one or two hundred. How about over a late dinner? I'd even step us up from pizza. Steak frites and a bottle of Beaujolais?"

I was unnerved by the offer, and the kind expression on his face. He was the closest I ever had to a big brother, and I knew I could trust him with everything on my mind. He might tell me I was doing something stupid—in fact, he had already done that, and more than once—but he would be in my corner no matter what.

"Sorry." I had some real regrets. "I have work to do tonight. A lot of work. I'm getting into some serious trouble on that."

"Another time," he replied without undue disappointment. "You know, one of the things Chris has confided is that she wishes you would have more of your own social life."

"What? No way."

He nodded slowly, with an expression I couldn't quite read. "She seems to feel you need more to think about than her."

"I have plenty to think about. Too much. School, house, supporting us, my future, her future. How could she…."

"What have you told her about that slick looking guy I met the other day?" Now I could see he was teasing. "See what she says then. Yeah, yeah, I know you said it was just business."

"It is. So I have nothing to tell her." Was my face turning pink? "And how is your current social life?" The best defense is to turn the tables.

He only smiled mysteriously. "I've got to get going."

His crew left shortly after and the house was quiet. I dug myself in for a long evening of work, trying to smother any questions I had about Rick. Or anything. By the time my weary eyes started to cross, I had written a long memo for my boss, with attachments. I thought—I hoped—I had redeemed myself on that front.

◇◇◇

The phone rang and rang, but when I finally got to it, it went dead. I squinted at my clock, three a.m., and looked in panic at the caller ID. Brooklyn. Leary I thought, but he did not answer when I called back and the machine did not pick up. I tried again. It rang and rang, and still no machine pick up. Then there was a kind of click and a hard breathing sound.

"Hello?" I said. "Hello?"

More gasping.

"Leary, is that you? Come on!"

More gasping and I finally realized he was groaning.

"Leary? Is that you? Are you all right?"

A whispered "Not all right."

"Do you need help? Should I call 911?"

"No. Please come…." and the line went dead.

I swapped jeans for my pajama shorts, pulled a shirt over my tank top and was pointing my car toward his block almost before the thought had formed in my mind. Luckily for me some idiot had left the outside door of his building open a crack and I slipped in. Last time, pounding on his apartment door worked but this time I had no response to my fist or my shouting.

I heard a faint sound, a moan.

"Leary? Is that you? Open the damn door!" I was already fumbling for my phone, ready to call 911.

Another moan, then a whisper. Something I could barely hear. Door? Is that what he said?

I shoved the door and it opened. He was lying on the floor, his face bruised, his skin the color of paper and clammy to the touch. 911 it was

I was already dialing as I knelt beside him, ignoring the filthy floor. "Help is coming." I said it softly but very clearly. "What can I do for you?"

He opened his eyes, seemed to struggle to focus and whispered, "Orange juice." I jumped up to get it and he gasped, "Wait." He finally forced the words out. "Add sugar." He closed his eyes again.

Was he going to die right there? I poured the juice with shaky hands, ripped open coffee shop packets of sugar lying on the counter, and was back in the living room, holding up his head to drink, in a fast minute.

Holding onto consciousness by a thread, it seemed, he sipped slowly, and slowly, his color returned from this death-like pallor to something more like his normal unhealthy tone. His eyes began to focus. He gradually moved from looking almost dead to merely looking exhausted. It was a substantial improvement. I talked to him, trying to keep him from drifting off again, talked about anything I could think of. I asked questions and when he couldn't seem to respond, I babbled. The weather, the park, my new kitchen.

He finally said something back, in a shaky whisper. "There were men. They wanted something. Don't know...." He stopped, seeming too tired to continue. He flinched when the downstairs buzzer broadcast static into the room. I pushed the intercom button, a voice barked, "EMS" and I pushed the button that would unlock the lobby door. Thank you, I whispered to someone and went back to Leary.

He was trying to tell me more. "Just took my shot and didn't get to eat. They got in—shoved me around. Hit me. Dunno.... something happened. Too much insulin."

The ambulance crew burst in, I told them who he was, who I was, how I had found him, and then had to get out of their busy way. A few medical procedures later, they told me orange juice was what the doctor would have ordered.

"Lady, you might've saved his life," were the exact words. They asked me a few questions I could not answer, but Leary was able to mumble, "In my wallet," and they were off, talking to me over their shoulders as they wheeled him out. "Kings County Hospital." "Don't follow. You can call later." "You'll be in the way, and if you're not family, no one's talking to you anyway. We got HIPPA rules."

I managed to tell them this had maybe been an assault and they said, "We already figured that." Their voices disappeared as they entered the elevator, and suddenly all was quiet.

I sat down—no, I collapsed—onto his scary couch. When my heart finally stopped pumping so loudly I could hear it, I began trying to understand what had happened here.

Leary had a medical episode because some men interrupted his bedtime routine? He had too much insulin in his system, because he needed a snack? The men did something to him—the bruises on his face could not have come from a fall—and then what? Fled?

Or was he imagining some of it? All of it? Were hallucinations part of this kind of diabetic situation? I had no idea. But the EMS team had seen something to make them think there was an assault. Would the hospital report that?

I wanted to do something useful. Clean up here? I had a pretty strong feeling he would not like that. Pack him a bag for the hospital? I flinched at rummaging in his clothing. I could at least lock up when I left. Where were his keys? They did not seem to be near the door. I could try his dresser top.

The room was the same disaster as the rest of his apartment, and no keys were in sight. I would try his office.

One look at that room told me the mysterious men were no hallucination. His pristine files were all over the floor, drawers were open, and paper was everywhere. Oh, yes, someone was certainly looking for something. I wanted to look myself, but I knew better than touch anything. I could look, though, couldn't I? Walk carefully into the room and see what they had focused on, if anything?

It was such a mess, this could have been completely random, not a search for something in the files, but a search for something else entirely. Drugs. Perhaps people had seen him with needles and misunderstood. Or money. Not that he appeared to have any, but who knew what a desperate, stupid, drug-addled criminal might think? This wasn't the best neighborhood.

I tiptoed over the papers on the floor, squatted in the middle and looked without touching. I used a pencil to lift a few things and dropped them right back where they were.

Every file that I could see, meticulously labeled with subject and date, was from the early 1970's. Damn. It was everything we had been talking about. So then, it was no random break in, and no hallucination, but it also made no sense. A retired reporter's random notes, written a lifetime ago?

I left the room, very carefully, to collapse again on the sofa. Maybe my mind was racing, but my eyes still focused, and there were the keys, on the floor where I had found Leary. They must have fallen from his pocket.

What should I do now? If the hospital found signs of assault—and I was now sure they would—they would contact the police. They would talk to Leary and look at the scene, I thought, but I didn't know how to tell them about the threatening phone calls Leary had mentioned to me. He said they were prank calls, harassment from young problem neighbors, but now I was sure they weren't.

Suddenly I had to get out of this apartment, a creepy place even in normal times. I was alone in a place where, it seemed, someone had been attacked. Was I crazy to be here? I was. What if they came back?

It was still almost dark outside, gray pre-dawn. My hand was shaking so badly I could barely get the key into my car door. Even in my exhausted fog, I kept thinking about the files all over Leary's floor, and the files he had given me. Was it possible that I had what they wanted? And could they know that? Whoever they were, these mad history-pursuing thugs, they were certainly thugs. Who beats an old man over old news stories? None of this made sense and all of it was scary.

I caught a parking space near home, as someone was leaving for an early morning job, all but ran inside and gratefully collapsed back into my bed.

The next thing I knew, bright sun was poking through my window shutters. I hid my head under a pillow, but last night came back to me and escape was useless. It was well into the morning. No. It was no longer morning at all.

I had barely made it to the shower when the phone rang. News about Leary? No. Dripping wet, wrapped in a towel, I took a call from Steven. Who I should have met that morning at ten for an update on my work. Damn.

"What happened? We were getting together, weren't we? Breakfast and business? This morning?"

I briefly thought about saying he had the wrong morning. He sounded concerned in a polite way. Not angry about the missed meeting. Puzzled, perhaps.

"I had a crazy experience." His polite tone made me feel like I needed to explain. I didn't want him to think badly of me, and without ever intending to, I poured out the whole story. Sentence by sentence, his replies became warmer, until at the end, I felt like I was once again talking to the guy from the concert. Then he said something a friend really would say.

"Maybe it's none of my business, but I'm thinking you've stumbled into something that is way over your head here. Any chance I'm right?"

"You aren't the first person to say that. "

"That doesn't surprise me. Can I help in some way? I could be a sounding board for you, someplace to talk it over. I am considered fairly bright."

"I don't...I have no...." I took a deep breath. I would not dither. "I don't think so." I hoped I said it firmly. "I am handling things." Was that true? I hoped it was.

"I have no doubt about that." Though the words were supportive, the tone expressed nothing but doubt. "Look. I am back in my office now, in downtown Manhattan. Can you come here, and have our missed meeting this afternoon?"

Another surprise, but I did owe him a meeting. I had to say yes, and we arranged it for late afternoon at his downtown office.

I called Kings County Hospital but could not get any information about Leary except that he could not yet have visitors. I could try again tomorrow. I needed to dress, eat, and hustle myself into Manhattan.

I have one business suit for summer and one for winter. It would have to do, with my one pair of business heels and the only intact hose I had. My neglected work could go with me on the subway. I didn't get much done though, because I could not stop thinking about Leary. I would read a page or two, make a note, then remember his dreadfully pale face. I wondered with a pang if that was how Rick looked. I read a little more, and then started trying to make sense of what had happened to him. A complete exercise in futility, of course.

When I emerged from the subway at Bowling Green, right at Manhattan's southernmost tip, I had a few extra minutes to wander the twisty streets of the financial district. I always loved the layers of history here, the street names from the Dutch, when this was New Amsterdam—Maiden Lane, Beaver St., Wall Street, Bowling Green itself—the commodity exchanges going back to the days of the clipper ships, the cobblestones on a few narrow side streets lined with buildings right out of an antique print.

Then right around the corner there would an assertive glass office tower, occupying an entire block, covering the site of something like the Dutch city hall, and here and there, the ordinary twenty-first century sandwich shops and chain drug stores and nail salons to serve the thousands of workers of those towers.

Here was the cemetery where Alexander Hamilton was buried, the church where Washington prayed, the cathedral-like granite towers where the old robber barons worshipped Mammon. There was Delmonico's restaurant, a reconstruction of the place where Diamond Jim Brady cavorted with Lillian Russell. There were ghosts everywhere, most of them old enough, centuries old, to seem benign.

The most painful downtown ghosts, the most real to me and every New Yorker, were not right in front of me today. The site of the World Trade Center was many blocks north from where I stood right now.

None of it quite banished the dreadful scene at Leary's apartment. I feared the emergency room would never tell me anything; I would have to go see him as soon as I could.

A few more twists and turns brought me to the address Steven had provided, right on Battery Park, an impressive yet subdued stone building, a home for movers and shakers who preferred a more discreet profile. Inside, though, the soaring lobby was all polished marble, in several colors, inlaid floors, and elaborate brass trim, the epitome of Gilded Age décor demanding attention and awe.

It gave me the same feeling I have looking at Renaissance art. I had to admire the beauty even while I remembered the questionable fortunes that paid for it.

I spotted a discreet, handsome sign saying Hoyt Enterprises and it confused me. Wasn't James Hoyt Steven's uncle? I thought this was Steven's office. Before I could even step to the lofty reception desk, a man in a dark suit came over to me, said "Ms. Donato?" and when I admitted to it, said, "Right this way."

We bypassed the reception desk, the ID checking, the signing in, the visitor's tag, and went directly to an elevator. It was waiting for us, doors open. "If you please," he said and ushered me in.

The doors closed smoothly, and when they opened again, seconds later, we were at a discreetly elegant reception area and Steven was waiting for me.

"Thank you," he said to the silent man, and to me, "Right this way."

It was a comfortable office, handsomely furnished, with his nameplate on the door, "I don't understand. I thought we were meeting at your office. "

"We are. I have an office at my own firm, of course, but I keep one here, because Uncle James is an important client of ours. What do you think?"

"I think I would never do any work at all if I had that window." We looked right out over Battery Park, a scene of soothing greenery and constant activity, and past it to the ferry terminal and the harbor.

He smiled ruefully. "Note that the desk chair keeps my back to the window. Not an accident. Have a seat? Can I ring for anything for you? Water? Coffee?"

I barely had my folders out, with period photos and useful articles, on his desk, when someone else rang for him.

"Excuse me, I need to take this."

He turned away from me, and I heard him say softly. "Yes," "Now?" and "Yes" again. The caller was doing all the talking.

When he turned back, he stood up. "Let's leave the work for now. We have an invitation to meet someone" He held out a hand to me. "I promise it will be interesting."

We went back to the elevators, and twenty floors later, with no stops, we stepped directly into an office suite so huge it might have occupied the entire floor. Or at least, it seemed that way to my overwhelmed first glance. In the enormous inner office, bright golden late afternoon sun slid between the bands of a closed silvery shade.

Pastel leather sofas were placed in small groups on the thick Chinese rugs and there was no clutter on the huge glass desk. The sole object was an abstract marble sculpture precisely placed at one corner.

"Ah, Steven. So this is your guest?" The elderly man sounded like Franklin Roosevelt and he had silver hair, a deep golf-course tan, and on this hot summer day was perfectly dressed in a charcoal pin-striped suit, pressed shirt with cufflinks, silk tie. No lounging around in business casual in this office.

"Come in, come in. I am happy to meet you. Erica, isn't it? Please call me James. It's a beautiful day. Let's take a drink out on the terrace, shall we?"

No one needed to introduce me. This was James Hoyt, the man whose name was on the building. I swallowed hard and looked at Steven with, I'm sure, a question in my face. Lots of questions. His expression didn't answer any of them.

We paused at a bar that seemed to cover one end of the room, and there he poured from a cut glass decanter. "Will you join me in a small pick-me-up? I am having excellent aged Scotch, Highland Park, all the way from the Orkney Islands. Steven, for you? Or I have bottled water here."

"Water, please." I did not need liquor adding to my confusion, however exotic a drink it was.

The terrace was landscaped with planters and furnished with solid teak deck chairs, comfortably cushioned, and solid wood tables. I thought fleetingly of the rusted wire mesh seats on my tiny deck. We stood at the stone railing, looking out over the harbor, the bridges and the boats. From that height we could see past New Jersey, past Staten Island, right out to the ocean. I was definitely not in Kansas anymore. It did feel like an old movie, though, a different one with Cary Grant or Humphrey Bogart playing a tycoon.

James spoke from behind us. "I've been here forty years and I'm not tired of the view yet. Sometimes I am able to look down over the storm clouds."

"Uncle James has Zeus fantasies." Steven's voice was teasing and James waved a dismissive hand.

"Now, young lady, Steven seems to think you have just the skills to help us with a little problem on our project."

Our project? I sent a sharp look in Steven's direction. Was James the mysterious client? The one I was working for? Was there a reason he had not mentioned this? Behind James back, Steven put a discreet finger to his lips, and poured another drink.

"Why don't you have a seat and tell me all about yourself? Steven tells me you are from Brooklyn yourself?"

Did I really hear an undertone in his voice that added, "Of all exotic places?" Or was I being defensive?

Looking at me steadily, as if he was reading my mind, James added, "I understand you've acquired the local insights we find so useful from your work at the Brooklyn History Museum. I know it well. The president of your board is an old friend of mine."

I had never even met a museum board member.

"And do you also live in that lovely neighborhood, my dear, where the museum is located?"

"Brooklyn Heights? Not a chance. I could not possibly afford it." I suddenly felt compelled to establish exactly who I am. Aggressively. "I live in Park Slope, also old and charming, but I live in the less charming part, in a very little, undistinguished house that needs a whole lot of work. I grew up in East Flatbush, actually." Not so old and not so charming, I thought.

There. It was all in the open. Of course I hadn't yet mentioned that I went to public schools and still went to one, and I had never met a debutante. All this luxury was making me prickly.

"Ah, Park Slope indeed. Now there is a neighborhood that gives new meaning to urban change. I'm sure your house is charming, as they all are there. Why don't you tell me all about it?"

All right, I haven't had a lot of job interviews in the business world. Actually, I haven't had any, but this one, if that's what it was, seemed decidedly odd. Unless he was trying to find common ground. Or he had a subtle interview agenda I was not able to recognize. This was not my world.

"Where should I start?

"Why choose an old house that needs work instead of something clean and perfect?"

"I like old things with stories. I am a historian, after all, or will be when I finish my Ph.D. I have to admit that my parents asked me the same thing." More than a few times, I thought but did not say.

"Does that mean your parents aren't historians?"

"Exactly. My dad is a retired cab driver, and my mother was, well, she was a mother, and then a secretary at a school."

"Ah, I see."

I wondered if he did.

"Of course renovation is a creative act in itself. I've put a few renovations in motion in my time."

Behind him, Steven winked at me. "On a somewhat different scale."

James waved a hand to dismiss the difference. "Several spacious country houses in my various marriages. Of course they were usually the current wife's project. I imagine a brownstone has a whole set of preservation issues."

"Not mine. Everything worth keeping was ripped out long ago."

"I see." He looked at me with serious attention.

"Steven has explained to me that the useful work you have been doing for our little venture has been sidetracked by some disturbing problems." He patted my arm with one almost transparent, trembling hand. I wondered if he was older than he looked. "How can we help you? We consider you a new member of our team, and we do try to take care of our own. Why don't you tell me what is on your mind?"

I had a feeling people did not often say no to James Hoyt. I didn't. I couldn't. It never even crossed my mind.

I began slowly, fumbling, and was appalled to hear my voice turn shaky several times as I described the series of strange incidents in my life and the lives of people around me.

"Is it saying the obvious to suggest you cease asking questions? Someone seems unhappy about that."

"Yes. All right, yes, maybe I should, but I don't seem to be able to."

"I see." James was nodding thoughtfully. "Please accept my condolences on the untimely death of your friend. I sympathize with your desire to understand it, and on that, I may be helpful. I have friends. But I wonder if there isn't also a clear issue of your own safety? Maybe we can help directly with that."

I nodded slightly.

"You have a child, don't you?"

Off guard, I stammered. "Yes, but she's fine. She's not here, in fact I sent her off to camp because I was a worried…."

"Probably you should be. If someone is harassing you, it is not impossible that he could go after her too."

His words sent a chill right into my body. I must have shivered, because he said gravely, looking right at me, "I don't mean to alarm you unnecessarily but too much caution is surely preferable to too little, don't you agree, where a child is concerned?"

I didn't want to talk about Chris with this smooth, enigmatic man. My child was entirely too personal a topic for this company and this place. I remembered what Steven had said about his cousin JJ.

"You speak as if you know." I was very politely turning the tables. "Do you have children?"

He put his glass down so quickly, whisky splashed out. "Not any more."

He used his monogrammed pocket square to awkwardly blot up the spill, then he turned back to me with an unreadable face. "Ms. Donato, please believe that we are trying to help you. Indulge me if you will and allow an old man to feel useful. Steven can take you to meet my most excellent security director and he will come up with a plan for your safety. And you will exercise more caution in your activities?"

As I started to protest, he patted my hand, "I am sure you will do the intelligent thing. I am sure you see what it is."

He seemed confident that he had made his point. I was guessing that most meetings with him ended with him making his points. He made a call and exchanged a few quiet words. Next thing I knew, another silent man in a dark suit was in the office to escort us down in the elevator.

James shook my hand, then bent down to kiss me on my cheek. "Ms. Donato, use your friends; that's what they are for."

Chapter Eighteen

It was another swift, silent ride. Steven put a reassuring hand on my elbow, but only said, "We are going to meet Rob McLeod."

My questioning look was answered with, "He handles buildings, corporate, personal security, everything that needs doing. Relax. He's a good man, very capable."

Our escort took us to a door with no information on it, punched a code into a keypad, walked us to a modest, comfortable office, and left.

The tall, trim man at the desk stood to shake our hands. "Steven, good to see you. Ms. Donato? Please be comfortable. I'm Rob McLeod, Mr. Hoyt's head of security. This is my private office."

McLeod's suit hid his physique, but something about the way he moved told me there would be muscles under the Brooks Brothers clothes. He had the erect posture and short hair of an ex-military man. Or an ex-cop. After we were seated, I asked him which. He smiled, briefly. "Both. Marines and Chicago PD. Now tell me why Mr. Hoyt sent you to me?"

McLeod didn't take a single note. He only nodded at the end. "Oh, yes, you are deep in something ugly and even without knowing what it's all about, there is clearly risk for you."

I flinched and Steven put his hand over mine for a second.

"First, Ms. Donato, do the obvious and lay low. Stop asking questions. Why take chances? And you've told me everything, and have no idea who you are ticking off so dramatically? You're sure?" He looked thoughtful at my heated denial of any further knowledge. "We can look into that if it seems necessary, but let's talk first about how we can throw some safety around you until this blows over, shall we? Steve, that's what you and Mr. Hoyt have in mind?"

"Exactly."

"Of course we have all levels of security from house alarms to bodyguards, and twenty-four surveillance. Mr. Hoyt didn't specify; he's leaving it up to my judgment."

"I'm thinking she needs..."

"Excuse me!" I interrupted these smooth men with their smooth executive conversation. I said it like a woman who knows how to push her way out of a crowded subway train. "Excuse me! Am I still here?"

Both men looked startled and then smiled. Steven quickly apologized, and McLeod said, "Maybe I was getting carried away with my job here. I'll ask it differently: when do you feel the most endangered?"

"That's impossible to say, because it has been so random. And then people I know seem to get in trouble. The not knowing what the hell is going on—or if anything terrible is—is what is driving me crazy. But are we discussing bodyguards? We can't be. That is ridiculous. I'm not some rock star with a huge ego."

"Ms. Donato," McLeod said gently, "I was just laying out some options. That's the level we provide for, say, one of our executives in a foreign country with a high crime rate. Perhaps what makes sense right now is to do a full security assessment. Someone did break into your house. Let's figure out how to make sure that does not happen again. And then we spread ourselves further as we see the need."

Steven started to protest, but McLeod went on. "In the meantime, we can make a few efforts at digging into what this is all about. When can we send someone to your house for a look around? We can also think about a home alarm system. That's not unusual and not a big deal to do. I'm sure Mr. Hoyt meant for me to include it as an option."

"Without a doubt."

"No, but that's too much...I can never repay that kind of favor."

Steven looked at me very seriously. "It's nothing to James, you know. No more than subway fare would be to you. And I can assure you he would be insulted at the word repay."

McLeod smiled. "Why don't we figure out how to install a basic one? At the very least, it would protect you and your home from another intruder. That's not a small thing for a woman alone."

I knew that made sense but I felt as if my life was spinning into some surreal zone. How could this be me, Erica Shapiro Donato from East Flatbush, talking to a high-powered security expert?

"I will think it over and get back to you." I saw their faces, and added, "Soon. I will get back to you soon. I promise. I need to think a little."

McLeod nodded, slightly. "We will accept that, and hold you to it. Say the word and I can have a team there right away. Deal?"

"Deal." I stood up. I was exhausted. "I am going home now."

Steven stood up with me. "I'll put you in a company car. You've had a long day."

As he walked me to the entrance, I finally had the chance to ask my pent-up questions. "But what about our work? Isn't that why I came here? I have all this material, too. And your uncle! What is his role here? I am so confused."

His expression was amused, but all he said was, "More questions? I have to be somewhere now and I'm tied up tomorrow. Let's reschedule our meeting for day after? Breakfast? Don't worry about the material you brought. I'll take good care of it."

He had not told me a thing and all in all, I was too tired to really care anymore. I would make a list of all my questions, and day after tomorrow, over breakfast, I would confront him without mercy to get some answers.

The short drive home was extended by traffic everywhere. I drifted. Afterwards, I could not have said if we took the tunnel or one of the bridges to Brooklyn. I knew nothing until the car stopped in front of my house.

Upstairs to my room, to change out of my only summer business outfit and hang it up carefully. Out of my heels and hose,
and into my comfortable gym shorts and t-shirt. I was home at
last, back in my cave for the rest of the night.

My phone rang and I let it go to the machine. I was not in the
mood to rush to answer it. A voice I didn't know began, "Don't
you learn? Stop asking questions. Stop talking to cops. Stop
talking to reporters. Stop meddling." I sat down, legs shaking,
and listened to the rest, telling what would happen to me if I
did not stop. It was vile, unbelievable, unreal. I was too shocked
to move; I was too shocked to turn it off.

They were right, those smooth corporate men, Steven and his
uncle and McLeod, and even Rick. I was caught in the middle
of something ugly and dangerous. One thing after another had
happened around me. This one was aimed right at me.

I had two immediate choices. I could make that call to the
polite, tough Mr. McLeod or I could have hysterics. Hysterics
was a tempting, but with hands that shook, I dug into my purse
for McLeod's card.

McLeod was calm and entirely reassuring. He would have a
security team there within the hour.

I was too exhausted to think anymore. I waited for McLeod's
team, curled up on my sofa under an old baby quilt of Chris',
with the TV turned to very old comedy programs. I would have
cuddled up with Chris' old teddy bear if I could have summoned
energy to walk upstairs to get it.

I knew I should have been scared—oh, all right, I was plenty
scared—but I was also angry. I was tired of someone messing
with me and those around me. Furious, actually.

McLeod's team arrived in less than an hour, three awesomely
competent looking men in neat, anonymous work clothes. I was
surprised to see Steven with them.

"I know you are stressed by all this so I thought you might
like some company while they work." He hesitated, then put a
gentle hand on my shoulder. "For support, physical and moral
both." I was touched by his thoughtfulness.

The team moved around my house with great efficiency, taking measurements, looking at outlets, assessing my window locks. They hammered and screwed and Steven joined them. I escaped into television; I could not have said later what was on. When they were done, they showed me how to use my brand new alarm system and left, while Steven came back to talk to me.

"Would you like to get out tonight? Maybe it would be good for you?"

I was again on the sofa, wrapped in Chris' quilt. How impossible would it be to get up and go out? I was too sad about Rick, too worried about Leary. Really, too overwhelmed by my life.

"You have to eat, if nothing else." And then in my mind, I heard Joe quoting Chris on my pathetic social life. "Why not? Give me a minute to change?"

A quick look at my e-mail before we left showed me a note from Chris. "You called? How R U? I'm fine. Really. Stop worrying. Miss U. Write me a letter about Rick and our lost girl and everything!!! Have fun or something!" Timely advice.

Once again I was in Steven's luxurious car, and the hour was late enough so traffic was only a problem and not a torment. Over the bridge and then we were wandering around the brute masonry of bridge ramps and foundations. The street patterns, running up against the bridge, made no sense to me. Though we were near the original City Hall, Police Plaza, and the city government office towers, there was no possible reason to be there in the evening. There was no neighborhood there.

"Where in the world are we going? "

"Be patient. One more turn around a block and—aha!—here we are."

We were in front of a tiny, three-story clapboard building, painted barn red with black trim. Overwhelmed by the massive structures all round, it looked like it belonged in very old New England. Salem, perhaps, or Cape Cod.

Steven looked as pleased as if he'd built it himself. "Behold Bridge Tavern, the oldest drinking establishment in New York.

They serve food too. The right place to take a historian? You like places with a story."

It certainly had one. The menu told us it was more than two hundred years old, and it was as charming on the inside as the outside, with a nineteenth-century pressed tin ceiling, and walls covered with art from all eras and styles, depicting this same building.

"I love it. What a wonderful idea."

"I'm glad. My plan was something or someplace so captivating it would distract you right out of your difficulties for an evening. And they do have excellent real cooking, not bar food."

"If bar food means burgers and pizza, it would work for me. I'm not really so sophisticated." I felt sheepish, saying it.

"Want to discuss the menu?" It was a kind offer, not condescending, and I was grateful. Mussels, duck and bluefish, wonderful sauces and garnishes, and a bottle of wine with a shocking price tag. At least it shocked me. Everything tasted delicious and luxurious

We started out talking about the charming restaurant and its wild history over the centuries. It had been a bar, a grocery that sold liquor, a brothel. Before the building of the bridge, this had been one of the city's worst neighborhoods in one of its most lawless periods.

Then we went on to talk about almost everything except my current disturbing life, or Steven's marriage or mine. We stuck to pleasant topics, as if we had made a deal without saying so. Steven's stiffness melted away and so did my stress and exhaustion, at least for now.

The fish we ate led to my memories of fishing on day boats off Sheepshead Bay with Rick and my dad, and his memories of learning to cast for trout on Adirondack vacations. The Adirondacks led to Chris at camp and my hope she would get to travel more than I had. That led to hilarious stories about his post-college trek through Europe. We talked about favorite travel books, and then we talked about beloved childhood books, which took us to dessert.

It was clear we had almost no experiences in common and it didn't matter; we never stopped talking except when we were laughing. I admitted silently that Darcy was right about him after all.

After dinner, he said, "Surprisingly they have one of the best collections of Scotch in the entire city. I think I should teach you how to drink quality Scotch. What do you say?"

"Ouch. Did you notice I didn't drink any in your uncle's office?"

His smile was teasing and challenging but not mocking.

"I'm game." I smiled back. I might even have giggled. "But I might still prefer beer."

He had a quick conference with the bartender, and brought back four full shot glasses.

"Now pay attention, Ms. Donato. School is in session. Please observe that the colors vary slightly. Very discreetly, take a sniff of each."

I almost choked.

"Take a little sniff! Can you tell the difference? No? Try again?"

He played professor and walked me though the names, the origins, the subtle differences. When I asked if I should be taking notes, he told me not to be impertinent.

I looked up at him, laughter in his expression, and thought, "I am having fun tonight." It was such an unfamiliar emotion it had taken all evening for me to recognize it.

Finally I said, "My mouth is all Scotch tasting. I need to stop. I think I've had enough for now.

"Any favorites?"

"I still like beer better."

He laughed. "You are a waste of first-class alcohol, but the cure for that is more tasting another night." Driving tonight, he had not been sampling, but he finished off one before we left.

We walked back to the car arms wrapped around each other. It seemed natural by then. I wasn't drunk, but I was a little happy, a little relaxed. I was grateful, and I stopped before we opened the car to tell him so.

He kissed me then. I think it surprised us both. He didn't pursue it, just smiled and said, "You taste like Scotch. Very nice."

We were quiet in the car, all talked out, but he held my hand under his on the gearshift, another entirely new experience for me.

At my house, Steven made sure I knew how to turn the new alarm off, saw me in, and kissed me good night. We ended up kissing each other good night for quite awhile. He put his hands on each side of my face, and searched my eyes.

"This is…something, isn't it? Not just any night out?"

I nodded, speechless. It had been a long time since I had been kissed like that. And since I kissed back. It felt good. It felt too good.

Arms tight around me, he whispered into my ear, "Go get some sleep. I'll call. I'll see you day after tomorrow. Lock the door behind me and make sure the alarm is on." A few more kisses, and he was gone.

I was breathless. I was smiling. I was confused.

There was a voice message from Chris and even that did not rattle my smiley state. Yes, it was a late night call from my child, but I was incapable of worrying at that moment.

I didn't need to. She quickly assured me that she was fine, but she had been given access to the camp office phone and wanted to see how I was and find out what was happening with the research on the skeleton and any news about Rick. She told me I could send e-mail to the office, and the staff would get them to her. She added, "But nothing too private, please! And please, no mushy stuff!"

It was my first task in the morning, before shower, before coffee, before work. I had to figure out how I could possibly tell her all that had been happening. Then I revised my question. What was appropriate to tell her? And then I had to ask myself if I knew what she would consider too private. I missed her so much, yet I was also so glad she was not home in this complicated, confusing period of my life. And then too, maybe I was having, or was about to have, a private life now, for the first time in a long time, and I was glad to be conducting it without her watchful eyes.

I had a note from my boss at the museum. He liked the material I had sent recently, and added, "Keep it coming! We have deadlines. And when are you coming back to work?"

Damn. I thought the big pile of information would keep them happy to a few days at least, a gigantic bone for the dog. No such luck. I had an idea, though, for a move that would stun them into giving me some breathing room. I remembered James Hoyt's words, to use my friends, and went to find Nettie Rogow's phone number.

"This is Erica Donato. I don't know if you remember me," I began, but this was immediately stopped with, "Why of course I do! You're that charming young historian. And we talked about my Harry."

"Yes. You were extremely helpful."

"And I served one magnificent brunch, too. Don't forget that."

I laughed. "I could never forget. I still have the memory around my waist."

She laughed too, and then said, "What can I do for you?"

"Well, I had an idea. You may not know this, but we historians are really excited by archives. All those boxes of boring, everyday business records actually can add up to telling us a lot. So, I got to wondering if you—I mean the company—have records that go all the way back to the early years."

"Why, of course we do. My Harry was of the 'you never know' school. He kept it all, even his old report cards. I finally had to threaten to leave him if he didn't get the cartons out of the basement of our house. There were mountains of them."

I held my breath. "And where are they now? Is there any chance I could take a look?"

"As to where, that's easy. It's a warehouse in Brooklyn, down near the docks. As to looking, well, dear, trust me, a nice girl like you really doesn't want to. Those warehouses are foul places, damp and nasty—I mean, there's vermin—and no decent facilities, either, if you know what I mean. I was there a few times, years ago, and swore nothing would drag me back. And nothing has."

"Mrs. Rogow, you make it sound pretty scary, but I need to wow my bosses with my initiative. I'm a historian on a quest, you know, like an archaeologist. It might even be the start of my dissertation. So I'm not going to be turned away by some water bugs."

She surprised me by saying, "Indiana Jones, are you? Yes, I'll set it up. Why not? They'll want permission in writing, which I will send, but you can go ahead and tell them what you need. Probably they'll have to dig out for you so give it a couple of days. My memory might be shaky but I recall it's Dock Storage, and I think it's on Van Brunt, maybe near Snyder."

I was sure it was right there if she said so. I knew there was nothing wrong with her memory.

"I used to deal with Rosemarie there, but of course, that was years ago. And dear? It's not at all a nice neighborhood. Visit only in daylight and park right there so you don't have to walk around on your own. Please be careful. I would never get over it if you got into trouble because I said yes to this."

"Of course. I am always careful. You know I do have some street sense. And thank you so much."

"I'll tell you how to thank me. Come entertain an old lady. I want to hear all about what you found, and any discoveries you make. All right? In person and over a meal. Do you like pot roast? And if you write something—that's what you scholars do, isn't it?—say good things about my Harry. He would be so tickled to be in a scholar's article. It's such a respectable thing."

Of course I said yes to everything. I hung up, thinking, if I could look at the records for my own block over the years, I would have a perfect little picture, a microcosm, of neighborhood change. And maybe, with luck, I would find something that would be a clue about our dead girl. Two birds with one stone: I would be keeping my promise to Chris at the same time.

Chapter Nineteen

I turned away from my desk but didn't get more than a step before the computer pinged at me.

Damn. It was a message from my ditsy cousin Tammy. She's the only cousin I have a sort of friendship with. It's pretty thin. A few years older than me, she moved way the heck out on Long Island, the true 'burbs, even before I moved further into the city, and our lives diverged as much as our geography.

"Hi, little cuz. ?4U Still MIRL today? CM ASAP SYS?"

A grown woman sending e-mail in text-speak. Ridiculous. I could translate it, of course—I live with a teen. "Are we still meeting in real life? Call me as soon as possible. See you soon?"

About twice a year something causes her to venture in to "the city" and she remembers how to find her way to Brooklyn, where, incidentally, she was born, raised, educated and married. I had forgotten today was one of those times; we had a lunch date.

I had too much to do and too much on my mind and too little tolerance but it was already way too late to cancel. I called.

"Hey, honey. What did you think of my message? I am learning how to text! Are we still on? I could really go for girl talk and some of that fancy pizza I heard reviewed on the news. My treat."

Trapped, I told her where to meet me. I had to eat, after all. To tell the truth, I had a soft spot for Tammy. We might have zero in common as adults, but she was the cousin closest to my age when we were kids. She defended me from her tribe of brothers and taught me how to put on mascara and shave my legs. I had warm memories of sleepovers, staying up late reading her copies of *Tiger Beat*, discussing who was the cutest brother on *Home Improvement*, and would we rather grow up to be Brenda or Kelly from *90210*.

The problem was that she was still that person. True, she didn't read *Tiger Beat* anymore but she did avidly follow celebrities in *US Weekly*, *People*, and the *Daily News* Page Six gossip feature. I expected that today, reality TV stars, the hot actors du jour, and Brad and Angelina would likely come up. How could I keep myself from telling Tammy I could not care less? That I had a real life of my own to contend with?

She hugged me in a flurry of shopping bags and teased out hair. "I'm so glad to see you! And I am starving." She wore high suede boots, and a sequined t-shirt and she tactfully did not comment on my non-outfit.

As soon as we had wine in hand, she said, "Tell me, how is your dad? He called my mom from the hospital."

"He did what?"

She giggled and shrugged. "I know. I guess they must be speaking again."

We both giggled. Discussing the eccentricities of our respective parents is a bond that never frays.

"So do you think they're starting over, or what?" And we were off and running with speculation and reminiscence. We discussed our children. She assured me Chris would be less moody in a few years, and then admitted her youngest son was home from college, living in her basement, with a life plan that went no further than a job at Trader Joe. We congratulated each other that we had allowed them to continue living. Then I told her about Chris and camp, and that led to Rick.

The giggling stopped.

"Dear lord. Your dad knows?"

I nodded.

"Then my mom does, now that they're talking again. Ya know, I remember him from barbecues and stuff at your house? Was he the guy who always organized the water fights?"

I nodded again, unable to speak.

"Now, none of that." Tammy poured more wine. "You gotta keep remembering those good times. That's something grandpa taught me, that holding onto the good memories are what get you through the bad times."

"Tammy, you know, that sort of helps a little." It was actually the smartest thing I'd heard her say since she told me a boy who didn't treat me right was a waste of oxygen.

My surprise must have showed because she smiled. "In the immortal words of Marilyn Monroe, I can be smart when it's important."

She patted my hand, and changed the subject. "Now, with Chris away, I hope you are managing to have a little fun? Getting out more? According to the *Daily News*, there are some hopping clubs around here now. Wait!"

She dug a tabloid paper out of her bag and turned to photos of, yes, genuine celebrity spotting nearby.

"See? So just tell me that you are taking part in this new local glamour?"

"You want me to lie?" She made a face at me, and then I had an idea.

"Actually, I did meet someone you might know about from reading those trashy rags." I'd had enough wine by then to not care if I teased her. And she'd had enough not to care either.

"Pfft. It's harmless entertainment and you know you love to hear all about it. So tell me."

"What do you know about a guy named James Hoyt?"

"You met James Hoyt? YOU met James Hoyt?" Her eyes opened wide.

"Yes. Yes I did. I, um, know his nephew, sort of, and he introduced us. He's pretty famous?"

Her look was beyond exasperation. "This has even been in what you call the 'real newspapers'"—she used fingers to put that in air quotes—"that you read now, Miss Highbrow. He is one of the richest men in New York and was all over the news when he had a messy divorce a while ago. You living in a cave?"

Before I could respond she dove back into her gigantic purse, pulled out a tablet computer and next thing I knew we were online searching for gossip.

Could I have researched James myself? Oh, yes, But this was so much more fun. Like she said, harmless escape. Even if I felt a little cheap later.

Tammy, being Tammy, zoomed right in on juicy details of the most recent divorce. That wife, his third, was apparently famous for being a serial spouse of powerful men. Could that be a career choice? Tammy assured me it could, with the right combination of looks, ambition and luck. I thought an absence of morals probably helped.

The rags shared all the public details, and also helpfully included pictures of wife number two, a voluptuous minor opera singer, and number one, a cool blond ex-debutante.

There was a glamorous home décor article about wife number three and the glamorous house they were decorating in glamorous East Hampton. Of course that was when they were still glamorously happy together. Or so they told the writer from *Vogue*.

"Tammy! Hey." I had to get her attention. "This is fun but I'd love to see something with a few more facts?"

"Sure, sure." She took over on the keyboard. "Here. I'll send you the link to all this, you can look again at home. And here"—she turned the screen back to me—"here is a long, juicy profile, exactly what you ordered. Whew, I'm done with this. Going back to stuffing my face."

The article was from *Vanity Fair*, the perfect source for pages of solid information mixed in with the gossip and photos. I was about to learn exactly who James Hoyt was.

So. He had taken the very comfortable fortune his father had left him and turned it into billions by arcane financial wizardry. Reading about it, I concluded no ordinary person could understand how.

With that fortune, he had taken over failing companies, astutely invested in new ones before anyone else knew about them, was active in politics, and gave both time and money to worthy cultural and educational institutions.

There was plenty to suggest he had enjoyed every minute of it—the battles with regulatory agencies and corporate boards; the homes in Aspen, Bermuda, and Provence; the movie star girlfriends and the three marriages. Or perhaps he hadn't enjoyed those so much.

There was an unmistakeable undertone that he had been brilliant, charming, and ruthless and remained so even as he grew old. It sounded right to me.

Aha. With three marriages, he had only one child, long dead. There were hints of tragic circumstances but I could not find more details, or an obituary. Was his death not newsworthy, I wondered, or had it been covered up? It was decades ago, long before there was the ability to put every rumor and scandal out in cyberspace.

I sighed, rubbed my eyes, thought about what I had learned, and what I had not.

"Do you want to fight me for that last slice?" Tammy pulled me back to the here and now. "I won't lie. I'm a believer now. Twenty-five dollars for pizza seemed ridiculous but boy, this is great."

"Help yourself. I assume you don't have room for dessert?"

"Who says?"

We put the computer away and returned to the business at hand, which was eating, but I couldn't wait to get home and take another look. I wanted to know more about this man that I now seemed to be in bed with him. With him and his nephew. Whoops. Interesting metaphor to come crashing into my mind. I was very glad I had not said it out loud. Tammy might be ditsy but as she said, she could be smart. I would have been answering questions I did not want to hear.

When we parted, it was with promises not to make it so long until next time. This time, I think we meant them. I had forgotten how relaxing it could be to spend time with someone who knew me when I was young and stupid.

I made it home in time for my ringing phone. Chris.

"Mom, mom, you're there." She sounded very up. "Where have you been?"

"Lunch with Tammy. I do have a life. "

"Whatever. I have good news. A counselor needs to go to the city soon, and they said I could drive down with her. Cause, you know, it is a special circumstance."

"What? Say that again. You're not making sense."

"Mom, what's up with you? Here, talk to Katherine."

Katherine the camp director repeated Chris' news, and added, "Chris seems to be very worried about how you are doing, and so we are a little concerned about that. It's against normal camp policy but you've had a special circumstance. She could go and then come back a few days later with the same counselor."

Chris suddenly home? The idea took my breath away, but this time in a good way. I said yes, and then immediately swung into mom mode. Were there clean sheets on her bed? Should I stock up on food?

I certainly was not forgetting why we had sent Chris away— Rick and I—in the first place. Was it really safer now? Safe enough, with the help of Steven and his uncle? Dammit, yes, I told myself. Yes. For a few days, I could surely keep her out of trouble, even if it meant keeping her on a short leash. Perhaps the short leash was unrealistic but there was no way I was going to tell her not to come if she needed to.

And if she was coming home, I needed more time off my job—I knew I was on thin ice there—I would have to swing into action right now. I needed to score a home run before asking for more time off. No post-pizza/wine/fun relaxing for me now.

It was time to dial up Mrs. Rogow's warehouse and get some work done. A cheerful woman's voice assured me that Mrs. Rogow's request had been received and everything would be ready shortly.

When I thanked her, she said, "I'd do anything Mrs. Rogow wanted. She has been a customer here for sixty years, and she is lovely to deal with. The best. Not like…um, not like all our customers. When you come, just ask for me, Rosemarie. All the men know me."

The warehouse wasn't far away as the pigeon flies, but I crossed worlds to get there. As I drove downhill toward the harbor, I left behind stable residential blocks and lively streets, moved through blocks of depressed small buildings with no street life, and into a low-end business area. There were storefront tire shops, sleazy body shops operating out of two car garages, tiny groceries hanging on by the grace of God and the sale of cigarettes and lottery tickets. Then it became an industrial area: stone and marble and tile dealers, importers of Middle Eastern food, contractors' warehouses.

When I crossed the last avenue the street ended abruptly at a chain link fence. On the other side there were hulking shells of buildings scarred along their dark sides with broken windows. Between the elevated expressway and the buildings blocking the sun, it was dark down here, even on this summer day, and I suddenly wished I had brought a companion.

When I finally found a small through street, the parking lot proved to be full of cars and trucks, with men walking in and out pushing hand trucks. It was reassuringly, normally busy. I found unmarked doors, the colors faded to generic metal. After I walked back and forth a few times, baffled as to how to find Rosemarie, one of the drivers saw my confusion and pointed to the small door between two large barred windows.

Rosemarie turned out to be hefty and very blond, with a face that was meant for smiles and joking around. She wasn't smiling now. Her office was filled with a stack of storage cartons and Brenda Petry. Petry was definitely not smiling.

She was impeccably dressed and coiffed as always, almost comically out of place in the grimy warehouse, but her face was missing its usual glazed perfection. She looked stressed and tired, and for the first time, middle-aged instead of permanently preserved. I wondered if the designer clothes and shellacked hair and glittering jewelry were meant to be armor.

She looked at me with a new expression. For a fleeting moment I thought, absurdly, that it was fear. She said, "Why are you doing this to me? Why can't you leave me alone?"

I stammered, "Not you. My research…your mother." I took a deep breath and started again, in a voice I willed to be firm. "Would you like me to explain?" It couldn't hurt to be polite. At least, that's what my mother always told me. I'd give her the edited explanation with my professional and scholarly goals. Chris' interest did not need to be part of that story.

She stared at me with a grim mouth, and yet, still, that fugitive look in her eyes, and finally said, "I suppose it might be useful for me to hear this. Talk fast. I'm stealing time from my very busy day."

I did talk fast, all about my museum assignment. I added the persuasive—I hoped—point that with access to a complete company archives, I might even use it as a key part of my eventual dissertation. It could be an opportunity to tell her father's true story and how much her mother supported this. My own shamelessness would have bothered me if she had not been so unpleasant.

I finished with an attempt to build a more personal connection between us. "Everything seems to be pointing to my own neighborhood, and even my own block, as the subject of my dissertation." I added, "I'd love to interview you and add your memories to this—this mosaic I have in mind."

"I told you before: I knew nothing about the business back then. My parents kept me tucked safely away in the suburbs."

"But some people remember you." I added quickly, "It came up by accident. It would be so—so—so—enriching, to have your own personal take on it all. You would be an incredibly valuable source." Ah, flattery. She certainly looked like the kind of person who would be susceptible

Her sharp intake of breath was almost a hiss.

"Your sources are quite mistaken about my past in the business and your trivial research is a waste of time to me. It's gone, that past. Can you tell me how it matters for your future?"

Her face set into its glossy mask, and I was never sure, later, that I had seen anything else.

She turned her anger on Rosemarie.

"You cannot give everyone off the street access to our company records. That is a complete breach of your contract."

"Mrs. Rogow gave me the permission." Rosemarie's arms were folded, her frame massive. She acted remarkably unimpressed by the demanding woman in front of her. "Her word is good enough for me."

Petry flushed. "If anyone around here was well informed, you would know I run things now. As to my mother's permission, she is not the person who pays your exorbitant monthly bills. You can consider this business arrangement terminated as of today."

Rosemarie snorted. "You got sixty years worth of records here. You want us to dump them in your fancy office? 'Cause believe me, I could arrange it. It would be a pleasure. You'd better secure another facility before you make these types of threats."

"Be sure that I will. You can start pulling the paper work today." She turned back to me. "As for you?" I had some of my own armor in place. "Give it up now and stop harassing my mother and me or there will be legal actions. Trust me that I have far more resources to do that than you have to fight it."

I certainly did trust her on that.

She stalked out, and I was forced to watch the boxes—my boxes!—being hauled away after her. I imagined throwing myself in front of the carts, driven by the belief that they were filled with scholarly treasures. I was shaking with anger and shock at being the target of so much fury.

Then Rosemarie and I looked at each other and started laughing. It began with a giggle and ended with us wiping tears from our eyes.

When we finally stopped, she gasped, "What was that all about? She's always a pain but I hardly have to deal with her in the flesh. She doesn't get her manicured fingers dirty. Usually it's her little slaves…" She shook her head. "And Mrs. Rogow was always such a nice lady."

"I don't know what it's about." I looked around the empty room. "So much for my brilliant academic plans. That idea is down the drain."

"Don't be so sure, kiddo. I'll put it in our system to tell me to give you a call as soon as the boxes get checked back in."

"But she said..."

"Yeah, yeah, wait till she finds out what it would cost to move all their stuff. Ha. No break from us for good will either. She can count on that. Betcha anything the boxes will come back and that will be the end of it. And I'll call you the day they do. No worries on that."

Chapter Twenty

Back in my car, I remained shaken, even though laughing with Rosemarie had cleared my head. The sheer senselessness of Petry's rage scared me. I didn't fear physical danger; I didn't know what I feared. Merely being in the presence of that storm was scary.

I knew it would be all wrong to confront Mrs. Rogow and say, "Why is your daughter a crazy bitch," but it was tempting. Instead, I thought if there was one person I knew who would appreciate this crazy story, it was Leary. Kings County had had long enough to patch him up; I was already out in my car; I was going to see him. And if he was difficult, that little scene had my adrenaline in overdrive. Let him try giving me a hard time, I thought. Let him try

He was sitting up in bed, eyes open, skin still pale but no longer deathly pale. "I don't know how I got here, but they tell me you're the one who called in the cavalry."

I nodded.

He looked annoyed. "I suppose that's a good thing, so I have to say thank you."

"Don't put yourself out too much. I figured you wanted to have a few more years in this world, but forgive me if I got that wrong."

"No, no, you didn't get it wrong. I'm not too good at this making nice stuff, but yeah, thank you."

I grinned. "Don't take it personally. I'd have done it for anyone."

"Good. Now I don't have to be so grateful." He closed his eyes as if the brief conversation had exhausted him. Then he opened them again. "Now that we're done with the small talk, tell me what the hell happened? I don't remember any of it. I don't even know why I'm here."

"And to think I came over to get information from you." I told him what little I knew.

"Sounds about right. I took my insulin shot, and before I could eat, someone came in." He considered that. "Maybe two someones. Wait…" He seemed to be pondering something. "How the hell did they get in? Was the door busted?"

"Not noticeably."

"Ok. I must have let them in."

"That doesn't sound like you."

"Nope, it's not, but sometimes I'm a little confused before I eat. So all right, for now we say I let them in." He got that confused look again. "I'm still blanking about what happened. Anything about what happened. They tell me—the docs, the nurses—that I was beat up pretty good."

"Have cops been here?"

"Yeah, they took a statement, asked me if it was a break in, did they want money? They said they'd look into it, but who the hell knows? An old man gets beat up in a building with lousy security on a block that's getting worse every day? It's ordinary life in the big city. Who cares?"

"Was it money they looking for? Or something else? Your files? Do you remember that at all?" Come on, Leary, I thought. Something useful has to be in there, somewhere in that hard old head.

He looked puzzled. "Not money. I'm sure—pretty sure—it wasn't a robbery, but I can't even say why I think that. I have little pieces in my mind—they kept asking me questions, but they weren't—I don't think they were—about money, or drugs. I don't know what else a robber would think I had. Certainly not family silver." He gave a tiny sly chuckle, like the ghost of the real Leary.

I didn't know how much to tell him. He was better but a long way from all right. What I had seen would certainly upset him. Would that put him in danger? There was no one there I could ask, but he solved the problem for me by saying, "Come on. You're holding something back."

In spite of his condition he gave me a shrewd look. "Don't you know patients need to be kept calm and contented? Like cows. Worrying about what you're holding back could cause a medical crisis. You appear to have a conscience, so I'm sure you wouldn't want that burdening it."

"Well, it sounds like either the neighborhood has really gone downhill or you really pissed off someone, hard as it is to imagine such a thing." I hoped to sidetrack him.

"Those days are gone for good," he said with obvious regret. "That was my job, back then, pissing people off. Now…." His voice trailed away and I stood up.

"Where do you think you're going? You never answered my question."

"Which question was that?"

"Come on, honey," he said sarcastically "You know. I want to know what you are hiding. Spit it out. Being in the hospital doesn't mean I've become completely stupid."

Apparently not. By the time I was done telling him, the little color that had returned to his face was drained away and his eyes were closed. I was reaching for the nurses call button when Leary opened his eyes again, and muttered, "I hate anyone messing with my files. It's worse—it feels worse—than getting beaten. It's…."

"Yes. Yes, it's your best self in there, your work. You're violated. I got it. But, you know, it's just paper. You are here, getting good care, and the papers can be put away again."

"No, no, maybe not. Maybe I'm too old, maybe I won't remember things, and maybe they took something." His voice faded, and I saw—I thought I saw—something like tears in the corner of his eye.

Then he blinked a few times, and said, "Well, damn it all to hell. I want to know what they were looking for. Nervy sons of bitches. And I want to know who they were."

Leary was back. I almost cheered.

"Here's what I'm going to do," Leary went on. "The cop who was asking me questions left a number, so I'll give him a call and tell him all this. Tomorrow, maybe. I dunno—maybe he'll understand why it matters, maybe not. You." He looked fiercely at me. "When they're done there, you might as well go take a really good look at those files. Sounds like you messing with them can't make it any worse than it is. Maybe something will add up for you that doesn't add up for the cops. What the hell could I have that matters to anyone, anyway? All that old, old junk. Jesus H. Christ."

He leaned back against the pillows, but now there was a small gleam in his eyes.

It was time to tell him about my encounter with Brenda Petry.

When I was done, he chuckled. It wasn't the real Leary guffaw, but it was a faint echo. "Time sure hasn't improved her personality. She's a real chip off the old block. I know something new about her. I heard something. TV maybe? Ahhh, my mind is not right." Then he made a large effort to sit up, refused my help, and looked straight at me. "Come on, kiddo. Use your own head, which did not take a beating like mine, and add it up."

"I have been using my head!" I snapped it out. "I wanted to look at records for my own block, for those years when that body—that poor girl—was hidden there. I hoped to find some little thing that would be a clue about her. Or maybe I was just fantasizing there, but at the same time, the general information could help my own work, both job and school. Petry seems to want to hide the same information but I can't imagine why. And someone else was looking for whatever you had at home from around then. So there."

"Good girl." His voce was fading. "One plus one plus one is always three. Not real good at math, are you?"

"Four. It makes four. My old family friend, the ex-cop who was killed…he worked in the neighborhood at the same time. I keep trying to add it up some other way but it's about my neighborhood and about that time. Maybe it's even about my house, and finding the body."

I had been fighting it now for a long time, as far back as the last time I had seen Rick. It was about my house. It all began with Chris discovering a body.

I had said to Rick, that last night, that I feared random chance more than anything. Or something like that. And he had said that didn't mean you stopped looking both ways when you crossed the street. Had I been stepping right out in front of a truck barreling down the street at me? Rick tried to tell me that then, and Leary was trying to tell me now. I didn't know who was driving it, but I had to stop acting as if it wasn't coming.

Leary's eyes were closing, but he said clearly enough, "Reporters don't get to choose facts. Keep doing the math. You got to take the facts you have and make them tell you the story. You should know…." Then he was asleep. He looked almost as difficult as he did when he was awake, but I couldn't resist giving his hand a little squeeze before I left.

Now I had to finish working out the puzzle on my own. If that grumpy old fox thought I could, maybe he was by god right.

I drove with my mind full of Petry's anger, Leary's still precarious state, and the math he had recommended. I ran a stop sign and almost went through a red light. On my block, a tiny piece of my mind noticed that plumbers van was still parked in front of my house, taking up what could have been my space. I circled the block a few times, found a space around the corner, walked home, still thinking.

Tomorrow I would see Steven again, and it would be—what? A business meeting? A breakfast date? Even I knew that usually implied a night before, which was not happening. So maybe it was just a meeting? I pushed it out of my mind, with some effort. That was tomorrow. Tonight, I was working on this puzzle my life had become.

I ate leftovers straight out of the refrigerator, standing up, and contemplated Rick's life. Not for the first time—maybe the fiftieth—I wished Rick was here to answer my questions. I thought he had the answers, and the only person who came close to Rick, my second father in my own mind, was my real father in my own life.

I dialed Phoenix, hoping he was down from his pharmaceutical high by now.

"Hi, Dad. It's Erica."

"Hey, toots, how are you doing?"

"So-so. More important, how are you doing?"

"Better. Up and about a little. Can't wait to get out. You know I'll be back there as soon as the docs spring me."

He sounded like himself.

"I hear you and Aunt Sophie are talking again."

I was wandering. I didn't know how to get into my real reason for calling.

"Oh? Where'd you hear that?"

"I had lunch with Tammy."

"Yeah, well, Sophie called, and we got to talking. It wasn't so bad. You know, she's not as nutty as she used to be. She's kind of mellowed, believe it or not. How's Tammy? Still the fashion queen?"

"You would say so, yes. We were talking a little about Rick, she actually remembers him, and so I got to thinking." There I was, easing in.

"Yeah?"

"Last time we talked, I asked if you know about him working here, right here in my neighborhood, way back when."

"You did? I don't remember a thing."

"No surprise. You were high as a kite on pain killers, I think."

"Oh, yeah." I could feel him smiling through the phone. "Let me try again. Rick? Park Slope? I'd forgotten all about that. It is way, way back."

"How come he never said anything to me when I moved there? I think that's weird."

"Ah. That, I do not know but I'd say 'cause they weren't good memories. Something about it…I always felt like something bad happened to him, but we were guys. Ya know? We didn't really talk. He might've met a girl and got stomped on. That sounds sort of right to me. Anyways, he was glad to get out and then he was rising up the ranks pretty fast."

I hadn't learned much new from my father, but it did confirm what little I already had. I would keep digging but now it was too late at night to call anyone else.

Sometimes though, the gods smile down on us.

I turned on the New York news before bed, and there she was, Brenda Petry, Mrs. Rogow's demon-seed daughter, looking perfect as always, and a lot happier than when I had last seen her. It was a replay of an earlier broadcast.

She was with the mayor and someone from one of the big investment banks and they were all beaming at a press conference, announcing an agreement to develop a big chunk of derelict waterfront property.

She was thrilled to have completed the deal. It was thrilling to take on a project of this significance. The mayor was thrilled with the vision of magnificent, much-needed housing in our crowded city, and thrilled that his administration was making it all possible. He used the word "legacy." The banker was thrilled to be the lead financier of such a significant project. And the site was right here in Brooklyn.

That's why she was so touchy. With the backing of the city, and buy-in from a prestige lender, her reputation as a reliable business woman was more crucial than ever. But what in the world was she hiding? The old scandal about her father? That was public record, there for any antagonistic journalist or business rival to bring to light. And there would certainly be antagonism. Her plans were not good news for everyone, no matter what the mayor said. Or was she hiding a wild hippy youth, as Leary claimed? She wasn't the only one. Why would anyone care after all these years?

Did I care about Brenda Petry and her life? No, not one bit, but I found her intense animosity puzzling. More important, she was around here when Rick was around here and I had a photo to prove it, the hippies on the steps of my house. Leary had told me the girl with the flowing hair and the flowing dress was Brenda. What if she also knew Rick? Or knew about him? Or knew Leary? Maybe she thought I had found another, bigger secret about her? Whatever that big, scary secret was?

I knew the NYPD was never going to let me near the puzzle of Rick's recent life until they were done with their own investigation, but the Petry puzzle was mine to solve and it all connected in some way I hadn't yet uncovered.

The truth is, I was not ignorant, I would not be bullied, and I had the skills to find out what I needed to know about my house and then about Rick if I needed to. Who wanted to keep me from knowing? Why? I felt safer now, due to James Hoyt's kindness, and I wasn't going to roll over.

Petry would certainly not talk honestly to me, though I had a happy moment imagining her face if I showed up without warning at her office. However, I knew someone who might talk to me. True, I could not ask Mrs. Rogow why her daughter was a lunatic, but I could tell her I had seen the news conference and I could say congratulations. And see where that could lead.

She was happy to hear from me, accepted my congratulations and was delighted by the idea of another conversation. In fact, she said, she would be in the city tomorrow for an appointment at the Time Warner building. Did I know it?

Well, yes, it was hard to miss, a shiny monster of a new office tower plus extremely upscale mall, right across from the western edge of Central Park. We could meet for coffee at a lovely café on the second gallery.

I was far too wired to go to bed. It was too late to make more calls but on a lovely summer night, there were still plenty of people out and about. I needed an ice cream, I thought, and milk for breakfast. And a little walk. It was comfortably cool outside. On my block the night was dark and quiet and mysterious. In the moonlight, if I could delete the cars, it could almost be a hundred years ago.

One young couple came into the circle of a streetlight, arms wrapped around each other, stopping to embrace every few feet. And up the block, a cab sat double-parked in front of a house, letting someone out. Down the block, someone opened a car door, reached in, loudly closed it. In the late night quiet, the slamming of the door sounded like a cannon. That plumber's truck was across the street now.

That truck struck me now as very odd. Not threatening, but odd, to be here all the time. Or had so much happened I was becoming paranoid? I made a mental note to really notice it later, tomorrow and see if it was really such a constant.

Aside from that, it was a peaceful scene, familiar and lovelier in the dark than in daylight, but it felt strange and off to me. I looked up and down, but there was no one who looked out of place or threatening. No drunk teens, ready to do something stupid. No dogs out alone as a city dog should never be. No one loitering with intent. Yet a shiver ran down my spine.

I shook myself, and headed at a very brisk walk up to the avenue where I would find lights, friendly social noise and fancy ice cream. As I turned the corner, Mary stopped me. There was no escaping and I was ashamed of my desire to. I knew she was lonely. I was too.

"How are you, my dear, on this lovely summer night? My, you are up and out late."

"I felt like a walk." We were in front of the news stand/snack bar/tobacco shop. "Uh, would you like a coffee?"

"Oh that's lovely. I'll take a doughnut, too, if they have any left," she said, pointing to the stale remains of the day. "That's very kind. Where is your lovely daughter? I haven't seen her in ages and ages."

"She's away at camp. But where have you been yourself? You're the one who hasn't been around for ages."

She smiled shrewdly. "Here and there. I get around, here and there. But now your daughter, I'm glad she's there and not here. They take good care of the children there, don't they, at her camp?"

"Oh, sure," I said absently. "She's having a wonderful time." Then what she actually said sank in. "Mary, is there some reason you say that? About Chris being safe? You've said it before."

"Yes, there is." She looked alarmingly alert for about a second and I thought I might learn something real. Then her face faded back into its usual blur. "It's this. This is what I want to say—those precious girls, such sparkly eyes, so pretty with their silvery necklaces and silvery earrings and silvery hair." She smiled encouragingly and patted my hand.

For once, I was really listening to her. "Mary, do you have children? I mean, I wonder because you always ask so nicely about Chris."

She nodded. "I did have children. Daughters and sons both. Back then, a long time ago." Her eyes clouded. "Sometimes people lose them, you know." She turned away, still holding her doughnut, and then said, over her shoulder, "Say hello to her for me."

Nothing else happened on my walk there and back, absolutely nothing, yet I spent the time on high alert, watching the dark patches on the street between the street lamps, looking over my shoulder, resetting the house alarms and locking my door behind me with a sense of relief. I told myself I could not be rattled by Mary's words. Of course, she was a mentally damaged old lady with a shaky grasp of reality. Of course, her words were completely meaningless. So—of course—I wished I could go straight to the phone and call Chris' camp.

Then I checked all the locks and all windows, twice, before I was ready to go to bed.

I was up early, thinking about Chris, thinking about Steven, thinking about Mrs. Rogow, thinking about Rick. I made up my mind to think about Steven first, as he was first on the schedule. A practical choice. I needed make both myself and my downstairs presentable. I had asked Joe for no workmen this morning, even though I knew it might set the work back.

Steven arrived, juggling muffins, coffee, my newspaper from my stoop, and his attaché with, I assumed, my files.

I tended to forget how attractive he was, as he really wasn't my type. That is, assuming I had a type. Then I remembered when I saw him again. An affectionate kiss on my cheek. What did that mean?

After I assured him the security system seemed to be working and nothing unusual had happened, he spread breakfast and files on the table, opened his computer and we got to work, He read quickly, checked off some points, and overall, was extremely pleased with the information I had gathered. We made notes about further data needed.

"Now," I said. "Now. Please explain everything to me.'

"You look cute when you're determined." He laughed. "All right, I'll stop teasing you. I do various jobs for James. He was the client that made it possible for my partners and me to start our own firm. And no, we are not his in-house consulting firm. We have a highly satisfying collection of other clients and our own offices."

"I don't think this development project is his usual type of investment, though. So what's up with that?"

He raised one eyebrow, a trick I've read about but never actually seen. I admit I found it rather attractive, and distracting.

"You've been researching Uncle James? Ah, well, it's not that hard, he's so public." He looked at me with an odd expression. "I shouldn't be surprised, not even a little. You are right. He's not normally a real estate developer. He prefers more abstract investing, moving the numbers around, but in this case, he is the financier I told you about, with the famous architect friend. He's excited about the creative aspect. It's a hobby, like Sunday painting."

We were talking about a man for whom a billion dollar project was a hobby. I had no words for my reaction. Of course that only lasted a few minutes.

"Plus he expects to make a lot of money?"

"Well, yes, of course. That's what James does, he makes money. It's a talent he has. Like you have one for asking uncomfortable questions."

We were done with business. At least Steven was. He leaned back with a smile. "You know, I could get to like this dating thing. That is what we are doing, isn't it? Dating? I was, let's say, out of practice, when Darcy first tried to get us together. It's been a long time. But this is starting to feel…right? Like the right thing to do, right now."

He looked like he wanted to kiss me again. I would not have objected.

Instead, he said, "How busy will you be before your daughter comes home? Glued to your work, or busy shopping for the fatted calf?"

I giggled. And then I told him about Mrs. Rogow, my bizarre encounter with her daughter, and my plans for a Manhattan get-together with her.

His expression changed from amused to unreadable. "You can't stop yourself? Is that it?" He put up his hands in a gesture of surrender. "I give up. I like you—there, I said it out loud, on the record—and I don't want anything to happen to you."

Then his expression changed back to amused, but not quite.

"Do you have any time for an actual date? Tonight?"

"Yes."

"Let's make it a real night on the town. What do you think? I know a great Latin dance place." He smiled, ruefully. "My WASP heritage means I can only do the fox trot and the waltz. I'm a lousy Latin dancer but it's fun. Care to take a chance?"

"Sure. Uh, what do I wear to this place?"

"Go for flamboyance."

"Flamboyance? Me? And look at you, Mr. Prep School." He was wearing chino-colored chinos, a light blue button down shirt and loafers. With tassels.

"And I will look the same tonight. But you have a chance to get wild if you want to."

Wild? That would be a problem. I would have to raid Chris' closet, and her vast earring collection. I hoped she would approve.

Steven stood up. "Till tonight, then. For now I must be pushing off to drab meeting rooms with boring middle-aged men in suits. This is a lot more fun."

At my door, his arms went around me, unexpectedly, and my arms went right back around him. That was all, except for a long, serious look into my eyes and a kiss that lasted after he was gone.

Chapter Twenty-one

I allowed myself to have a moment of interesting thoughts about Steven. All right, it was a few moments, very nice ones. Then I went back to Leary's math problem trying to add up one plus one. The problem was that numbers are stable and clear, and I was adding up facts that were slippery and foggy. The first one was our poor dead girl, a complete mystery. Maybe Rick could have shone a beam of light into the fog, but now he could not. Leary himself couldn't, much as he was trying. And Brenda Petry wouldn't.

Time to hit the subway. I had a coffee date in Manhattan with someone who would, I thought, if she could.

I spent my time on the train thinking about how to talk to Mrs. Rogow. Start with congratulations again on her daughter's success. Lead her into how her daughter grew up in the business, learning from her father, now walking in his footsteps and all that.

I would wonder if there was anything else she knew or remembered or even speculated on, about my immediate neighborhood. I grew up around cops. They were neighbors and relatives. They used to say witnesses often know more than they think they do. Ask again. And again.

I did have tiny pang of guilt about plotting to manipulate an old woman who had not been anything but nice to me. It was only a tiny pang. I had to keep pulling at all the threads of this tangle until something came loose.

It was another way of thinking about Leary's math problem.

We met in the very chic café with a dramatic atrium view. Her clothes were as colorful, her makeup as careful, but her smile was mechanical, pasted on for this social situation. I knew this, because I caught a glimpse of her face before she saw me. There was no smile.

"Sit down, my dear." She tried to expand the smile. "'I've ordered coffee and pastry. The pot roast I promised you will have to wait until the next time you come to my house."

"I want to say again how impressed I am by your daughter's new venture. I mean, it's great to see a woman rising that high in a man's game." I was burbling. "You must be so proud of her, continuing your husband's heritage and all."

She gave me a shrewd look.

"I don't think you came all the way here to tell me that. And I hear you have excellent coffee in Brooklyn now."

This was not the chatty, grandmotherly lady I had met before. My shock must have showed in my face, because she sighed deeply. "Forgive me. Motherhood is not my favorite topic today." I saw that her hand was trembling as she put her cup down. "Let me ask. How do you get along with your own daughter?"

"My daughter?"

She nodded, silent and unsmiling.

"Ohhh...It's hard, isn't it?" I was suddenly fidgeting with the sugar bowl, with my napkin, my cup. I had come ready to talk about her daughter, not mine. "Lately it has become hard almost all the time. I mean, we used to be very close, and now. Wow. We are on different planets one day, and then another, she's my baby. Maybe even in the next hour." I took a big gulp of coffee and barely noticed I had forgotten the cream and sugar. "Sometimes it's even in the next minute. It feels like a gulf, sometimes, this big." I moved my hands. "And I'm always, always, struggling to get across it."

Mrs. Rogow's jaw was clenched as she said, "Every day. Every day is like that with my daughter. It's exhausting. Yours will outgrow it..."

"If I am lucky."

"She will outgrow it. Remember, I heard her voice on my phone. I could tell from that, she's a good girl. But my daughter? Never. Never. It's too late."

This was not the conversation I had rehearsed but going along seemed the only choice. Besides, I liked Mrs. Rogow.

"Did something happen between you, recently?"

"Always. There is always something happening to break my heart. "

"But wasn't yesterday a good something? Something to be proud of? I mean, she was on TV! With the mayor!"

She was looking off somewhere, over my shoulder, not at me, but I could see her eyes were dry and hard.

"Yesterday is the day she signed papers to take my Harry's name off the company. It is time to move forward, she said. It is a new era. Complete crap, you should pardon the expression. Everything she is, and everything she has is built on his hard work. Who do you think he did it for? Her! And me! So now she wants it to be called Petry Limited, the name of her whitebread, no-good second husband she hasn't spoken to in ten years." She stopped, the line of her mouth grim.

"Mrs. Rogow? You said she learned everything from her father. Did you mean that? She told me she was never involved."

"Of course she was. When she was a little girl, she would dress up in a nice coat and ride in with him and carry his account books. She called it going to work with Daddy. And she wrote those accounts too, when she got older. All that about not being involved? Ha!" The dismissive gesture was not quite an obscenity. Not quite.

"And did he love it. I never gave him sons but he saw how smart she was, and decided she would be the heir. Rogow and Daughter, instead of Rogow and Sons. Why not? And then…." For the first time, the angry voice faltered.

"And then?" I was holding my breath. Mrs. Rogow was doing my work for me.

"Ahh, she got a little wild. It was the times. Wild times. And then too, her father…what happened to him. Did your daughter do that wild thing? Did you?"

I shook my head. "My daughter is a little young so not yet. I just dread what might be ahead. She'd better not!"

Mrs. Rogow shook her head. "If she wants to get in trouble, nothing you do will stop her."

"Military school? No, no, I'm kidding. I didn't get into trouble much myself, because I fell in love young. I wasn't out running around, and yet." I remembered the screaming fights with my father. I was out too late, I was with Jeff all the time, my skirts were too short, he didn't want me driving at night. My poor mother was caught in the middle, trying to keep the peace. "The truth is, I was a good girl with a smart mouth. Dad didn't take it well. We could fight about anything. Or nothing."

"Harry never knew what she was up to. Sweet as could be, she was with him. Quite the daddy's girl. She was sneaky even then. But I knew. She thought I didn't. But mothers know. She was hanging around with those dirty hippies. She would say, so sweet, 'I'm going to the city, mama, with my friends. We're going to the Metropolitan Museum for an art assignment.' But I found the hippy-dippy clothes in her laundry basket, when she had a closet full of sweet dresses from Saks. And they smelled." She gave me a full look. "I didn't know then but I do now, that it was drugs."

It was a scary picture.

"Was she going to Brooklyn?"

She shrugged. "I thought so then. I told you about the groups in our houses. One of the few mistakes Harry ever made. I heard. People told me. And I didn't believe it, at first. My own daughter. After awhile she stopped pretending. Long dirty hair, late nights, bad grades. There was a boy, maybe lots of boys. I think, lots of boys, and maybe an older man, too, a working man. My sweet little girl playing the tramp."

"Is this her?" I put the little photo on the table along with the magnifying glass.

Her expression softened and blurred, just for minute. "Yes, I believe it is. Dear lord, I remember that dress. And it is one of our houses."

So. Two numbers just added up. My house plus Brenda Rogow on my steps. Around the time a girl disappeared into my fireplace. Around the time Rick was at a party next door.

That's when I knew. I didn't know if I could ever prove it, but I knew, in my heart, that she was there at my house when it—whatever it was—happened. It was the only thing that made sense, a secret ugly enough to threaten everything she had built.

Now I knew she would never talk to me.

"What happened next? I mean, did she drop out of school? Run away?" I thought of Leary's file of runaways' notes and thought I would not wish that life on anyone, not even Brenda Petry.

"No, no, none of that. I have no idea what happened, but something, because she changed her mind."

"What do you mean?"

"What's not clear? She changed her mind. Something happened, and she changed back. Cut her hair. Took bubble baths. Got rid of the hippy clothes—I saw her sneak the trash bag out one night. She went back to cashmere sweaters and Pappagallo shoes. And got herself into Barnard."

'When was this?"

She looked right at me, and said, "1971, if my memory serves. 1972. The time you wanted the company records." She stopped then. Her expression said, "Make of it what you will."

"About those company records?"

"I know, I know. Rosemarie phoned me."

I kept quiet. I had no idea what to say, so I waited.

"She was quite upset, Rosemarie was. She couldn't do what she promised."

"It wasn't her fault. She seemed to be very helpful but your daughter..." Whoa. Thin ice. I shut up.

"Yes, my darling daughter." The sarcasm was intense. "That's what all this is about, isn't it? My daughter. She's forgotten what happens when she tries to override my orders so disrespectfully." She smiled, not happily. "I am actually on my way to my lawyer to discuss this company name change. I'm not as old and helpless as she thinks."

Could Petry possibly think that? I certainly didn't.

"My driver will escort me up to my appointment." She motioned to a nearby man in a uniform. "But not to forget about Rosemarie's call. She had pulled some of the files from the cartons to give you directly. She thought maybe you did not realize how big a job you would have to take them all. She's not sure it's really what you wanted most, but of course I explained it very well to her. You can go back any time to pick them up; she only wanted the OK from me. Is that good?"

"Good? That is great! I am so grateful."

She refreshed her lipstick, stood up with the help of a brightly painted cane, and draped her elegant silk stole around her shoulders with the help of the man in the uniform. "I'm off to battle. Wish me luck. Lipstick on straight?"

I went in the opposite direction, toward the subway escalator, thinking that in a battle between a team of lawyers and Mrs. Rogow, I was betting on the little old lady. It would be no contest.

I checked the subway map. Was there any possible way to get to the warehouse on my way home? Ah, yes. It meant a few blocks walk through the area Mrs. Rogow had described as very questionable, and questionable it was, an almost abandoned industrial area, with no foot traffic and no stores. I walked fast, with that attitude which says, "Bother me at your peril," and nothing happened at all.

Rosemarie had folders packed in a large cardboard envelope with a tie, and accepted Mrs. Rogow's greeting with a laugh.

"Now I don't know if it's exactly what you need. These old self-made guys? Think they had a system? They were making it all up as they went along. The boxes were kind of by neighborhood, then year, and then block. So who knows if it's exactly the right files? But hopefully, it's a start."

"I am really grateful. But won't you get into a battle with Ms. Petry, if she finds some things missing?"

She assumed an innocent expression and Betty Boop voice. "Oh, my goodness. Things get lost over the years. And I'm an ignorant office worker. It's soooo unfortunate."

"I get it. Thank you again. I'm off to the subway."

"You hold on. I have drivers going out all day. Someone can drop you at home, if you don't mind riding in a truck."

In a few minutes, I was climbing into a truck cab with a driver who had a delivery of documents for the Brooklyn Museum. She handed me the envelope, winked and said, "Happy hunting."

As I left the truck, I heard the silly burst of music that signaled a text message. "Mom. You're not picking up. Y? Am on way home now! Ride had to leave today. See you dinner time-ish. Yay."

Chris as soon as tonight? I felt all the free-floating tension of the last few days melt as a big smile grew across my face. Would it be replaced by Chris-induced tension right after she walked in the door? Maybe, but right now I couldn't wait to see her. It took me a few minutes to remember I had plans of my own for tonight. First things first. And that would be my daughter, always, and especially now, after my talk with Nettie Rogow.

I called Steven. There was no answer; I left a message. I texted. No immediate response. I went grocery shopping. Not quite the fatted calf, but at least I could provide Chris' favorite chips and dips and soda.

I came home to find Steven on my stoop. He came in with me.

"I'm sorry to barge in, but I had bad reception, saw that you called but couldn't get the whole thing. And I was nearby, meeting with some people, so I came in person."

I explained about Chris, apologized, explained some more about how I'd love to reschedule but could not do it until I knew when she would return to camp. He looked genuinely disappointed and I was absurdly pleased by that.

We seemed to have settled down on the couch and we seemed to be holding hands.

"Let's visit here instead. A mini-date." He put his feet up on my coffee table, made himself comfortable and invitingly patted the cushion next to him. We sat close, and I told him about the productive day and unusual day, about the unusual Nettie Rogow, the unexpected help of getting documents for my work, my hope that I could learn about Rick indirectly by learning more about that right time and this place. It was so comfortable, and comforting, to have someone to tell, I lost sight of the fact that he did not actually think my asking questions was a good idea. The increasing chilliness of his expression brought me back to reality.

"Why can't you stop? How can you pretend that this isn't serious? Come on! A man was shot to death and another was beaten up. You've been threatened. Your daughter is coming home. You don't want to be close to this."

My voice was ice cold. "Are you trying to tell me to forget about it all?"

"Yes! Yes, I am." He held my chin gently, getting me to look right at him. "Erica, I was trying to say it this morning. I care about you. Who knows how it happened, but we have something, just beginning, and you know it. I can't stand on the side and watch you keep wading right into these deep waters. People drown."

He took a deep breath. "I'm sorry but please, let the police department deal with all these incidents. You cannot be involved."

"Cannot? Are you saying 'cannot' to me?" I jerked away. "God help me, I was kind of liking you too, but I don't now. My world feels upside down to me, and I'm not one to sit around and let that continue. And you don't get to tell me what I can and can't do. Whatever gave you that idea? You're not my father and I wouldn't listen to him anyway. You are not my husband, or even my boyfriend."

His face was white and rigid. He half-smiled, bitterly. "Well, I had high hopes on that for this evening." He stood up, stared out the window, then turned back to me. "Look. Everything I say is coming out wrong. I don't mean to hurt you."

I stood up.

"I think you should go."

"Erica, I…"

"Please go now."

I stalked through the house to the front door, unlocked it and held it open. He followed me but stopped there, put his hands on either side of my face, and said, "I'm not giving up."

I closed the door behind him with a satisfying slam. Then I sat for a long time in my dark living room, on my drop-cloth covered sofa, unable to move. I was right. I knew I was. I had to do this, get some parts of my life right side up again, and Steven was completely out of bounds.

Being right was not actually much comfort, though. What was I thinking, anyway, sliding into a cozy relationship as if it was a warm bath, when I had so much else on my mind? It was turning into just one more complication, the last thing in the world I needed in my increasingly confusing life.

Chapter Twenty-two

My best cure for sad musing is work, but I didn't get very far.
There was insistent pounding on my door. Steven, back? No,
Chris was on the top step clutching a backpack, and waving to
a very young woman in a car at the curb. There was hugging,
squealing, a shouted "thank you" to the counselor. My daughter
was home.

"Oh my god!" She flopped down on a drop cloth-covered
sofa. "This place is still chaos."

"Yes, well, I guess Joe slowed down without your help."

She giggled. "I should yell at him. Right now what I want is
a hot bath with at least half a bottle of bubble bath."

"Well, let me look at you first. Tan, mosquito bites, sun
streaks in your hair?"

She grinned and shook her head.

"Ah, late night experiments with cosmetic products?"

"Cool, isn't it?" She turned her head in all directions and said,
"Like my earrings? I made them in a class."

"Macramé and glass beads? Very creative."

"OK? You've seen everything. Tub is calling my name."

I fiddled, doing nothing at all, until she emerged wrapped
in a terry robe and clouds of lavender.

"That felt great. So now, catch me up on everything? I feel
like I've been gone for months."

"What do you want to know?"

She looked at me with something like suspicion.

I fumbled an answer and her eyes opened wide. "You're blushing. You've been dating someone! Is that it? Wait. Is it Joe?"

"What? What in the world are you talking about?"

"Well. I was thinking about this while I was away. You need to get more of a life. You know, I have to start getting on with my own life and I'm going to college in a few years. You need to start getting ready for that."

She was so earnest, I almost laughed, but she went on. "And Joe is actually pretty hot, for a guy his age. You should hear what my friends say when they see him here."

"Your friends are just…"

"Young women with eyes in their heads! And he's here a lot."

"That doesn't mean a thing. He's my friend and that's what I am to him, too." What it's always been. I was not in the mood to think about this any further.

"If you say so. But if you were dating someone you would be…."

"What else is on your mind? My social life isn't exactly my favorite topic."

"Humph. I'll get you to tell me before I leave." My face must have showed my emotions, because she suddenly said, "Oh, Mom. Is it Rick that's been on your mind? I've been worried about that. I, you know, I didn't want to leap right into that."

She jumped up and hugged me.

"Oh, honey. I've been managing, but it kind of grabs me every so often. Know what I mean?"

She nodded. "I totally do. Me too."

"I still don't have any real information about what happened. They don't know, or they aren't telling." And I certainly wasn't telling her what they think they know. It was hard enough for me to know it. She didn't have to. "And I need to write a eulogy and plan a service, and…" I imagined the protest in her face. "No, no, it won't be until after you are back. I know you would want to be here. But it's all hard."

"It seems impossible not to see him again, or say good-bye."

"Hard, isn't it? He bugged me so much, sometimes, but now that he's gone...."

She nodded. "Kind of like grandpa being so far away. I guess I adopted Rick for another grandpa, sort of."

"He adopted us, too. Me, when I was little, and then you too."

"He taught me how to smoke so I wouldn't make a fool of myself when I tried."

"He did what? Smoke?"

"Yeah. He said I was sure to try sometime so I should do it right. Then he told me after I try it, I should never do it again or I'd answer to him."

"That's not the only thing he did behind my back. He used to sneak you bags of candy at Halloween. Months later I would find them stashed in secret hiding places in your room."

"You knew about that?" There was indignation all over her face.

I laughed.

"Were there ever any aunt Ricks? You know what I mean."

"Oh, there were a couple of them. The last was when you were small. There were girlfriends, though. You're old enough to know it now—Rick was definitely a player."

She considered that. "I can see it. He was a big flirt and he had—hmm—that kind of something. Even for an old guy."

I looked at my daughter, already more grown up than the last time I had seen her, and told her about Wanda. I left out the part about the cops. "Wow. She sounds interesting. Why didn't he ever introduce us?"

"I do know the answer to that. He thought of you as too young to know about this part of his life." She began to protest until I added, "Hell, he always thought of me that way too."

She laughed. We shared some more memories, and I realized I could write a eulogy now. It still felt all wrong, telling all this without being able to finish the story, to tell the secrets, and the way it ended. But it felt right too. It would be the truth, what I was going to write, even if it was not the whole truth.

"What happened between him and grandpa? Grandpa only said they grew apart."

"You've asked him? Grandpa?" I was astounded.

"Sure." She looked at my expression and said calmly, "Well, we do e-mail, you know. Kind of every few days. We talk about all kinds of things. He's out of the hospital and says he's coming home soon."

"Wait. Wait! I'm a few steps behind you here. He said you write but I had no idea you were really discussing things."

"Mom! He's my grandpa! Of course we do. Even if you are both too stubborn to." Her expression radiated disapproval.

I ignored that. "If he's out of the hospital, and not home, where is he?"

"He's home, there. He's coming home, here. Don't know when yet. When the doctor says he can fly."

This was all too much for me to process.

"Hey! Come back to earth. I'm starving. Aren't you? You have a hungry child to feed."

"What do you want? Our kitchen isn't quite ready to use."

"I've been at a healthy camp *forever*. I need grease!"

I had to laugh. "Fortunately the neighborhood still has a few greasy spoons. Bacon and eggs? Or a burger and a mountain of fries?"

"Oh, heaven. Both, please!"

She asked me about our lost girl as we walked to the coffee shop, and I told her about my meetings with Leary, omitting the recent events. "I haven't gotten any further than that. And please don't fuss at me about it. I have had a few other things to deal with. Way too many other things. And finding anything on our own was always a long shot."

"I know, but I haven't forgotten her. Maybe I'll call those detectives while I'm home?"

"And you can look at the files Leary gave me, if you want to. They're in your room."

We had a meal with no redeeming nutritional value whatsoever, and a slow meander home. Chris ran into a gaggle of her friends and they greeted each other with screams and hugs and several minutes of breathless catching up. I tried to drift off, and not seem to be listening, but I caught an involved anecdote that either described the complicated love life of their most advanced friend, or the current storyline on a favorite vampire soap opera.

After they moved on, we made a quick stop at the corner grocery to stock milk, juice, and soda. The refrigerator was working, so we could get some basics.

We ran into Mary in the dairy section. She was muttering to herself and making heavy work out of selecting a single container of yogurt. She saw us and looked confused for moment. Then her mind seemed to clear, and she said, "Ah you have your sweet girl home with you."

"Visiting from camp."

She put her hand on my arm. "They grow up when we're not looking, don't they? That's what happens with little girls, right behind our backs. My little girl learned water safety at camp. That's what they called it."

She turned back to Chris and stepped closer, peering at her. "You have my girl's same pretty hair. Ah, nice necklace." She reached her hand out and tapped it and Chris moved back, alarmed. "She had one like that, that Egyptian thing you have."

Chris mumbled something but Mary, absorbed again in her yogurt selection, did not notice. We left that aisle, made our purchases and turned toward home.

"Where did that interesting necklace come from? Did you make it too?" I was making friendly conversation.

"A friend. It came from a friend." She snapped it out, and then didn't say another word all the way home. In the house, she said, "Mom, do you have to know absolutely everything?" and stomped straight up to her room.

I didn't understand what had just happened. We were fine a few minutes ago, just like old times. Maybe the necklace involved a boy, and she wasn't ready to tell me about it. I repressed my desire to snap back. I reminded myself teens are all moods all the time. I reminded myself of Darcy's mantra for parents of teenagers. "Whatever it is, it will pass. Probably in the next sixty seconds."

And her sulking at least allowed me to listen to my phone messages in privacy. Steven had left two. I hardened my heart and erased them both.

When I went up later, she was sitting on her bed, surrounded by Leary's files and so absorbed by the stories she could barely look up at me. Or maybe she didn't want to. She responded to my presence with a grunt and went back to reading.

Oh, well, I thought. It's late; this day has been a lot for both of us.

"I'm turning in soon, and I suggest you do the same. Joe's crew will be here at 8:00."

Another grunt, then, as I was leaving, she said, "What if she was one of these kids? What if?"

"She could certainly have been someone like them, a lost runaway. I suppose that's why Leary gave me the files. It would explain a lot, but I don't know how we'll ever know for sure, unless those cold case detectives turn out both to be geniuses and to have second sight."

She moved the files to the foot of her bed, and got up to comb her hair. "Guess I have to give it up for now. Maybe she'll tell me herself, if I fall asleep thinking about her tonight?"

"You mean like in a dream?"

"I don't know. For now, I'm going to meet my girls, the ones who are home. See you later. Might even stay over with Stacy."

"Call me to say. You have your keys?"

"Mo-om! I've only been at camp, I haven't had brain damage."

Whatever. Sunny Chris had visited a few hours. It was nice while it lasted. Now she was back to teen brat. I could go back to work and not even miss her. I told myself that.

I opened up the file from Rosemarie at the Dock Storage, opened up a spreadsheet on my computer and went to work. Dry as each document was in itself, they added up to something, a portrait of my own changing block in real time.

It was an unstable era, at least for rental buildings. People moved in and out constantly. The ethnicity of the names shifted from mostly Irish to almost anything. Low-end businesses also went in and out: corner grocers, candy and news shops, cheap lingerie. Buildings deteriorated but I didn't see bills for thorough renovations, just stopgap repairs. The documents were arranged by year, and then by property, so I had to do some digging to find my own house. It was not the only address that interested me. My job was to look at everything and add it all up but my desire was to find my own house's history and show it to Chris tomorrow.

I spread the house papers out, year by year. There were multiple leases for some years, as people moved in and out. There were group leases with multiple names. I made a list and then I could see more clearly how often the tenants seemed to come and go. Was anyone there for any extended time, and could I find such a person? I tried a few of the names with the phone directory, but no luck. I hadn't expected to but one can always hope for a miracle.

As the hour got late, and my eyes got tired, I began to feel it didn't, after all, add up to a damn thing. And then it did. I looked at one name again. And again. And then I went scrambling through my piles of papers. That glossy, gossipy magazine article about James? Where was it?

It confirmed what I thought I remembered and could not believe. One of the names on the lease was James' first wife, the mother of his only child. I read it again, compared the spelling, and read the article again while my stomach twisted into knots.

And then I dug out the Pastores' old photo of the house with the crowd of young people hanging out on the steps. I used the powerful reading glass I had borrowed from Leary, and looked closely at all of them. I saw the girl in flowing prairie dress and long African earrings, who Leary told me was the very young Brenda Rogow. And the boy with the silky hair over his shoulders and the sly grin, holding up a pipe. He had James' face, and Steven's.

I put my hand out to call Steven. When I jerked it back I saw that it was shaking. What was I doing? I no longer knew who Steven was, if I ever had. Smart and fun and attractive, yes. A thoughtful date, yes. It had been—what, exactly? A beginning, that's all. Why on earth was I calling him right now?

Because I wanted to have him tell me there was a perfectly reasonable explanation for everything. And because I also wanted to yell at him, to ask if he had been lying about everything, was there a deep game here I was unable to comprehend? No, I should definitely not be calling him right now.

I took a few deep breaths and reminded myself that I was not, in fact, stupid, even if I had been—only temporarily, I assured myself—swept away by whatever the hell it had been. No, I was a smart, tough woman. I was certainly capable of set-ting everything aside—yes, I was—everything except my ability to think, and make connections and pull pieces of evidence together. Making connections and analyzing facts was what I'd spent a lot of tuition money and study time learning how to do. I needed to keep doing it right now, for my own life. Facts now, and nothing but.

James' son JJ must have lived in my house. Was that possible? I was pretty sure James' first wife, the society princess, could never have been a tenant here, but she might have signed the lease for her son. It was around the same time a girl's body had been buried, or hidden, in my fireplace. A chill ran down my back.

I had a photo that put Brenda Petry right on my steps. She was involved. And Rick must have been involved, somehow.

I knew. I knew I was on the point of understanding it all but I could not think out how to explain it to Detective Russo. Was it enough? Would I have to include my personal connections? I didn't want to talk about that at all. Ever. As I was thinking it through, my personal life came to find me.

Steven stood at my front door and rang the bell, looking determined, handsome, and grim.

"You're not answering my calls or messages, and we have to talk. I know Chris went out so I'm here. Let's go in."

'You know about Chris? How?" The light dawned. "Have you been watching me?"

He lost his poise for the first time since I'd met him. "I, no. No, it's not important." Inside, he cupped my face in his hands, gently and said, "I'm so sorry. I never meant to quarrel with you."

"That doesn't matter now." I moved away from him. "It's time for you to tell me the truth."

He went from staring into my face to not looking at me at all. He fixed his gaze on the wall behind me. When he finally met my eyes again, the warmth was gone.

I met his eyes, arms across my body, head steady, mouth set, hoping the pose would stop the tears I felt forming. "Your cousin lived in this house, didn't he? Dammit, how could you not have told me that?"

"What are you talking about?"

I pulled out a copy of the lease, and slapped it into his hand.

"Explain that away. I'm pretty damn sure it wasn't the first Mrs. Hoyt who was living here. Try telling me the truth this time."

He didn't look at it. He was looking at me. He knew.

I sat down, trembling, and he sat too, a cautious distance on the sofa. He had turned pale under his tennis tan but his expression was furious and calculating at the same time.

"I was afraid you would find this eventually. I tried to keep you from it...."

"You underestimated me."

"No, I didn't. Not for a minute." He smiled, so briefly I almost missed it. "That's why I was worried. I desperately hoped I would succeed in sidetracking you."

"Have you been watching me? And listening? Was the oh-so-caring security system an excuse to keep an eye and ear on me? That scary call that pushed me into it right after you and McLeod made the offer?"

He looked embarrassed.

"We had to know how much you knew. You don't understand! It's a story that absolutely has to be kept secret, and it was never even my story to tell you."

"It was all a game." My voice sounded as wobbly as my hands felt. "I told you all about what was happening in my life and you knew what it was all about, and you pretended to be worried…."

"We were trying to stop you. That's all."

That momentary desire to throw myself into his arms and have him tell me it was all a misunderstanding—that was gone.

"You have to understand—"

"Have to?"

"Damn it, Erica, just let me get it out." He looked as angry as he sounded and I felt scared for the first time, but not of him, not exactly. I was sure he was not a man to physically threaten me himself, then and there, but I felt like I was caught in a whirlpool.

"I looked up to my cousin. He was a dozen years older than me. I adored him when he was that tall guy who threw me in the air when I was little and I wanted to become him when he was a man of the world to my doofus teenager. He knew how to order a drink and roll a joint too. I was the first guy in my class to have a fake ID for bars—he got it for me. He told me what to say to girls—it worked. He didn't have a boring job like all the other men I knew. He didn't seem to have any job, he did crazy, amazing things, like an Amazon River trip because someone bet him he couldn't take the climate or drive to Maine for a lobster dinner. He surfed in Australia."

"So he was some kind of idol?" I wanted to scream at him to get to the point, but I didn't want him to get mad again and stop talking.

"He was the golden boy—you've got to understand that!—and then he wasn't. Something happened. In college, after college, I never knew. I was too young then to know about it, and I had to be pretty grown up before I got it that the trips were only sometimes rafting on the Amazon. The rest of time, they were to hospitals and rehab centers."

I was all ears.

"James was busy with his career as a billionaire and his mother, well, she was making the Best Dressed list her career." He stopped. "By the time I was old enough to know what was going on, he was in and out of the best treatment facilities money could buy. Drugs, alcohol, maybe some bi-polar, for all I know. The works. When he was thirty-seven, he OD'd in a flophouse in Harlem."

He could hardly get the words out.

"And you are telling me this because…?"

"Because I need to give you the background. When I'm done, you'll be convinced that you should burn all your information. Forget you ever cared. For your own good and everyone else's."

He went on. "I became James' other son, the good one. I became the golden boy. He'd make fun of me for saying it but I know I was his second chance. He's certainly the closest to a father I ever had. And I would do anything for him he ever needed me to do, anything at all, no questions asked."

I believed him. His voice was hard, and my heart seemed to be beating in double time. Where was this going?

"One time, when I was an adult, but young still, I found him, my cousin, at James' place, working his way through a bottle of very good Scotch, with another waiting next to his glass. All by himself. First time he ever let me see him like that. He had a lot to say about how he'd been high most of the time since he was in high school, and that it had all been a great ride."

He shook his head. "Of course his hands trembled when he tried to pour, he smelled, and his skin looked like he'd crawled out of six months in a POW camp." Steven looked as if he was seeing a very old picture, certainly not one he would have chosen.

"He rambled on about living in righteous houses—that's how he said it—all over the east coast. Maine, then Berkeley, somewhere in the Smoky Mountains, and then Brooklyn. In our world, that was falling off the earth as much as moving to a cabin in the woods. Maybe even more. We understand the woods part, if not the cabin. But a crummy house in Brooklyn?"

"This house?"

"This house." He met my eyes with a face carved in stone. "It didn't sound like a commune with a philosophy. Actually, to me it sounded like a vision of hell, but he insisted it was great. For a while. People drifted in and out. Some were his more rebellious prep school buddies, some were roommates, some were crashing. His landlord's underage daughter was one of them. Nobody worked or went to school or did much of anything, just slept and partied and ate junk and got stoned. High times, he said. But then something happened. Here."

I could barely force the words out.

"The body we found?"

He nodded, one quick movement. "It all came pouring out that night, as if he'd been waiting for a chance to make a confession. She was a crasher, a young teenager from the mid-west somewhere. Someone in the house picked her up somewhere and they shared house, food, and dope in return for housekeeping and sex."

I felt sick to my stomach. This was my worst imaginings, the cards in Leary's file come to life. I almost couldn't bear to hear any more.

"It was pretty bad, the story he told me. That person I looked up to? That night he went up in smoke forever." He stopped, swallowed, stared at the wall above my head.

"I think you'd better finish this sick story, now that you've gone this far." I could barely say the words. I knew, in my heart, I had already seen the end.

"One night, they had the dumb idea to use every drug in the house, have a big party and mix it all up. She wanted in on it and had nothing to contribute, but she really begged."

"So he said."

"Yes, so he said. So she banged each of them—sorry to be so crude, his words I never forgot—and got to try some different substance each time. Then she passed out. They were so stoned, they thought it was funny and laughed and tried to wake her up. Then they decided she was no fun any more, and they partied some more, and when they noticed her again, she was dead."

I could hardly breathe. "You mean, they watched her die? They had sex, and she died, and no one did a thing to help? Called an ambulance? Tried CPR? Nothing?"

He nodded again.

"They watched? They watched? And laughed? Those lousy, stupid...." Words failed me, and then words exploded that I hadn't used since I was trying to be tough at fifteen. It took me a minute to be able to ask another question.

"So they must have covered it up? Buried her in the fireplace?"

He swallowed hard. "He never told me exactly what they did, only that they hid her. I never knew, until...."

"Until you met me."

"All he said was that next morning, when they woke up and understood, they panicked, and hid the body, and bailed out of the house as soon as they could. They felt bad, he said...he wasn't saying it was high times by that point in the story...."

"A sort of a burial, wasn't it?"

He nodded. "He said they hid her away with her favorite things, and tried to say some suitable words, but they were so scared. They got out of the house as fast as they could and simply...disappeared."

Mrs. Rogow's words floated back into my head.

"The tenants who left a mess and disappeared. Garbage everywhere to cover up the carpentry. And the smell! They were a group of cold-blooded little s.o.b.'s weren't they? Or worse..." Light dawned. "They had help, didn't they? To hide it? Your uncle?"

"I didn't know about that until recently." He stopped, then added, "JJ never talked about it again. I tried a few times and he said he didn't know what I was talking about, I must have had a bad dream, nothing like that ever happened. And then he was dead."

I pictured that lost girl, and thought that he had it coming. Poor child. She could have grown up out of her troubles. Found some kind of life. Found her family again, or a better one. I thought of Chris.

"You knew it was my house."

He looked at me, mouth set in line, eyes as cold as marbles.

"Oh, god. Darcy must have told you about what I found. She was chatting, the way she does. Filling in the background."

More light. "You bugged my house, didn't you? So easy when you install a security system. And that scary phone call just after we talked about installing some security. How did I not suspect the timing?" I felt like an idiot. More light. "That van that keeps parking near my house. That's you too. Spying on me! That thug photographer too? And the threatening note? Dear lord. It's all been a sick undercover game."

He said, "Don't you know better than that?"

I could feel my face turning red.

"I was attracted from the start. Darcy was right about that. She said I'd be fascinated, that we would connect, that you were not at all like anyone I knew. She was right."

"But you said yes after you knew about the body in my house."

One nail at a time, I was hammering together a cage. Or a coffin.

"Hell, no, I'd already said yes. Then she told me, in passing, really. It was one of those weird coincidences that happen in real life."

He finally raised his voice. "You don't know how hard it's been! I knew you were stepping into a hornet's nest. James would do…I wanted you to leave the past in the past, where it belongs. I was worried about you, up in the night worried, wanting to kidnap you and take you out of the country worried."

"You have to go." I stood up quickly. "You have to, right now. I am either going to be sick, or I might start throwing things at you. I don't want you here in my house."

"Erica…"

"I mean it. Right now." I was blinking back angry tears. "And call off your spies, too. I'll be watching to make sure you do."

I had the door open by then, and he finally walked through it, brushing my mouth lightly with his fingertips before he left. "Erica, please. I'm begging you. Be very careful."

After that I was really and truly, thoroughly sick. When I was done, and wiped my sweaty face and brushed my teeth twice, and drank some soda, I didn't know what I needed to do next. Throwing everything breakable felt appealing, but not, finally, useful. Words slipped into my mind.

"If you're troubled, keep moving. Makes it harder for anything to catch you." Rick used to say that. Damn it, Rick, I thought, why aren't you here to tell me what to do? I remembered his words, that the strange events in my life must be related to finding the body, and I wondered if everything that had happened was connected, the threatening note, the attack on Leary, Brenda Petry's insane behavior. Rick.

It all might have been—must have been—but I couldn't think anymore. I could barely take in what I had learned from Steven. My brain was in shock, overflowing with horror about that poor girl, crushed by the truth about Steven, appalled at how foolish I felt.

Was I Chris' age, to get so swept away? To entirely lose my Brooklyn attitude? To be such a dope to think he felt something for me? And all mixed in was the anger—no, the rage—at those trashy young bastards. Prep school friends, he said. Rich young bastards who treated everyone like a toy. Break it and there would always be more.

I wrote down everything Steven had told me. I would make a file with those notes, the lease, the photo, all my research, and give it to the police as soon as possible. I hoped it would be enough.

Keep moving. I knew they might never figure out who she was, our girl, but with all that I had, maybe someone would be made responsible, finally. That was not nothing.

Chapter Twenty-three

Then it was 3:00 a.m. and I couldn't sleep. I had collapsed into a dreamless stupor, but something woke me up later. I wasn't sure if it was a noise from outside or the streetlight coming in or my own racing thoughts. Steven's words circled around in my mind on an endless loop, with other thoughts drifting in and out around edges. Memories of Rick, Chris being home, Chris sulking, Leary in the hospital. Everything.

I went downstairs as quietly as I could on our creaky old steps. I wandered out to the deck, leaving the lights off, hoping that the night air and scents from the Pastores' garden would ease me back to sleepiness. I remembered sitting out here with Rick, shortly after we had found the skeleton in the fireplace. We talked about that, and Chris was especially interested even then. And one little piece fell into place.

I went in and stood at Chris' doorway, watching her sleep. Her long legs now almost filled the bed we bought when she was two. Makeup and CDs from some group I had never heard of cluttered her dresser top and stuffed animals covered her bed. The last hours showed me the gutsy girl she was becoming and the kid with bad judgment she still was.

I hesitated. Things that loom large deep in the night become trivial in daylight. Memories haunt me and then melt away in the sun. Brilliant insight turns to gibberish in the morning. I finally gave in to the suspicion that was floating around in my head, and woke her up.

"Mommy? What?" She burrowed her head back into her pillow. After I shook her softly and shook her again and switched on the clown lamp that had been in her room since she was born, she opened her eyes.

"What? What?" She sat up abruptly. "Is something wrong?"

"Maybe. You tell me." I touched the silver charm around her neck, a cross with a loop at the top. "I need to know where this came from. There was something a lot like it in the fireplace where you found the skeleton."

She squinted at me. "What time is it?" She squinted at the clock. "You woke me up at 3:30 to talk about jewelry???"

"No, honey, not jewelry. This piece of jewelry."

"Well, we have a workshop at camp and I…" I drilled my eyes into her face and she faltered. I was right.

"I want the truth this time. No more stories. Did it come from the fireplace? I finally remembered where I last saw something like this."

One quick nod and then a dive back into her pillows.

"Oh, no, Chris. We need to talk about this. Sit up. Right now."

She straightened up but would not meet my eyes.

"I'm not yelling at you—not yet," I said very quietly, "but I do need to know about this. Talk now so I don't have to yell. What were you thinking?"

"It was…it was…." She shook her head, and then went on, still not looking at me. "It started out like, an impulse? You know? It was such a strange thing, and so scary, but when I realized it was a girl. I don't know—I wanted something to keep."

"You mean like a souvenir?" I couldn't believe my ears.

"No! Do you think I'm some kind of ghoul? I don't know, really, I only wanted to have something to—you know—remember her."

"A keepsake?"

"Yes, that's it! I've worn it every day. So, you know, she would know someone remembers her. I mean—I don't think she's a ghost, not really, but she shouldn't be, like, lost and forgotten."

My warm-hearted daughter. With the judgment of a little kid. Or a magpie, even, hoarding bright objects.

"What is the matter with you? Didn't you understand that it was evidence? The cops said don't touch anything."

"But they had everything else. They didn't really need this too. What difference could it make?" She had that look with the set jaw. The look that said, she knew what she knew and she was sticking to it.

"Well, it does matter! I'm pretty sure this is illegal, which certainly matters, and it's wrong, which matters, and it's dangerous, which also matters." I couldn't stop myself from adding, "How could you have been so stupid?"

She didn't even try to argue.

"If I restrain myself from yelling at you, however much I feel like it, will you promise to take it in first thing in the morning? Full confession to that Lt. Russo? I have the number downstairs."

She had her hand wrapped protectively around the charm but she whispered "Yes." And then added "Will you come with me?'

"I don't know about that—you're not missing how angry I am, are you? And I'm not making decisions in the middle of the night, either." I shook my head. "Nope, not now. Back to sleep for both of us."

She slid down, turned her back to me and returned to hugging her pillow. I went back to my room and stared out the window, looking for some kind of comfort, I guess, from the moon or the streetlights. Had I handled this well? Should I have come down harder? Should I have taken the necklace from her tonight, for safekeeping?

The moon wasn't much help. The whole street was fast asleep, and finally I was ready to be too.

Sunlight streamed in through the shutter slats and there was pounding on the front door. I woke up with a start, checked the clock and saw I had overslept by an hour or so. I tumbled out of bed, made sure I was decently covered, and stumbled into the hallway. Joe's voice was coming up from the kitchen and there were welcome sounds of life from behind Chris' door.

Joe and one of his men were hauling in slabs of synthetic counter tops. I had a second of regret for the granite I could not afford, and then suppressed it to admire the sleek, clean surfaces they were manhandling into the kitchen.

Joe grinned. "As promised. Bet you didn't know how scary you can be."

"I'll take that as a compliment."

He promptly replied, "Exactly what I intended."

I rubbed my eyes, trying to wake up. "Joe, this is great."

"How are you doing? Happy to have the princess home yet? No offense but you look a little frazzled."

"Not so much to the second question, I don't know to the first, and not enough sleep to the last comment."

He put a cardboard container of coffee into my hand and led me to the chairs in the living room.

"Joe!" Chris screamed as she came in, bare footed, still in her sleep shorts and t-shirt.

"Hey, baby!" He threw one arm around her shoulders and planted a kiss on the top of her head. "I brought bagels—I heard there might be a growing girl on the premises. Your mom can have one too, if she behaves."

She giggled. "The house is coming along great. When is my new bathroom going in?"

"It would be that much faster if you hadn't bailed on me." He saw her face and said, "Hey, I'm kidding. Kidding!"

"Could we talk?" she said more soberly. "Friend to friend, like we did when we were tearing down walls together?" He pointed toward the deck and Chris went with him, meek as could be. I saw them talking intensely. Chris looked ready to walk away at one point, but then she seemed to be nodding, and they ended with a hug.

She came back, said only, "Joe explained it all to me," and headed toward the kitchen and muffins.

Joe said to me, "She gets it now. She already did, but there's something about hearing it from a non-parent."

I wanted to protest but then his kindness got through to me. I clutched his hand a little harder, and said, "Thanks, buddy. I know. Rick used to be that person for me."

He let go and stood up, "Kid meet that preppie yet?" He added quickly, "I know, I know, he has a name. And it's only a work relationship for you, too. So, what did she think?"

I looked away quickly, trying to hide from him that my eyes were filling with tears, but he knows me too well.

"Hey! What's wrong?" He turned me around. "Come on. Want me to straighten him out, Brooklyn style?" He faked a tough-guy accent that almost made me smile.

"She doesn't even know?"

Chris walked in. "What don't I know?"

"It would fill a book."

Joe said, "I've got to hit the road, now. Other clients call. I squeezed you guys in today." He rumpled my unbrushed hair, a gesture he knows I hate, and left whistling.

Chris disappeared too and came down in a few minutes, fully dressed. Standing up very straight, she said, "I still had his card and I called and he's there now. I'll go by myself. I can walk over and back." Her face was serious. "I've womaned up to it. And I am going to ask about their progress solving the whole thing too. I don't care if you don't want me to." She looked both defiant and determined, and a little scared.

Now that she was taking on some responsibility, I wanted to rush in and deny it all, to say, "No, no, you're my baby and I am coming to hold your hand," but what I actually said was, "Call me if you need me, anything at all, if those cops scare you or…or…just anything,?"

She let out a long sigh. "I will, I promise. Actually he sounded fine, like he was glad to hear from me, so maybe it won't be so bad." She swallowed hard, gave me a weak smile and said, "Off to the lion's den."

"Call me as soon as you're done? Got your phone? Is it charged?"

"Mom! Stop it! Don't worry."

Of course I would worry, every minute, until I heard from her. What would they say to her? How upset would they be? Would she be in real trouble? I would cope by chaining myself to work, up in my room, away from the construction noise. I brushed my hair, made the bed I had barely slept in, and I was ready to begin a productive working day. No calls. No net surfing, get something done while Chris was out. I plowed ahead on my work project, but when I had not heard from my daughter in an hour, my concentration trickled away.

I calculated. Fifteen minutes to walk there. Maybe some waiting time before Russo could see her. Fifteen minutes to talk? Time to get home. But she was supposed to call as soon as she was done. On the other hand, this would not be the first time she had forgotten a promise like that.

No, it was too early to be reasonably worried. Not that I wasn't anyway. After another half hour I decided it was time. I dug out Russo's number and braced myself for two separate conversations. First, where was Chris? Was she in trouble there at the station; did she need me, if so, why hadn't she called? Or was she on the way home?

I called Chris, leaving a pointed message about people who don't keep promises to call. Then I called Lieutenant Russo, leaving him a message asking him to call me as soon as possible, that I had important information for him. I thought that would get a faster response than leaving him an anxious mother message. What I really wanted to know was what he had done with my daughter.

And then I called my father.

Chapter Twenty-four

I had no idea why I was calling him. Over the years, we had a contentious relationship, but it used to be that he was the dad who would always be there for me. Then he turned around and went off on his own. Moved across the country with his new woman friend. He was the one who left, not me, and I had decided I would manage without him.

Now my own new thing in my life had blown up in a particularly ugly way. Rick, my dad *in loco parentis*, was gone forever and I still did not know what really happened to him. Maybe I never would and that felt like losing him a second time. A lost young girl had died in my house, and right now I was becoming more antsy by the minute about Chris' whereabouts.

Oh, hell. Maybe I wanted someone else to be the grown-up for a while. I wanted a dad.

"Hey, cookie," he said. "I knew it was you—I got caller ID on this new cell phone."

At the sound of his voice I lost my own. "Oh, dad," was all I could say.

"What's wrong there? Something with Chris?"

"Not, not Chris. Well, I don't know. Maybe…no, she's. I…I needed…" I took a deep breath and told myself to stop dithering. "Please just tell me about some of the dumb things I did when I was Chris' age. Remind me? So I know she'll grow up and have some sense some day?"

As soon as I said it, I knew that's why I had called. Even with all the other dark things swirling around in my life, that was the one thing I needed to hear most.

He chuckled, then said, "How much time do you have? I have a list right here."

"It's not funny."

"I know, but I also know she hasn't done anything really crazy. I know. And all kids do something stupid. Didn't I ever tell you about the time when we were kids, me and Rick and some other guys hot-wired a neighbor's Caddie—and him a cop!—and went joy riding? Never got caught neither."

Somehow, across all those miles, he heard my need in my silence, or my breathing, and said again, "She will be fine. She is fine. You're doing a good job. I know, because we talk, her and me." He hesitated. "A girl needs her grandfather, even if a mother doesn't need her own dad anymore."

I almost took him up on that then and there—what nerve, when he was the one who deserted me—but I didn't have the heart for it at that moment.

"Oh, and speaking of dumb things, how the hell come you didn't tell me about the crime scene in your life? I had to hear all about it from talking to Chris?"

"What are you talking about?"

"The body Chris found in the wall. That's what."

"Well, you could have asked me if you were so anxious to know."

He sighed. "So I'm asking now. Why not talk to me about it?"

"Oh, dad. If I told you the whole story, it would take all afternoon. Between that and Rick...and that isn't even all..."

"So? I have nothing to do except physical therapy. You want to start with Rick?"

I told him all about my futile detective work, step by step; how I had tried to find out what really happened, had been blocked everywhere, had to plan a service for him and it probably should not wait any more.

He said, "I'm coming home to help with that as soon as the docs clear me to fly. No arguments, got it?"

I got it. I didn't even feel the slightest impulse to argue.

"Chris told me. I'll be glad to see you." I could hardly get the words out, and yet, once again, as soon as I said them I knew they were the truth.

"Now, tell me all about Chris. And about the body. Seems like it's on her mind."

I gulped. I didn't want to hear what he might say and then I didn't have to. Saved by the bell. Alexander Graham's bell. And call waiting.

"Dad? Chris is calling so I've got to go, I'll call tonight?"

"Be sure you do. I'll be right here."

It wasn't Chris. A hard man's voice said, "Mrs. Donato? You have something we want and we have something you want. It's about five-foot four and maybe fourteen or fifteen years old."

My house seemed to disappear around me and I stopped breathing.

"Good," he said. "I have your attention. I do, don't I?"

"Yes," I whispered.

"We want that file you are compiling, every word in it, every photo, every piece of paper."

"I don't…how do you…"

"We know, and it doesn't matter how, though I'm sure you will figure it out eventually. Here's what you do. There's an empty little store at 27 Gerry Place, a nice, quiet, out of the way block. You know it? Not much foot traffic. Brown paper on the windows, hiding the renovation work."

Through lips that barely moved, I said, "Used to be a cigarette store?"

"That's it. Bring the package we want, and if you do it right—all the material is in it, you come alone, no cops, no friends—maybe we'll give you the package you want. Clear?"

I jerked out of my fugue state, and said in a rising voice, "Is she there with you now? Is she all right? Let me talk to her right now!'

"Why, of course." He sounded almost genial. "Here, honey,' he said, away from the phone, "tell your mom to be good if she wants to have you come home."

"Mommy?" Her voice shook. "I'm so sorry, I'm so...."

The connection was broken before she could respond to my shouted, "Are you all right?"

"Of course she is," the voice said. "We don't trade in damaged goods. We just want to get your attention about the price you'll pay, if you don't follow instructions. Let's set up a time. Let's say thirty minutes? Long enough to for you to get everything together and get you over here, not long enough for any side trips. You understand that?"

"Yes," I whispered.

"Could you make that a little more emphatic so we don't have to worry about any misunderstandings?"

"Yes, yes, yes. Of course I'll come alone! And with everything! You hold all the aces."

"Yes, we do, don't we? Looking forward to seeing you. There's a little alley alongside the building with a side door. Just give it a tap—we'll be expecting you."

The phone went dead.

My heart was pounding so hard, for a moment it was all I could feel or hear. Nothing around me seemed real. I felt like I was sleepwalking. If I woke up, and really thought about it, this would be worse than any nightmare. The only thing that was clear to me was that they wanted my papers. Well, they could have them if they would give me Chris unharmed.

I put the folder into a shopping bag and, almost without seeing, I tipped in the entire untidy stack on my desk. Clippings, Leary's old notes, the Pastores' photos, warehouse papers. Everything I could find.

They had Chris. They could have the deed to my house, the key to my car, my ATM card. My right arm.

I saw Mr. Pastore in the garden and didn't say hello. I saw Mary running up the street, and ignored her wave. Later, other

people told me they had seen me that day and worried when I
walked by like a blind woman.

I was going out of the neighborhood, to the raw no man's
land almost under the expressway entrance, and it took a few
minutes to get there. I could not move my legs fast enough; I
felt as if I was walking against a strong tide.

The storefront was where I remembered it. It used to be a
shop for smokes, Lotto tickets, and—maybe, probably, in the
back—illegal substances. Though it was a bright summer day,
there was no one on the street of mostly empty storefronts and no
reason for anyone to be there. The alley was dark even in daylight,
deeply shaded by taller buildings, the cracked pavement covered
with rubble and oversize beer bottles. Probably worse, too.

The back door swung open before I even touched it and I
stepped into a dark room. It was not dimly lit, it was completely
pitch-black dark.

A voice came out of the darkness. "Thank you for coming,"
a man's voice, not at all as grateful as his words. "And be aware
that there is a large, armed man near you."

"What do you want from me? And where is my daughter?"

"She's right here, as promised. Young lady, assure your mother
of that."

"Mom...." And then she was cut off.

My knees buckled at the sound of her voice. She was right
there and I could not see her or touch her. I tried to keep my rage
out of my voice when I said, again, "What do you want from me?"

"That package in your hand, of course. Yes, we saw it as you
came to the door. Put it down and don't look behind you. For
obvious reasons, we do not want to be seen by you, but when
you put it down, someone will take it into another room to look
over. If it's all there, we will disappear and leave your daughter
behind. A nice neat plan. No one gets hurt and no one gets into
any trouble."

I put the shopping bag down. I heard footsteps behind me
and I sensed a little light. Then there some noise moving away
from me.

"I want to talk to my daughter." I knew I had nothing to bargain with, and so did he, that voice. He didn't even respond,

I stood and waited, trying to calm my raggedy breathing and telling myself, again and again, that it would be all right in just a few minutes.

I heard a noise in the alley, and sensed alertness behind me. Then it was gone.

I called out, "Chris," but there was no answer.

"Chris, honey, are you there?"

"Yes." Then she was cut off.

I was still trapped in that nightmare. Nothing could compare to this.

"Have any of you thugs offered Ms. Donato a chair?" It was James' voice, distorted a little, but unmistakable. I was simultaneously both shocked to hear it and yet not even surprised. Of course. It had to be his.

There was soft movement behind me and I felt a seat press against the back of my legs. I collapsed into it.

"Please forgive them. You don't get the highest class of help for this kind of work. This isn't exactly routine corporate security. And please forgive me for putting you through this. I am not a thug, but you left me no choice."

"Are you here?" I could not believe that.

"Aha, so you think you know who I am. No, of course I am not there in the flesh. I am on a remote connection so I can keep on top of what is happening. You will not be seeing me, and you will never be able to prove that I was even talking to you. Oh, by the way, I suggest you not even use my name, assuming you are correct about what it is."

"I don't understand…"

"What don't you understand?" He sounded almost concerned, though that seemed highly unlikely. "That I am not there? Or that I am involved?"

I couldn't even begin to list everything I didn't understand, so he stepped into the silence, as if he too was uncomfortable, impossible though that seemed. "I shouldn't even be talking to

you—I have been so advised—but I don't want you to think
too badly of me. Your daughter has not been harmed; I don't
attack little girls. If you have done what you were told, this whole
situation simply disappears into the air like a mist."

"But why?"

I spoke into the dark, focusing on the voices in the room
since there was nothing I could see. There was a tiny thread of
light down near the floor. A door, I thought, into another room.
That was all.

Chris must be there, in that other room.

"Ah, Ms. Donato you are still your inquisitive self. Surely
you know all about this. Loving a child, protecting them when
they make mistakes, catching them when they slip and fall. We
all owe them that, don't we?"

"Your son."

"My son. I did nothing but make mistakes with him, but
I could not let him go to jail for that one judgment-impaired
night, the one at your house, now could I?"

"You helped him…"

"I had people who helped him. Yes, at my request. And I had
people who helped keep it a secret all those years. People who
knew, and learned it was to their advantage to forget. People I
could help, through the years. People who didn't ask questions
when they might have. I saw to that in the earlier years, when
it surely would have mattered. You must have guessed at some?"

"Brenda Petry? She was so scared about what I was finding,
protecting her reputation? Was she there that night?"

Silence.

"She kept quiet and you helped her with business connections? And investing, maybe?"

More silence.

"Rick? Did he know something happened there? Or guessed?"
I knew it as I said it. No one had to tell me. It had been in front
of me all along. "Leary's notes. Rick was on a missing child
investigation. And he knew something? And he didn't look?"

"Ah," was all he said. All he had to say. "All along I knew someone might show up who would take the house apart, but as the years went on, it mattered less and less. I felt sure no one was still looking, no one would still care and certainly no one could find those old puzzle pieces." He stopped, then went on, "I must have been losing my talent for outthinking the other players. You, my dear, turned out to be the wild card."

"I don't care about any of it now." Perhaps I shouted it. "Let me have my daughter and as you say, the whole story becomes so much mist."

"I made sure of that by telling you to bring every piece of information you have unfortunately dug up. Foolish of that old reporter to give you files. You could go now and spin this wild tale about an abduction and who would take you seriously? I have other people—they would destroy your reputation with just a few hints in the right places. Keep that in mind…after."

I had to try not to scream at him. I had to try not to sound accusing.

"It was a long time ago. Why does it still matter to you? Keeping it a secret, I mean?"

"Well, I'm a businessman so let's call it closing out my books. The doctors tell me the time for that has come, and I don't have much of it left. The best doctors money can buy and all they can get me is a few more months. You understand? I may not have been much of a father—the one failure of my so-successful life—and my poor JJ wasn't much of a son, but I can't bear to end my life with the entire world learning that my boy was even more of a disgrace than everyone suspected. I've covered it up all these years. Do you think I was letting someone like you, a student, a nobody, wreck that?" Even through the speaker I could hear his voice shake.

"Here I am, the famous financier and philanthropist, and the only thing people will be talking about will be this new scandal about my boy. Just like my poor friend Brooke Astor with a public scandal on her deathbed. Making sure that story remains buried where it has been and still belongs, in the past, is the last thing I can do for my son."

It sounded more like the last thing he would do for himself. I couldn't say that. I couldn't say, "What about that poor girl, and the people who loved her?" I couldn't say anything. Not until I had Chris safe in my arms and out of this black hole.

There was the sound of the outside door scraping along the floor, and then a bright beam of light was cutting wildly into the darkness. I was almost blinded when it hit my face. Then as it danced crazily across the walls, I had glimpses, like flashes of old, jerky film, of a cellar-like room and of a large man moving quickly. Then, suddenly, the light stopped flying around the room and landed on me, and Mary's voice was saying, "Why, Mrs. Donato, what are you doing here?"

I could barely see her face, not enough to see an expression, but her voice was confused. "Did I invite you here? It's one of my hangouts but I don't remember doing that. How careless of me. Not that you aren't welcome. And this other man? Your friend?" She swung the flashlight back to him where he was planted in front of the door.

He looked nervous and confused. And familiar. He was the man who took photos in front of my house. Of course.

"A gun?" Mary was saying. "My, my. Not a very polite way to make a visit. Not at all. Let's get some more light in here." The clicking sound of a switch and suddenly there was a bare, dim bulb overhead, hanging from a string. The man held up a gun, moving it back and forth from me, to Mary, to me, as if he could not decide who was more dangerous. I was way too frightened, then, to see that how ridiculous that was.

She sighed. "Boys and their toys. You want to play a game?" Then she started flicking the light switch on and off. On. Off. On. Off. He was shouting at her, and in the flickering, I could see him frantically waving his gun. The erratic light didn't give him a chance to aim it anywhere.

I stood up, prepared to take any opportunity. The light went on for a split second and I was ready. The chair was light enough to lift, heavy enough to do damage. I heaved it at him and heard a satisfying crash, and then a deep moan.

Then the light went on and stayed on. Mary shouted, "Ha!" and smacked him on the side of his head with her flashlight, while I picked up his gun. We were both breathing hard.

There were noises from the other side of the door, scuffling feet, a shouted "What the hell…"

I stood behind the door, gun up. Did I know how to use it? No. I hadn't touched a gun since I had a friend who was a rookie cop. I hoped I had seen enough cop shows on TV to look competent and scary. Really scary.

Mary was daydreaming, admiring her long silver flashlight, so I reached over myself and turned the light out. I would open the door into—I hoped—a bright room, and coming out of darkness I would be safer and scarier. I hoped.

I took a deep breath, prayed to the deities I don't believe in, held the gun up in a way I hoped was threatening, and pushed the door open. In a split second I took in Chris, handcuffed to a chair; two men with guns pointed at me, and Steven. I pointed my gun right at him, locked eyes, and ignored everything else. "Drop the guns to the floor. I mean it. James, if you hear me, tell them. I am pointing a gun at your other poor excuse for a son."

At the edge of my vision, I saw Chris' eyes open wide.

"And I mean it too," Mary piped up. "I have your back. My gun is right here." I thought it was just her flashlight but I could not look.

James calmly said, "Better listen to the ladies."

The sound of hardware hitting the floor told me no one was taking any chances on my gun or Mary's.

"Erica," Steven stood up, "This is all a misunderstanding. You must know…I couldn't stop this….but I made them include me…to make sure nothing happened to Chris…."

"Go to hell, Steven. Here you are, and here is my daughter. There is no misunderstanding." Without turning my eyes away from him, I added, "One of you untie her from that damn chair." When she was free, I said, "Chris, honey, get up, and move away, behind me. Can you take my phone out of my pocket ? And call Russo? Call 911 AND Russo?"

"No need," Mary sang out. "Cavalry is on the way."

"What?" Several voices said it all at once.

"I followed you here. I wanted to tell you something. This is not a nice place at all, very creepy, this block, so I called from the phone at the gas station. Lucky I had some change on me, safe in my shoe! I was a secret caller. I said I heard gun shots." She smiled a loopy grin. "Figured that would get some fast attention."

A minute later, or a second later, the room was full of men in blue windbreakers with real guns in their hands, and Chris was in my arms. There was a kind of organized chaos all around us, questions, shouting, protests, but we just held each other, crying, while Mary looked around with satisfaction and a vague smile, repeating, "Like I said."

Chapter Twenty-five

It took a few hours to sort it all out. And then it took a few more days, a few more weeks, and a few more months.

At the moment it all happened, I was insisting they call Lt. Russo. Steven and the other two men were insisting it was all a mistake. They were assured they would have an opportunity to explain it all to someone higher up the food chain.

Chris was alternating between insisting that it was not a mistake and she had been kidnapped, and apologizing to me. Mary was sitting on a chair suggesting drinks all around to celebrate.

The uniformed cops kept us all there and told us to keep quiet while they asked questions and made phone calls. I turned my back on Steven when he tried, again, to talk to me, and I held Chris tight. In short order, all three men were bundled into a police car and Chris and I were more politely ushered into another. When we left, Mary was insisting she had no interest in talking to anyone and wasn't getting into anyone's car, police or otherwise.

At the station, Chris talked to Russo alone, in spite of my doubts. I talked to him, while a young cop offered to get Chris a slice of pizza and another took her off to clean up.

Russo looked exhausted by then, though no more than I was. He would not tell me anything, not even where Mary was, though he assured me she would be fine. He let me go at last, with only a, "We'll talk further." And then he added, "Those two punks will tell us everything. I'd bet my pension on it. Don't worry about anything." I caught a gleam of satisfaction in his eyes.

I was glad because, though I had plenty of questions for him too, my adrenaline surge was long gone, and in the aftermath, I was too exhausted even to ask them. I was past running on empty; I was running on fumes. All I wanted was to take Chris home and hold her, and then collapse.

Someone was delegated to drive us home and see us safely inside. Someone was told to park a car outside the house for the night, and keep his eyes open. Someone else was called to take a look at our probably bugged phone and our probably wired house.

While the de-buggers worked we sat together in a stupor, Chris and I, holding hands and nodding off into the sleep of the terminally overstressed.

The phone rang. Chris answered it, said "Grandpa?" and walked into another room. I heard her faint voice saying "You won't believe this. I got kidnapped. No, yes...it's all fine...."

She was gone for a long time, and when she returned she said, "He wanted to talk to you, but I said you were sleeping. I figured you didn't want to talk. Is that OK? And I told him everything is fine now, we're both safe." She stopped and then added, "But I think he was going straight to call about getting a plane ticket home, as soon as he said good-bye."

"That's fine," I mumbled. "I can't even think about it right now." But I could, for a minute. "Do you think she's coming with him? That friend of his?"

"Mom? They broke up a while ago? Maybe you two should talk more."

◇◇◇

I woke up on the sofa. A line of pale sunshine was slipping through the shutters, crawling in across the living room floor. Six a.m. My back hurt and my mouth tasted awful. And where was Chris?

My panic subsided when I found her collapsed on her bed, fully clothed, breathing the deep breath of one lost to the world. At least she had made it up to her bed, unlike her mother.

Cold water and a toothbrush helped me wake up a little. I would make coffee somehow in my almost finished kitchen. Looking for the newspaper, I opened my front door to the quiet, early-morning street, where the only sound was cooing pigeons out hunting breakfast. It was almost dark under the trees, the street almost empty, and the air almost cool before the summer heat hit. There was a cop car watching over us, and there was Joe on my steps, reading my newspaper and drinking his own coffee.

I sat down next him on the top step and he handed me a second cup. "I talked to your daughter late last night."

I braced myself.

"How are you doing?"

He didn't look at me. I didn't know what to say because I didn't know what Chris had told him.

"I...well...things have been very weird...I...."

"You know," he said conversationally, "you really are an idiot." He still wasn't looking at me. "Chris told me the whole story last night."

"Oh."

"Why didn't you call me? How could you walk in there alone..."

"I had to go alone. They insisted. I couldn't risk Chris."

"So I could have been somewhere close. Or going for help. We could have figured something out. You're five foot nothing. You didn't think you could use some back up?"

"I didn't think at all. I was..." My voice shook. "If you say one word...if you lecture me...I will never talk to you again. Ever." Now I was the one who was looking away.

He turned me toward him. His face was a mask. None of his usual amused expression. No warmth. Not even anger. "I am only going say one thing. Don't you know you can count on me when you are in trouble?"

He stood up. "I'm going to work now. I figured you and the princess needed a quiet day so I sent my guys on another job. They'll finish here tomorrow, looks like."

He went down the stairs and out my gate without another word, without even looking back at me. He was halfway down the block before he turned and said, "Try to stay out of trouble." He still wasn't smiling.

Then he was in his truck and gone.

I left the paper and the coffee on a table and overwhelmed, went straight up to bed. I curled up under the covers, still in my clothes, and slept until the room was filled with sunshine. I was ready to start the day a second time.

I found a note on Chris' door. "Didn't want to wake you. Some of my girls are coming by to take me to breakfast. Going to get a haircut, too. Really grubby after camp. Back later. Love, C. PS Yes, my phone is on. Yes, I will stick to the neighborhood. Yes, I will be careful. I'll even look both ways before crossing the street."

What? She was going out alone, after everything that had happened? I certainly did not consider her posse of friends to be any more safe than being alone. I wanted to call and order her home right now, keeping her locked in the house until she returned to camp, and then to send her to school in the fall with an armed guard.

It was not a possibility. I might not be recovered from yesterday for some time to come, but she seemed to be on the way. I wondered if she would convert the very real terrifying experience into an adventure story for her friends. Would experience with an actual crime make her seem glamorous?

Of course I called her anyway. I wanted to be sure she was safe. And told her to get used to it. She said, "Wait," and next thing I knew a waitress was on the line, saying, "Yeah, Ms. Donato, I got Chris right here with a coupla friends, eating an omelet. Gonna put it on your credit card. You good with that?"

I tried to wash the whole experience away with a very long shower. Freshly scrubbed, freshly shampooed, in fresh clean clothes, I finally settled down with leftover sesame noodles and the coffee Joe had given me. It was now the same temperature as my summer living room, neither hot nor iced, but it was still sweet and caffeinated. It would do while I finally read the paper and then worked out which of my many responsibilities came first.

I flipped on the local news while I ate my breakfast or lunch or whatever it was and promptly spilled my coffee. The talking head on local news had just said something about "the late James Hoyt."

Now there was a doctor on the screen, confirming that James had been very ill, information Mr. Hoyt insisted on keeping private. His death had come sooner than expected, but they had known for some time that he only had a few months left. There was a parade of famous faces, discussing how much he had given to the life of the city.

I didn't believe it then, and I have never believed it since. Oh, I believed he was dead, of course, but I always thought he had found a way to evade his own consequences, just as he had helped his son evade his, all those years ago. He'd taken extra pills, or mixed pills with alcohol, or had a special brew from a bribed pharmacist. Something. And if anyone ever found out, they would call it "depression over ill health."

Maybe he willed himself to let go now instead of later. I firmly believed his will was more than strong enough to succeed at that.

There was a bit mentioning that his nearest relative, his nephew Steven, was in seclusion. "Seclusion?" I thought. That certainly was a euphemistic word for it. I thought "held by police" might be more accurate.

With James gone, Steven would be left to clean up the mess. He deserved it. The fact that only a few days ago I had some feelings for him seemed less real to me than any dream I had ever dreamed. Less real than a dim memory of something that might have happened when I was a child. Or in another life. It happened a very long time ago, to someone else.

I hoped he would end up in jail. For the next few days, I kept a radio turned to the all-news and read all the papers, from the newspaper of record to the sleaziest tabloid, to see if there was anything more about how James died, or what was happening to Steven. In all the verbiage about James' life and times, I could not find one word.

I had another meeting with Russo, to fill in some details for him, and give him notes and answer more questions, so I tried to ask my own too. When I asked about Steven, he shook his head and said only two words, "Ongoing investigation." I hadn't expected anything better, but it was worth a shot. When I asked if I would have to testify at a trial, or if Chris would, he only shrugged and said, "Wait and see."

When I pressed him about Mary, he said, "Safe in a psychiatric facility, getting help." I must have looked horrified, because he laughed and added, "Calm down. It's no snake pit, believe me. She's getting good care. We need her to get better so we can ask her some more questions. Not that we haven't tried, but the answers don't always relate to what we're asking. Or even this planet, sometimes."

"I don't know what would have happened without her...I owe her...I can't even say how much. Please. Please take care of her."

He nodded. "We owe her too, loony as she is. Someone, somewhere, knows who she is. We're gonna find them."

Amazingly enough, they did, though I didn't learn about it for some time. Deep in her filthy shopping bag of meager possessions, there were two pictures of a young girl, sealed into a zip top plastic bag. Much later, he showed me copies. One was a yearbook photo, and if you got past the too-wide smile and the Brady Bunch curls she did look a little like Chris. The other was from a dime store photo booth. She was gaunt now, her hair string-straight, her eyes surrounded with black eye liner. She wore ankh shaped earrings.

Russo told me that the plastic bag also held a Minnesota birth certificate. They used it to make some connections, tracked down people still in the town who told about the teenage cousin who ran away decades ago, about the parents who followed a trail to New York and then hit a dead end, the heartbroken father who came home and the disturbed mother who refused, who insisted she'd stay until she found her, no matter how long it took.

So Chris had finally found her, behind a plywood wall in our house. I was sure of that now, and a few weeks later I found out that Mary knew it too. She came by my house with a middle-aged woman in a pink suit. Not a New Yorker. Mary looked shaky, but clean and less gaunt, and for the first time ever, her eyes were truly focused when she talked to me. Something had worked for her in the hospital.

"That Lt. Russo told me all about it. I thought I'd ask you if I could see where…where…you know. But maybe not. Maybe not." She went silent, lost in her thoughts.

"I'm Mary Margaret's cousin," the other woman said. "From Minnesota. I'm taking her back home. We're sure glad that policeman found us."

"Going back for a visit. Not so sure I'm staying."

"Mary," I said, "I have to say thank you, forever and ever. I've wanted to, but they wouldn't tell me how to find you. Do you want to come in? You are certainly welcome. We didn't…the fireplace is still there…it didn't seem right…is there anything I can do for you? Anything at all?"

I was babbling. I couldn't find the right words to tell her what I wanted to say, so I was using a lot of wrong ones.

She shook her head. "You don't need to say thank you. You found my girl and I found yours."

Close enough. I nodded, unable to speak.

"Cover up the damn fireplace and hang a pretty picture on it. She liked rainbows." She stopped, took a deep breath, started again. "We're taking her back home, my sweetheart, and saying a proper good-bye to her with a minister, choir, resting her next to her grandparents and her poor father. I'm thinking about writing 'Good Morning, Starshine' on the stone. She loved that song." She stared at my house. "Her name was Kristin, you know. Nice Norwegian name. Popular in Minnesota."

I hugged her hard and she hugged me.

"Remember me to your lovely daughter," she said as her cousin led her to the car.

As if, I thought. As if Chris would ever forget.

◇◇◇

My father came home. He took his house back from his tenant and we talk now. We don't talk a lot, not yet, but we talk. We began to plan a service for Rick, accepting that we might not ever know what really happened to him, but that we needed to remember and honor the man we did know.

Joe showed up at my house with a full crew a few days after our talk on the steps, and seemed like his old self. I was relieved. I could not deal with a lost friendship right now. I had too much else on my plate. I had to return to my internship and make myself useful—working overtime!—or I would not get the credits I needed. My father was back in my life. Chris would be coming home from camp, where she had returned to finish her summer.

Joe came to the party I had to celebrate my brand new kitchen. He looked over the tiles for signs of sloppy grouting until I told him to get a beer and leave my kitchen alone. He went into the living room, where I saw him straightening the picture on the wall. He was the same, but not quite.

Darcy came, still apologizing for introducing me to Steven. I told her to shut up and serve the potato salad. The Pastores came, with a restaurant-size pan of lasagna and some more old photo albums. They admired everything about the kitchen. Then Mr. Pastore got into a discussion with Joe about tiles and Mrs. Pastore immediately began cutting up the lasagna. The perfect guests.

Leary was there, unwisely eating everything in sight. We had fit some missing pieces together while he was in the hospital—he instantly recognized the two thugs in custody as the men who had invaded his apartment—and now he was eager to see where it had all started. To my surprise, he and my father hit it off instantly, trading stories about Brooklyn in the old days.

Chris had come back from camp a few days before, again starving and begging for a hot bath, with the results of her classes carefully packed into a portfolio. There were sketches and watercolor studies and a series of pictures she had taken in photography class, forest scenes after a rain. In one, the sun hitting the drops created a dazzling, multi-colored prism, a rainbow. I had the perfect place for it.

From deep in the duffle bag a turquoise bracelet emerged for me, agate earrings for all of her old friends, and a list of new friends who had to be invited to the party. At the party they immediately disappeared downstairs into the garden, and one of them was a cute boy who never left Chris' side. Was this a new parenting abyss opening up? Tonight I was too busy as hostess to think about it much, but I'd have to ask some questions tomorrow.

In the fall, Chris and I went back to school at the same time. By putting in killer hours I was able to finish my project at the museum, write my report and get my credit. They offered me a part-time job for the fall semester. A real paycheck would be involved. Of course I said yes.

Chris talked to the boy from camp every night. He lived in Riverdale, the other end of the city. He was a two-hour subway ride away, which was fine with me.

As the fall moved along, it became clear that there would be no trial of anyone involved in Chris' abduction, or the attack on Leary, or the various ways I had been harassed. The two men who had done it told everything they knew, to cut a deal for reduced jail time, just as Russo predicted. And when some small pieces of evidence they had overlooked put them in Rick's house, they owned up to that too, desperately insisting his death had been an accident. They were only there to make threats, they said, but Rick had objected to their presence and threatened them. They had the nerve to claim it was self-defense. They would spend some serious time in jail, even with their deal.

And no, they did not know why they were threatening him, it was Mr. McLeod's orders. They'd moved the body, tried to hide it, but in case it was ever investigated, they'd planted the bag of money to create confusion. Again, McLeod's orders, they claimed, though I thought it sounded stupid enough to be their own idea.

In the meantime, McLeod calmly asserted there was no proof whatever that he even knew them, let alone was involved with any of their activities. He kept asserting it, and though Russo cursed when he told me, it looked like he was correct, and he was going to walk.

Steven, however, would not. With the best legal counsel money could buy, he was only able to bargain down to a minimum sentence. He insisted he had nothing to do with Chris' kidnapping, he learned about it after the fact and was only there to see she was not harmed. Russo did not believe a word of that. I almost did—almost—sometimes—but I truly did not care.

All those years ago, when my husband was killed, I thought the worst thing possible had already happened to me, and there was nothing left to fear. Of course any parent knows that wasn't true, and having Chris in danger brought that home again with a smack on the head. I would never forgive Steven.

We finally had that memorial for Rick and as he directed, it was a party. The soundtrack was Sinatra and Ellington and Rosemary Clooney, and old cops took turns with the mike, telling stories both funny and touching. We all lifted a glass of Jameson's to the man we remembered.

The last piece of the story fell into place that day. Wanda showed up, escorted by her huge, silent brother. Her hair was a different color but her clothes were as eye catching as ever and she caught quite a few eyes. She mingled with old friends, joined in the toasting, and wept a little, but the story she most wanted to tell was not for the mike. It was for my father and me, no one else, and she told it in an empty adjoining room.

It was about a young, ambitious cop who took a bribe for the only time in his career. It wasn't money but a promise of introductions going way up the ladder, in return for abandoning an investigation on a drug-ridden block of Park Slope. It was a long shot anyway—the parents from out of town, the runaway daughter, and the few clues they had that led to that neighborhood. He knew the places to look but someone made it worthwhile for him to say he didn't, to not ask questions about the young people who had suddenly disappeared from an especially shady house, to make sure the parents went home to Minnesota without learning anything.

That was all it was. He had buried it in his memory until that missing girl turned up in a way that threatened someone he loved.

"He told me he told them he would never let you get hurt and they told him he still owed them and to keep his mouth shut after all these years. He didn't respond well to threats, so." Wanda shrugged, but there were tears in her eyes. "So they shut his mouth for him." Her brother came into the room, tapping his watch. "I gotta go now. Plane to catch. Anyways thought you'd like to know."

Dad and I went back into the reception, where someone was proposing another round to Rick.

To receive a free catalog of Poisoned Pen Press titles, please contact us in one of the following ways:

Phone: 1-800-421-3976
Facsimile: 1-480-949-1707
Email: info@poisonedpenpress.com
Website: www.poisonedpenpress.com

Poisoned Pen Press
6962 E. First Ave. Ste 103
Scottsdale, AZ 85251